THE INFORMANT

THE INFORMANT

Mary Burns

Copyright © 2000 by Mary Burns.

ISBN #:   Softcover   0-7388-4458-6

All rights reserved. No part of this book may be reproduced or transmitted in any form or by any means, electronic or mechanical, including photocopying, recording, or by any information storage and retrieval system, without permission in writing from the copyright owner.

This is a work of fiction. Names, characters, places and incidents either are the product of the author's imagination or are used fictitiously, and any resemblance to any actual persons, living or dead, events, or locales is entirely coincidental.

This book was printed in the United States of America.

To order additional copies of this book, contact:
Xlibris Corporation
1-888-7-XLIBRIS
www.Xlibris.com
Orders@Xlibris.com

CONTENTS

- CHAPTER 1 11
- CHAPTER 2 19
- CHAPTER 3 25
- CHAPTER 4 40
- CHAPTER 5 55
- CHAPTER 6 76
- CHAPTER 7 82
- CHAPTER 8 94
- CHAPTER 9 102
- CHAPTER 10 114
- CHAPTER 11 135
- CHAPTER 12 145
- CHAPTER 13 164
- CHAPTER 14 181
- CHAPTER 15 194
- CHAPTER 16 208
- CHAPTER 17 227
- CHAPTER 18 236
- CHAPTER 19 242
- CHAPTER 20 256
- CHAPTER 21 267

Many thanks to the members of the Edmonton Police Service, especially G. Alcorn, for the information and assistance they have provided. I also thank my readers for their valuable input. Finally, I would have given up long ago but for my husband's encouragement. Thank you, Eldon.

This first novel in the Edmonton: Life and Crimes series introduces many continuing characters including Mike Ceretzke, a police detective; Beth McKinney, a librarian and his love interest; Mary Carpenter, an elderly lady who loves solving crimes; and Richard Tanner, a manipulative reporter.

Friendship, work, and mutual acquaintances link these characters. They appear as minor characters in each other's stories and grow as they interact.

New characters are added with each story. Some play small roles in several stories, while others are promoted from minor roles to major character status.

The stories are located in Edmonton, a city of more than 500,000 located a five-hour drive north of the Montana-Alberta border and a four-hour drive east of the Rocky Mountains. It is best known for West Edmonton Mall, the largest mall in the world, and the Edmonton Oilers hockey team.

Edmonton hosts a summer filled with festivals to celebrate the arts and the diversity of our population. However, the aspect of the city that I relish most is the 7425 hectares of parkland bordering our section of the North Saskatchewan River. I have set several of my stories in that parkland.

The stories also flow through Edmonton's distinct seasons. The first features autumn's gentle change of foliage. The next includes a cold stretch of minus forty-degree weather and a death by freezing. Another has a rapid spring thaw deposit a body on the riverbank. Pounding summer heat and a severe hailstorm play roles in yet another.

I welcome you to my world.

CHAPTER 1

Stop.

Listen.

The whistle and chatter of birds; the rustle of wind dislodging leaves from nearly naked trees; the hum of vehicles speeding on the freeway; the sigh of a squirrel scurrying through dry grass.

No one around. Good. Move off the trail, into the trees. Don't disturb the bushes and tall grass. Where is the burrow?

A litany of predetermined steps played silently through barely moving lips.

First, pull on the gloves. Can't leave fingerprints.

Now reach through the brush into the burrow. Pull out the gym bag. Grab the coveralls. They're too loose.

Off with these shoes. Take the other pair out of the bag. Put them on. Damn it, now they're too tight. Too late. They'll have to do.

Next, the ski mask.

Pull it on. Roll it up like a toque. Don't want to look sinister.

Finally, the knife. Black and silver and sharp.

A strident laugh.

Someone's coming. Walkers. Wait for them to pass. No curious dog with them. Good.

Climb through the tangled underbrush to the top of the hill. Slowly, quietly, don't break any branches. Stay close to the path. The western approach is clear. So is the eastern. Please God let there be no witnesses. It must work today. Everything must work today. This is my last chance.

Coveralls are getting hot. Head's beginning to sweat. Hurry up.

Here she comes. Early today. What a good girl you are. A little closer. Any witnesses? Scan the trail, the road, the houses. No one around.

That's right, stop and stretch. You're beautiful, why couldn't you be loyal, too?

No. Don't think! Be cold. Be detached. There's no room for anger. Stay with the plan! Down with the ski mask. Move silently. Almost there. Get behind her. Arm around her neck.

She's trying to throw me! Watch her feet!

Her hands—don't let her grab . . Those damn self-defence lessons!

She's strong.

The look in her eyes. She recognizes me!

Stab her. In the chest. Stab her again. Again.

She can't stop me.

Damn pointy elbows. Control her arms.

She's weakening. Stab her in the back.

She's down, she's dead. So much blood. All over her. All over me.

How long? Too long? No, it was fast. No one in sight. Good. Pull her into the bush. Discard her. She's debris for the scavengers.

Get going. Can't get caught. Take her wristband, just in case. Down the hill. Watch that rose bush.

First, to the trail. Then, to the burrow. Off with this damn ski mask. Stuff the coveralls into the bag. Be careful of the blood. Change the shoes.

People coming. Freeze. Hurry up. Can't get caught now. Not when everything is on track again. Not when I'm safe again.

They're gone. Put the bag in the hole. Strip off the gloves. Remember to throw them in the river.

Start jogging. Get the hell out of here.

*****

Jogging is good for your health. Jogging is good for your health.

Beth McKinney repeated the phrase as she forced her long, fleece-clad legs onward in a constant rhythm.

Less than a half-kilometre to go. Her breath caught in her throat and the pain in her side flared. She grabbed her waist and tried to pinch the pain away. She was getting too old for jogging. Maybe she should stick to a brisk walk so she could enjoy the changing seasons and breathe the fresh air.

With each laboured breath she inhaled the smell of October in Edmonton with its hint of snow not yet arrived, but lurking only days away. The pounding of her heart synchronized with the crunch of dry leaves as her shoe landed on the pallet of red and orange covering the asphalt path. Bare trees lined her route, harbingers of winter's impending black and white landscape.

A dome of azure autumn sky cheered her on, urged her to push her body to its limit. The paved jogging path ran close to the street, avoided a toboggan hill, then swept around a tree-screened bend. The horizon opened outward revealing a meadow.

The leaf-covered grass stretched to the skyline, interrupted only by an octagon-shaped cedar platform complete with benches and a clear vista of the distant riverbank. The lookout platform stood sentry at the edge of a steep hill that fell into the river far below.

Beth felt the pain in her side ease and lengthened her stride. When she reached that scenic lookout she would rest against its weather-polished railing, stretch her screaming muscles, and admire the view. Lisette would be waiting for her and today she would learn what was bothering her friend. For the past week, Lisette had been distracted. Yesterday she'd missed their rendezvous, something that rarely happened. Beth squinted into the glare of the overly bright sunshine. When Lisette missed her run there was always a reason and it was never good news.

Lisette was reserved, though less now than when they had first met. She said there were things in her life others were better off not knowing.

Beth licked her parched lips and longed to satisfy her thirst.

She could wait a few seconds and about one hundred and fifty metres. Today, she would reach the lookout without pausing. She pushed herself, hoping to increase her stamina. Tomorrow, she would rest only long enough to catch her breath for the final three kilometres home. Today, if Lisette showed up, she would take as long as necessary to pry loose her worries.

Beth counted her strides. As she passed the larch, she began counting down from one hundred metres. No sign of Lisette at the lookout. Damn, Lisette had to be there today.

A movement in the stand of nearly leafless poplar trees encircling the lookout drew her attention.

Beth shaded her eyes, squinting to see more clearly. Whoever it was, it wasn't Lisette. Probably a hiker. The park was still full of them, though the cooler weather had already chased many away.

She focused on a splash of turquoise barely visible in the undergrowth. Lisette always wore turquoise. A premonition rippled through her mind like a shiver.

Why would Lisette be in the brush?

Beth stretched her stride as her unfounded fear grew.

Seventy-five metres. Someone was lying on the grass near the fringe of trees. Was it Lisette? Why was she on the ground? Lisette never sat on the ground. She hated bugs crawling over her.

As she closed the gap Beth's breathing grew laboured and her muscles trembled. At fifty metres, a pool of dark auburn hair identified Lisette lying crumpled in a fetal position.

Twenty-five metres. Beth gathered her strength for a final burst of speed. She called her friend's name, but dread rose in her throat and strangled her words.

Beth dropped to her knees beside Lisette. She reached out, then pulled her hand back at the sight of blood marking the bright turquoise sweatshirt. Beth forced her hand forward, pushed on Lisette's slender shoulder, and rolled her over.

The front of Lisette's shirt lay slashed and bloodied. Dark red cuts marked the pale skin of her exposed breasts. Sticky, discoloured blades of grass clung like leeches.

Beth touched Lisette's face in a light caress, brushed a loose strand of auburn hair from her porcelain cheek, and whispered her name.

Lisette's eyes fluttered open. Focusing her stare on Beth, she struggled to form words. In barely a whisper, she said, "Fun—time—Howard." She uttered the words as a final exhalation.

Beth pulled her friend into her arms and held her. She rocked Lisette gently. Lisette's blood spread to Beth's hands and clothes.

"Lisette, don't die. Hang on. I'll get help."

Blue jays echoed Beth's terror and confusion with their indignant screams. Magpies strutted in their black and white plumage, the concerns of mere humans beneath their notice.

Beth shuddered as the wind dislodged a solitary leaf, sending the brittle body floating downward in a feeble attempt to hide the evidence of the brutal crime.

She scanned the road and the houses for help. Semi-mansions bordered the park, cars in their driveways offered proof of human habitation, but no one was in sight. Beth prayed someone would come within shouting distance. She was not going to leave her friend alone.

Eventually, she spotted a tall man and a dog approaching from the west. Beth recognized them as Hendrick and his golden Labrador Retriever, Orff. They walked through the park daily, often stopping to talk with her and Lisette. Hendrick would know what to do, he always did.

Hendrick waved, then continued his steady march along the trail toward her, his head high, his back straight. He called out, "What has happened here, my friend?"

Beth saw only a grey halo outlining a featureless face until he came to rest in a squat that put them on the same eye level.

Orff nosed Lisette, then whimpered.

Through a thick haze that slowed her thoughts and muffled the world's sounds, Beth registered Hendrick's concern. She held Lisette and rocked her gently. Finally she spoke. "She is dead?"

Beth realized the dreadful words sounded like a question and hoped Hendrick would argue that Lisette still lived and would recover. He had been an army officer until his retirement twenty-five years earlier; he should know when an injured person was going to live.

She watched him fight the trembling of his bony hand and feel Lisette's neck. He shook his head.

"She is gone. I will go to find help."

His knees groaned as he forced them to straighten. He ordered Orff to stay and strode stiffly across the field to the houses facing the park.

Beth watched him cross to three houses before he found someone at home. Such effort was hard on an elderly man. She should have gone and left him to watch over Lisette. Still, she could not leave Lisette.

Beth followed Hendrick's pantomime as he spoke to the stoutly built woman who opened the door at the third house. He waved his arms and pointed across the field. Occasional sounds drifted to the tree line where she sat. He must have been convincing because the woman allowed him into her home. Hendrick reappeared, making wild gestures that Beth interpreted as directions to wait for the ambulance. He left the woman standing at the curb.

His hurried pace slowed to a cautious walk as he retraced his path across the open field. Orff whimpered and strained to run to his master, but his training held.

When Hendrick came within reach, he absently patted the dog's head, then pointed in the direction of the road where the robust woman paced.

"The police and ambulance are coming. Mrs. Arbutsom will direct them."

Mrs. Arbutsom pulled her pale blue sweater tightly across her abundant bust, then shaded her eyes against the brightness of the day. As a police car pulled to the curb, she rushed to the driver's side and pointed toward the park. The officer took a moment to extricate his long-limbed body from the vehicle. He bent forward as if fearing he would not hear the anxious little woman from his great height.

After listening and turning in their direction, he strode toward them, his hand on his holster. The officer's intense stare seemed fixed on them. Beth felt certain he was absorbing every detail of the scene.

Beth held Lisette tight while Hendrick walked forward, meeting the officer about twenty metres from her. They were nearly the same height, at least six-two, and carried themselves with a wariness that Beth had never before noticed in Hendrick. Did all military men cultivate that air, or did Hendrick's history include a stint in law enforcement in some Eastern European country? She knew little about him.

She forced herself to focus on the men, to hear and to understand what they were saying. "We have a lady here who someone has stabbed. The young woman who found her is Beth McKinney. I have been here several minutes and no other walkers have passed since I arrived. We have not disturbed the site." Hendrick related these details in his heavily accented monotone.

Beth held Lisette in her arms, unaware the men were approaching until their shadows blocked the heat of the sun. A shiver ran through her.

"Excuse me," the officer said. His voice caught then wavered into a stronger tone. "If you could put her down and step back, I'll see if I can help her."

Beth didn't move, so he gently liberated Lisette from her grip. Freed from the weight of her friend's body, Beth reluctantly accepted Hendrick's hand and pulled herself upright. They stepped back, but remained close, as silent witnesses to the officer's cursory examination.

The officer stepped away from Lisette, his face paler than when he'd arrived.

Beth gripped Hendrick's arm and was surprised at the firm muscle she felt. He seemed undisturbed by the blood, even unaware of it, and of her, as he studied the site. Eventually his expression settled into a blank mask and he put one arm around her shoulders, turning her toward the lookout with its solid bench.

"Officer, we will sit over here and stay out of your way. Beth needs to recover from this shock."

"Don't talk to each other about this," the officer said, waving his hand over the bloody patch of grass where Lisette lay. "A detective will take your statements."

"Of course, we will observe protocol," Hendrick answered over his shoulder as he guided Beth.

Overcome with dizziness, Beth collapsed onto the bench, rousing only when Orff nuzzled her hand, insisting she pet him. From what seemed a long distance away, Beth registered the increased activity that followed. Sirens blared; police officers tied tape around stakes and trees, forcing walkers, joggers, and the merely curious, to detour to the road. Disembodied, garbled voices mumbled from radios and emergency medical technicians arrived carrying a stretcher.

CHAPTER 2

She's late.

Sgt. Jack Pierce forced his features into what he hoped was a casual expression as he grunted and bent to retie his running shoe for the third time.

Damn, he was out of shape. The elastic waistband of his sweat pants rode lower each time he put them on. He really should work out in them, actually do the run he so often pretended to tackle. Still, his poor fitness level only bothered him when his clothes became uncomfortable. His weight like most other things had lost their nagging urgency after Marnie died.

The only things that cheered his otherwise workaholic existence were his grandkids and he saw them infrequently because work was his reprive against uselessness. As long as he had his work, he had a purpose in life, though he feared that when he finally retired his grandkids would be in school with friends to monopolize their days and would have no time for grandpa. He had to make time for them. Maybe after this case was wound up.

The noon sun was hot for the end of October. Jack pushed his bifocals back up to the bridge of his nose and wiped at the sheen of sweat coating his forehead. Where the hell was Lisette?

He felt conspicuous loitering about the tree-shaded parking lot. He had already stretched twice releasing some of the stiffness in his knees, now what was he supposed to do? Jack looked around, checking for watchers who didn't belong. Today would be the last time he had to play this game. Once Lisette arrived, it was over. However, the trail from the west remained empty.

Two women, with six kids between them, watched his every move as they unloaded their van. When the smallest kid, a cute blond girl about two-years-old started in his direction, the prettier of the women grabbed her. They gathered the picnic basket, blanket, chairs, and toys and hustled the kids to a spot far from the parking lot. He listened with approval to their lecture about bad people and checked his watch again.

Lisette was usually on time, within a few minutes anyway. Maybe she was still angry after yesterday's meeting. Maybe she'd decided not to come today. Damn, she couldn't miss today. It wasn't his fault she was mad. Yesterday he hadn't believed she was in danger. He'd been right to tell her it wasn't the time for her to quit. Things had changed since then. Now he understood her anger and her fear of staying in the house but damn, she had known going in what they expected in return for getting her and the kids to safety.

He wiped the sweat from his brow again, then tucked the handkerchief in his pocket. Come on Lisette it's already 12:10. You should have come swooping in here five minutes ago. She didn't have to worry about her fitness or her weight. He tugged at his sweat pants, squirming with discomfort at their tight fit.

Today wasn't the day for a show of temperament. He should have barged into Dorrien's house last night, as soon as he got the phone call. Was she safe? Had he been wrong to wait? Why hadn't he got her out immediately? Because he hadn't trusted the caller? Because he thought the hysteria he detected was a case of premature panic?

Late last night he had woken from as sound a sleep as he ever got lately to the buzz of his cell phone. A muffled voice had whispered, "Lisette's in danger. They've traced the info leaks to her. They're going to kill her. You have to get us out."

It had taken time to recognize the voice, for the words to register, and for him to react. Jack didn't like surprises, especially ones that endangered his people.

He took a deep breath, threw off the covers, and swung his feet to the plush carpet as he sorted through the barrage of questions swirling through his mind. He pulled himself into a sitting position, his toes burrowed into the plush carpet. Which question was the most important?

Lisette's cover was blown. How the hell had that happened? No, that didn't matter. Yet.

"OK, keep calm! When are they planning the hit?" Jack asked.

"Neil Karlek is arriving to chair the quarterly strategy meeting this Friday. They want her gone by then."

Jack felt a chill at the mention of Karlek's name. A chill that had nothing to do with the brisk breeze teasing his bedroom curtains. Neil Karlek was a name the Mounties knew well. He'd grown up in rural Ontario, then moved to Montreal in the fifties where he married his boss's daughter, only months before the boss died in a car bombing. Fingers pointed toward Karlek but his guilt was never proven. His wife stayed with him, either believing him innocent or not caring about his guilt.

After taking over his father-in-law's legitimate and illegitimate businesses, Karlek's drive for success and his ruthlessness in dealing with competitors paved his way to the top of the pile of shadowy entrepreneurs. The Quebec provincial police were convinced Karlek ordered the murder of a judge who gave a long jail term to one of his favourite employees. Unfortunately, they never proved that particular case or any other for that matter.

Ten years ago, Karlek started expanding his empire Westward. His power grew as officials opposed to his expansion suffered fatal accidents and sudden changes in attitude. The Mounties formed an Integrated Intelligence Unit to investigate him. The Unit combined personnel from the RCMP and various provincial and local police forces. It had a single purpose. Its mission was putting Karlek out of business.

Karlek recruited as he expanded. One person he recruited and moved into positions of ever-increasing importance was Hugh Dorrien. Dorrien was a businessman, not the type civilians associated with crime, but one who was currently the linchpin in Karlek's Edmonton operations. Lisette was Dorrien's wife.

Jack had worked on the task force since its formation, following Karlek's westward march, always hoping to receive damning information from one of his informants. Now they were close and Lisette's chance of giving him evidence was shot to hell. Would they ever get another chance to turn Dorrien?

Turning Dorrien and using him to gather evidence against Karlek was the second phase in the task force's plan of attack. With Lisette in danger, his chance of getting evidence against Dorrien would be more than halved. Still, he had no choice but to pull her.

"We can get her out tonight, if you feel it's urgent," Jack said.

"Only if you get me out too."

Jack switched on his bedside lamp. The informant sounded serious. He could not lose the entire set-up. It was too valuable and had taken years to put in place.

"It's not feasible to get you out now." Jack fumbled for his bifocals with his free hand.

"Then when?" The informant's voice rose, then fell to a husky whisper. "I've worked for you people too long already. It's my neck on the line just as much as hers."

Jack slowed his words and added every ounce of calm reassurance he could muster. Keeping his players under control was an ongoing challenge and he didn't intend risking the game because one person was spooked.

"This set-up is perfect. Maybe we can get you out in a couple of months. That's not important now. Let's deal with the immediate danger. We'll get Lisette to safety first. Then, we'll see what you learn during Friday's meeting with Karlek. Then, we'll talk."

Jack ran his fingers through his thinning hair, patting down the errant clumps. They would talk all right. No way, he would cut loose what was now his best chance of getting Dorrien and through him, Karlek.

Jack retrieved his housecoat from the floor and pulled it over his naked torso while holding the phone.

"Well." The voice coming through the receiver sounded calmer. "I guess grabbing her tonight would jeopardize my cover and the entire investigation. It'll hold for another day or two. I don't know the details, but I doubt they plan to move against her until at least Wednesday. If you change your mind though, let me know so I can bail out."

"Like I said," Jack repeated, "I don't want to wreck the investigation. We will get her out when we can do it without hurting your cover. If you hear anything more, call. And pick up what you can about Friday's meeting; it could be what makes our jobs worthwhile." Jack held the phone between his chin and shoulder and pushed his arms into the sleeves of his housecoat.

His source's voice changed back to a whisper. "I've got to go. Plan to get me out. If they're looking for leaks I could be the next one in danger."

Jack listened to the dial tone for a few seconds before punching the disconnect button. His options were damned sparse. He had to get Lisette out fast, but how? He had to get her kids out too. They were part of the deal. Hugh Dorrien might believe she ran off with their kids but he knew she would never leave them behind.

Struggling to loosen sleep-stiffened joints, he shuffled into his slippers and across the carpet to the hardwood flooring of his den. By the time he reached the walnut desk, his arthritic knees had loosened up. He squinted against the glare from the desk lamp. Marvin Brown's unlisted home phone number was recorded in his electronic DayTimer, hidden somewhere in the clutter of file folders, binders, and paper that covered his desktop. For this decision, he had wanted Marvin's official backing. If heads had to roll, they would roll from a rank higher than his.

Jack pulled his mind back to the present and looked west. The path was still empty.

Last night their plan had seemed simple. He would grab Lisette at the park, then intercept the kids when the nanny took them for their afternoon walk. They would take the nanny too if she made a fuss. What could go wrong? He grimaced knowing Murphy's Law rarely missed in its prediction.

Jack placed his hands on a tree trunk and repeated his stretching routine. Okay, so what was the worst that could happen? He could make the wrong move, expose his informants, and destroy a three-year investigation. It could not, would not, happen. Lisette would arrive. He would take her away to safety and the investigation would continue with only a small hiccup.

The shrill whine of a siren drifted to him on the air currents. Acting on instinct, he started running west toward the approaching sound, a prayer for Lisette's safety on his lips.

The kilometre took too many minutes to cover. His glasses bounced on his nose, sweat stained his shirt.

He rounded a corner and was confronted by the sight of emergency medical technicians carrying an empty stretcher. They trotted toward a clump of trees lining the riverbank where a group of people clustered around a turquoise-clad body.

A tall, uniformed officer intercepted the paramedics and spoke to them. Their pace slowed. The officer spotted Jack and with his hand in a halt position he left the technicians to their task and marched in Jack's direction.

Jack contemplated the crumpled body that had been Lisette Dorrien. He should have got her out last night. He should have known the situation was urgent.

Jack didn't identify himself but let the Park Patrol Constable guide him to the road. His breathing calmed from ragged gasps to steady panting. He tried slowing it further, deepening it enough to control the rapid pounding of his heart.

Damn, how was he going to explain this mess to Mike and worse yet, to Mary? This would kill Mary.

CHAPTER 3

Mike Ceretzke dropped his gym bag beside his swivel chair and looked across the narrow aisle to his partner, Evan Collins. The homicide detective spoke rapidly into the phone and gestured for Mike to stay standing.

After slamming down the receiver, Evan kicked back his chair, dropped his half-eaten ham sandwich beside the framed photo of his wife and infant son, grabbed his jacket, and lunged toward the door. Mike followed though he hadn't had a chance to shower and change out of his sweats.

"A body in Capital Park," Evan said as they headed to the parking lot.

Mike kept pace with his partner. His extra inches gave him a longer stride that made up for the younger man's speed. "What's the rush? It'll be a while before the M.E. finishes and I could do with a shower."

"Super Sam was clear, we get to the scene ASAP."

"Why?"

"She just told me it was our case and to get on it fast. And, she didn't sound happy."

Capital Park was a string of parks stretching along both sides of the North Saskatchewan River as it flowed through Edmonton. It incorporated pedestrian trails, bike paths, playgrounds, picnic areas, and boat launches.

The network of parks also acted as a nature retreat for the city's residents. Various types of wildlife were found wandering in the area, deer grazed the hillsides, beaver harvested the trees, and even the occasional coyote stalked the river edge searching for a wildfowl snack.

Sometimes it provided a home for Edmonton's homeless. When a body turned up it was an even bet whether it was a suicide or a homeless person caught on the losing end of an argument. Mike couldn't fathom why Superintendent Samantha Weisman had turned this into a priority.

The drive from downtown police headquarters to the park took them less than ten minutes. Steering his truck to the curb behind a police van, Mike took a moment to analyze the flow of people surrounding the cordoned area. Evan stepped out of the vehicle, but Mike held back as his cell phone beeped.

"I'll catch up with you," Mike called to his partner. His face grew serious as he recognized the voice coming through the receiver. It belonged to RCMP Sgt. Jack Pierce. He didn't need another of Pierce's distractions just now.

"Mike." The way Pierce said his name made Mike uneasy. "Your victim is Lisette Dorrien."

"Where are you?" Mike looked around, hoping to spot the dumpy little guy. Pierce had promised nothing would happen to Lisette. If this was tied into their investigation, Mike planned to strangle him, slowly.

"I'm close enough to see what's going on. I've been waiting for you to get here."

"How did she die?" Mike asked.

"Her cover was blown. My source thought there would be time to get her out but obviously, that information was incorrect. You're already involved in the situation so Police Chief Horban cleared you to handle the investigation." Then he asked, "Can you handle it, Mike? You two were pretty close."

"I admired her, that's all."

"Okay, just keep our involvement out of the investigation."

"Why, wasn't it your fault?"

"We thought we had time to get her out."

"It was your fault."

"Horban agreed that you must keep us out of it."

Mike disconnected the call without replying. If his investigation exposed Pierce and his group of undercover bumblers they'd have to live with it. Lisette was dead; the rest of them should get out while they could. Damn Pierce for forcing Horban to pull rank and have him assigned to this case. That alone explained the Super's attitude—Sam didn't like being told how to do her job. He slammed the car door and stalked over to where Evan was chatting with a constable.

"What's up?" Evan asked.

Mike held his reply until they were out of the constable's vicinity. "Complications. The Mounties are involved; the victim was one of their informants. Damn it! They knew she'd been exposed. Worse yet, guess who her husband is. No don't bother, it's Hugh Dorrien."

"The real estate guy, the ex-hockey pro?"

"The one and only."

Mike stormed across the field, leaving Evan hustling to keep up. He flashed his badge at the tall constable who met their advance.

"Detectives Ceretzke and Collins. Were you first on the scene?"

The constable's spine stiffened as he replied. "Yes, Constable Bob Harding. I work this section of the park."

The constable tried hiding his disappointment at losing his command of the situation so quickly. Mike recognized the look; he'd worn the same one a long time ago. More often now he wished someone would remove the responsibility from his shoulders, especially when it was going to be the high-profile disaster that this one threatened to become. As if he needed another bull's eye painted on his ass right now.

"Give me the details." Mike cast the words over his shoulder, just as if he didn't already know everything he needed to arrest Dorrien.

Pulling his notebook from his shirt pocket, the young man began. "Call came in at 12:05. I got here at 12:11. The old guy was the one who called. Said a woman had been hurt so they routed the call to me and Emergency Services."

"Names, Constable."

"Yes, yes of course. Sorry." Constable Harding pulled himself straighter at the rebuff. "Ms. Beth McKinney was holding Mrs. Lisette Dorrien, the victim . . the victim was dead when I arrived. She has multiple stab wounds to her chest, neck and back. Lots of defence wounds to her hands and arms; she put up a hell of a fight. Those two were the only ones on the scene when I arrived." He pointed across to the lookout where a tall, grey-haired man sat holding the leash of a golden Labrador Retriever. Across from him, a youngish woman rocked slowly back and forth. The dog sat close to her knee and occasionally nudged her.

"I told them, Mr. Domke and Ms. McKinney, to wait at the lookout until you talked to them. They were both really shook up. Ms. McKinney has blood on her from holding the victim. I got their names and addresses. Then I kept the scene clear of civilians until backup arrived; then we secured the area and routed people to the road. The M.E. arrived and then Ident."

His words spilled out, gaining speed as he spoke. "That's about it. Then you got here." He stopped speaking abruptly.

Mike glanced at the witnesses. Could they help hang Dorrien or had they arrived too late to see anything? He turned toward Lisette's body, sprawled where her husband had discarded it. The vitality she had radiated in life lay in the pool of stained grass surrounding her. He swept the scene with his gaze, gathering details, storing impressions.

"How long has the Medical Examiner been here?"

"She's just about finished. Ident got here a while ago."

Mike approached the barrier for a closer look at Lisette's body. One of her slender hands lay extended, grasping at nothing. The other was hidden beneath her. A knife lay about a metre to her left.

Her magnificent auburn hair had escaped the yellow band that she had used to restrain it. He preferred it swept up, exposing her long neck. She wore a turquoise sweat suit with yellow piping and white runners with turquoise and yellow stripes. Coordinated, as always. No jewellery, no watch. She seemed so fragile, like a discarded, red-haired Barbie doll.

The park constable cleared his throat, drawing Mike's attention back to the present.

"I'll talk to the witnesses now." Mike's voice was harsher than he had intended. He tried to soften his tone. There was no point in scaring the kid on what was probably his first murder. "You did good."

It was not the constable's fault she was dead. Blame a city detective who was too busy to help a friend, and a RCMP Sergeant who didn't want his sleep disturbed, and don't forget her husband. He would pay for killing her.

"Let's just get the formalities over with so I can go arrest the bastard who did this."

Constable Harding's eyes widened and his Adam's apple bounced. "You already know who killed her?"

The detective didn't answer. He was angry with Jack Pierce for his smug attitude, for worrying more about jeopardizing the case than keeping his people safe. This time his bureaucratic cover-your-ass policy had got the mother of two little kids killed.

Mike felt the old man staring at him like a frog tracking a fly. What was the codger's name—Domke? Damn, he was old. Probably close to eighty and the dog wasn't much younger. Tall, over six feet, but thin, like bones covered with rawhide. His steel-wool hair was thick, coarse, and cut close to his head. He'd be useless as a witness. A good defence attorney would have him crying on the stand.

The woman didn't look up as they approached, just continued rocking and stroking the dog's broad back.

"We have to ask you a few questions."

The woman, Ms. McKinney, lifted her head and narrowed her brown eyes; her crow's-feet deepened. She was shorter than Lisette, about 5'6". Heavier too, 130 was his guess. And a little older, probably in her mid-thirties. Her hair wasn't attractive like Lisette's; still, the curly, brown cap suited her.

Mike studied her reactions as she scrutinized the horizon, blinking her eyes as if trying to focus them. Then she turned toward the park, staring at the purposeful movements of the police department personnel, the removal crew, and the gathering flock of reporters.

Mike shifted his weight and waited for her to turn away. What was she thinking as she watched the crew bag Lisette's hands and head, and wrap her body? The woman noticed details. Mike approved. He had watched other people at crime scenes and knew she was etching a permanent record of the events. Would she let it fade or would it gnaw at the edges of her consciousness and twist her perception of the world?

Mike raked his fingers through his hair. Her reaction wasn't his problem. He had too many other things to worry about, like shoving Pierce against a wall and demanding—-what? It was too late for anything other than revenge.

And he was going to have to tell Mary before she heard the news on the radio. Now that was one psyche he had a right to worry about.

Evan spoke to the old man, guiding him and the dog toward the privacy of a police car. Mike focused his attention on Beth McKinney. Maybe her powers of observation would help him convict Lisette's husband.

Mike sat across from her, taking the spot the old man had vacated, and studied her colourless face. He touched her arm. She jumped.

"Ms. McKinney, tell me how you happened to find her," he said.

She recited the details in a detached voice, yet Mike could feel her shock change to fear and then to horror.

"There was nothing I could do to help her." Her voice trailed off as she bowed her head and stared at her hands.

"Lisette said, 'Fun time Howard'." Beth McKinney's voice was barely audible.

"She talked to you?" Mike heard the aggression in his tone and caught himself before he grabbed her arm to shake her into full awareness. He needed her help.

"I could barely hear her and that was all she said. Just 'Fun time Howard'."

"She wasn't dead when you found her?"

"Not when I arrived, she died after she said that."

"Do you know who she meant? Do you know Howard?"

Beth looked up, her brown eyes brimming, damp streaks marking her cheeks. Mike flipped the page in his notebook, trying to avoid the plea he read in her eyes. He controlled an urge to take her in his arms and comfort her, to tell her he would fix everything.

He looked across the field to where Lisette was being folded into a body bag. Ms. McKinney wasn't his problem. He simply needed to know what she had seen. Victim Services would cope with her suffering.

"No, I don't know who Howard is," she eventually replied. "Her husband's name is Hugh, so she didn't mean him. It might have been . . someone else."

With only a raised eyebrow at her pause, Mike waited for her to continue.

"We both ran along this path daily in the summer. Lisette lives across the river. Her house overlooks the park. She has a son and a daughter." Her voice trailed off, then picked up again. "I've never met them, but she talked about them all the time. She loved them a lot." She closed her eyes. Mike saw a shiver shake her shoulders. In a whisper, she asked, "What will happen to them now?"

Mike studied Lisette's body, now lying on the gurney, and the activity focused around it. That was where his responsibility lay. "Ms. McKinney, how well did you know the victim?" he asked, forcing her to concentrate.

A slight pursing of her full lips and a tightening around her eyes betrayed her effort at self-control. She closed her eyes, took a deep breath, and smiled what Mike interpreted to be a public relations smile. Her voice was slow as she carefully enunciated her words, reminding him of his tenth grade English teacher explaining for the umpteenth time the role of a verb in sentence structure.

"About three years ago I decided to get more exercise. I chose to jog through the park. By the time I reached this lookout, I was gasping for air and ready to give up jogging for life. Lisette was standing at the rail gazing over the river valley. She was very pregnant and very sad. We talked, introduced ourselves, and established an instant rapport."

Mike nodded, encouraging her to continue. He could have a real find here; maybe Lisette had confided in this woman.

She smiled her first real smile since he'd arrived and dismissed the school teacher tone from her voice. "Sometimes you meet a person who you know will be a friend for life. That was how it was with us. We met and we talked, provided moral support and advice."

Mike tapped his pen against his notebook, but then afraid of distracting her stopped the movement. He didn't need or want this soul mate, girlfriend stuff, at least not yet. Dorrien was his target and if Lisette had talked about him, Mike needed to know. "Have you ever met her husband?" Mike asked.

"No, never." She shook her head. "Not him or her children."

"Did she mention any trouble between them?"

She started answering his question, then hesitated. "She never talked about her marriage."

"Still, you suspected problems existed?"

"I had no reason for any suspicions."

Her defensive tone rang warning bells in Mike's mind. He let the subject drop. Maybe they could use her to testify to a pattern of abuse, if it ever became necessary. Odds were that the Mounties would barter Dorrien's release for his help getting Karlek, and Ms. McKinney's testimony would be irrelevant. All he could do was gather uncontroversial evidence and hope Dorrien chose to fight it in the courts. Still, if the Mounties turned him a call to Karlek might result in terminal justice. Mike filed that thought deep in his subconscious, knowing it was not only unprofessional but also criminal.

He had to find enough evidence to prove Dorrien's guilt. A good place to start was with Lisette's last words. "What does 'Fun time Howard' mean?"

"I don't know, maybe she was just rambling." Ms. McKinney chewed her bottom lip. She shook her head then continued speaking. "No, she worked hard to say the words so they must be important. Still, this had to be a random attack, though I don't understand why anyone would harm her. She didn't wear jewellery, at least not when she was jogging. Just her wrist pouch to hold her house keys and a couple of loonies. Besides, this is Edmonton, people don't get mugged here."

The searching schoolteacher look returned to her eyes. "It was a random attack, wasn't it?"

To avoid answering her, Mike asked, "Did you pass anyone on the trail?"

"Two women a few hundred metres away."

"Did you see anyone running in the other direction?" he asked.

"No."

"So, you saw no one near the scene?"

Her brow wrinkled as she concentrated. "I did see a movement in the bushes as I came around the corner. Something drew my eye to the trees, not—not Lisette." She stumbled over the words, then turned her head toward the removal crew that was wheeling the body across the field.

Mike followed her movements and wondered about her thoughts. He noted Constable Harding trailing behind the gurney, following proper procedure by keeping Lisette in sight until her body was locked up at the M.E.'s office. Maybe that young constable did have the makings of a good cop.

"I saw Lisette after that," Beth McKinney said. "I saw that movement first. It was someone wearing brown or grey clothing heading west along the hiking trail."

Mike looked in the direction she pointed. The hiking trail was a dirt path paralleling the asphalt-covered jogging trail and was used by nature lovers who braved insect pests and wild mountain bikes in their attempt to experience wilderness.

"I can't tell you more than that." She raised her shoulders and shook her head as if trying to clear it. "I can't think anymore. Can I go now?"

"A couple more questions before an officer drives you to the station so you can give a formal statement." As an after thought, he added, "We'll need to send your clothes to the lab."

Mike watched her look down at the blood smeared over the front of her jogging suit. The final tinge of colour drained from her face. She swayed slightly. He placed his hand on her shoulder to steady her. Damn, he couldn't have her passing out. In an attempt to distract her, he asked, "How was Mrs. Dorrien lying when you found her?"

"She had pulled her legs up against her chest, like a child with a stomach ache. I turned her over to see what . . she was still alive . . I wanted to help." Her voice rose, as the words spilled from her mouth.

Mike watched as the self-control that she had kept in reserve evaporated. She'd given him more than he had hoped for. Now if only she could identify Dorrien as being the man she'd seen in the park, half his job would be done.

"You couldn't do anything more for her, Ms. McKinney," he assured her as he replaced his notebook in his pocket. "You couldn't have stopped what happened here." Not like the others he blamed, himself included.

"Maybe I could have . . ."

"No, don't think that way. Where do you work? I'll notify them that you won't be back this afternoon." He hoped to distract her, give her time to regain her composure before they faced the gauntlet of media on their way to the station.

She straightened her shoulders and looked at him with a gleam of defiance. "I work evenings so I'll phone the Library later."

Mike studied her more closely. A librarian. That fit with what he'd seen of her reserve, her quiet demeanour, and even her blasé navy outfit.

"Please, I really must leave."

Life wasn't that easy. Though he was satisfied that he had explored every nuance of the information she held, she still had to write and sign a formal statement.

Mike sent a constable to Ms. McKinney's home to get another set of clothing to replace what she was wearing. Not that he remotely believed her responsible for Lisette's murder, but he would not let any possible lead go unexplored. No defence attorney would accuse him of focusing on one suspect to the exclusion of all others.

Finally, the formalities were finished. Mike accompanied Beth to the lobby where Hendrick Domke and his dog waited for her. Hendrick took her arm and guided her toward the door, but he stopped when Mike pointed at the street. It was lined with media vultures ready to descend on anyone connected with the story.

"I've asked Constable Harding to give you a ride home," he said. "Avoid talking to the media if you can."

Mike watched the couple follow the constable to a nearby patrol car and slide into the vehicle's back seat. They ignored the questions the press yelled at them.

Mike hoped Evan had had more luck with Mr. Domke. Like maybe, he was able to identify the assailant. Ms. McKinney had helped by providing Lisette's last words and setting the time of death. Not small details, but insufficient for a conviction, especially since she hadn't picked Dorrien out of the photo array. Without that id, her help amounted to nothing.

Even more depressing was the fact that according to her Lisette was happily married and at peace with the world. Had Lisette fooled Ms. McKinney or was she lying and maybe even involved?

*****

Beth felt the reporters' foolish questions battering against the fog that cloaked her emotions. Thoughts and fragments of thoughts chased each other through her mind, like children playing tag. First one leading, then the other.

Chaos was threatening to overtake her composure. She couldn't wipe the sound of Lisette's last breath from her mind. The weight of Lisette's lifeless body still tugged at her arms. The remembered image of the police putting a bag over Lisette's head forced Beth to stifle a scream of protest. She raised her hands to her mouth, stilling the impulse. She couldn't break down in public; she was stronger than that.

To distract herself, she visualized the details of Detective Ceretzke's tanned face, his straight nose, and square chin. His blue eyes were outlined by tiny creases but they held a desperate, shamed look she hadn't understood. Why was he so upset by Lisette's murder? The first constable was only a kid so she could understand his discomfort, but dealing with horrendous crimes was the detective's job. It wasn't as if he knew Lisette or felt pain at her passing. On the other hand, maybe she gave police officers too little credit for having human emotions.

She forced herself to remember how his hair suited his long face, how a wave of it fell over his broad forehead softening his features, how tinges of grey crept near his ears. Mostly she recalled his mesmerizing, sexy voice. It commanded trust and understanding, but occasionally his voice had hardened and betrayed anger. Why?

She tried desperately to use the image of his slender form, handsomely encased in navy fleece as a shield against the images forcing themselves into her mind. She wanted to think of anything but Lisette's violated body. Lisette had been her friend and now she was gone so quickly, so senselessly.

Beth knew she shouldn't have avoided the detective's questions about Lisette's marriage. Problems existed between Lisette and her husband; she knew that from what Lisette had said and what she hadn't. Hints of disagreements, unexplained silences, fearful looks, but Lisette had never confirmed her suspicions. Would telling the police what she believed be a betrayal? Still, it could hardly matter because Lisette's home life could have nothing to do with this slaughter.

The crime puzzled Beth. Random killings and muggings didn't happen in Edmonton, except in the rougher, inner city areas. It was not a crime-infested big city. Only last week the paper had quoted Police Chief Horban saying the crime rate was dropping.

Of course murders happened occasionally, but they grew from gang wars or disputes between people who knew each other, fighting over the things friends and lovers fought over. Edmonton was considered a smart city, full of research facilities, with science and technology of prime importance. It was also a government town and the capital city of the province, not the kind of place where muggers stabbed joggers in the middle of the day.

Beth shuddered and huddled closer to Hendrick. Eventually the constable stopped in front of a wood-sided bungalow on a tree-lined street. Hendrick turned to Beth and squeezed her hands between his.

"You must go home and have some brandy. Brandy is the best cure for shock. Do you have someone to look after you? You could stay with Freda and me, it would be our pleasure."

"I'll be all right." Beth loosened one hand from his grip and ruffled the hair on Orff's broad back. "You look after each other."

Hendrick squeezed her hand again, then stepped from the car. Orff bounded up the front step as the door to the sun porch opened and a tall, thin woman hobbled out. She leaned heavily on her cane, shielded her eyes with her free hand, and then lowered it to greet Orff. She looked from Hendrick to the police car, then back again.

Beth realized that she had not known Hendrick was married. Recollections of the many acquaintances who had passed anonymously through her life rushed in. Had she been so busy doing the things she loved and the things that had to be done that she had made so few close friends? Now she had lost the chance to know Lisette better. Still, Lisette had been the one who prevented their friendship from developing. No, Beth admitted she could have tried harder.

She vowed to try harder with the other people in her life. She would become closer to her family. She would cultivate the multitude of acquaintances that had filled the void left when she banished Richard from her life. It was time to end her pitiful, selfish existence. If she had spent more time with Lisette, pleaded with her to confide her fears, would Lisette still be alive?

Constable Harding interrupted her thoughts. "It won't be long until you're safely home."

Beth saw concern in his eyes as he peered at her in the rear-view mirror.

"I'm sorry you have to go through this," he said.

Beth couldn't force herself to answer, to make conversation. Even the word seemed blasphemous.

"Do you have someone to stay with you?"

"Don't worry about me. I'll be all right," she answered, fearing she would never be all right again.

When they reached Beth's two-story brick house, the constable followed her up the walk, past the attached double garage to her front door. Using the key on her wristband Beth fumbled with the lock, taking a long time to open the door. She automatically checked that the alarm was active before she entered.

She looked around for any sign that the police officer had disturbed her privacy more than necessary while gathering her change of clothing. She must remember to change the security code on the front door. Beth caught the flicker of a feline bolting into the kitchen. Her poor cats hadn't appreciated a stranger visiting them while she was away.

She turned toward the officer. Why was he hovering? Lisette was dead. She wanted to be alone.

"Are you sure you don't want me to call Victim Services? They're experienced in helping people handle grief," the officer said.

"Just leave, please."

"A cup of hot tea is the best thing for shock. Just add lots of sugar."

Realizing he would linger until certain she was able to cope, Beth pulled herself together, held open the door, and smiled slightly. "Thank you for the advice. I'll do that right away," she said as she pushed him from the house.

"Take my card in case you change your mind."

When she was finally alone Beth locked the door, leaned against it, and discarded her veneer of calm. As she sank to the floor, her threatening tears turned into a flood and her shoulders heaved with sobs.

Two furred heads butted her arm, offering silent, unquestioning condolence, and sympathy. She scratched the ears of the nearest cat, Magpie, a shorthaired mongrel with black and white markings. Splatter nudged her, demanding attention. Her name came from the riot of white, orange, and black specks decorating her head and the front half of her otherwise charcoal-grey body.

By the time Beth's sobs subsided to hiccups, anger had taken firm root in her heart. She stood, dislodging the cats from her lap. She would do whatever she could to aid Lisette's children and find her murderer.

Then her tears welled again. Why hadn't she seen that man more clearly? The detective had seemed certain she could recall some detail if she tried hard enough.

CHAPTER 4

With the witnesses' statements on file, Mike felt he could follow procedure and notify Dorrien of his wife's death. Then he would reconnect with Ident before searching the Dorrien house.

"Okay Mike," Evan said, intruding on his thoughts. "Give me the story on this investigation. Why are we getting it? Who pulled strings? The armed robbery task force is taking all of our time."

Evan followed Mike as he headed down the street to his truck. Mike had managed to change from his sweats into his usual attire of sports jacket and slacks. He had also grabbed a donut from a box sitting beside the coffee machine and called it lunch.

Mike focused on pulling away from the curb, resisting the temptation to rid the world of a few of the reporters blocking his path. When he completed that task with no casualties, he answered. "The request came from the Mounties, but Chief Horban pushed it through channels."

"Right, the Chief went against his cast-in-stone policy of non-interference and assigned a specific detective to an investigation. Since when does he get involved in the daily routine of police work?"

"When the Mounties ask him to. I can't tell you a lot about what they're doing, but we can't ignore their pull in this case. Their guy, Jack Pierce, will fill us in but don't count on learning much. He's a tight-lipped SOB."

"You're stalling, Mike. So the case is important and high profile, that still doesn't tell me why it landed on us."

Mike stopped for a red light and turned to look at Evan. Partners didn't keep secrets from each other, but Lisette hadn't been a partnership deal. Still Evan had a right to know.

"We got the case because I was involved in setting up and monitoring this fragment of the total plan. Mary Carpenter called me about six months ago, before you started in Homicide. Do you know Mary?"

His partner's blank look was his answer.

"She worked for the Department for years, but it must have been before your time. After she retired, she started teaching painting and Lisette took a watercolour class from her. The Mounties uncovered the connection and asked Mary to act as a bridge. Mary was uncomfortable about the set up and insisted the city police get involved and that they use someone she knew and trusted.

"Their people talked to our people and the result was an Integrated Intelligence Unit. My role was limited to attending a few meetings and sending progress reports up the chain. Sometimes Lisette attended the meetings, mostly she didn't."

"Doesn't that eliminate you from running this investigation? Being too close and all that?"

"Not this time. I know the case background so they think I'm ahead of the game and they want this case solved yesterday, with no mention of Mountie involvement."

"So how do we handle the robbery task force as well as this murder investigation?"

The light changed and Mike shifted gears. When Evan became his partner, Mike hadn't counted on being pulled back into the business of robberies. A string convenience store robberies had started about eight months earlier, eventually the gang graduated to trust companies.

When the crime spree started it was Evan's case. In early July, they became partners and when the first robbery-related death occurred in September a task force was formed and dumped into his lap.

Most of the employees in the places they hit followed their training and handed over the money without heroics, but Martha Simpson had felt the need to defend her employer's profits. Two other fatalities had followed.

The gang didn't leave clues and now, eight months later, the task force still couldn't identify them. A couple of security videos had aired on the nightly news, but since the gang came through the door with their faces covered and their shotguns at ready there wasn't much usable tape. Two witnesses had spotted a dark van, one got a license number, but the plates were stolen.

So far, the gang had had all the luck. The task force personnel went through the motions of searching both paper and computer files for similar modus operandi and matching physical descriptions. Calls to other communities had netted them nothing but dead-ends.

About ten days ago, a customer of Harmony Trust tore the Balaclava from the head of the taller robber. That Good Samaritan now had a pulverized shoulder, though he would retain some use of his arm. His sacrifice might yet pay dividends because the surveillance camera captured the robber's face before he blasted it to pieces. It wasn't a great picture but it was the best they had.

They ran the picture in the newspapers and on TV but no valid leads had resulted. Mike hoped the gang's streak of luck would end when a Crime Stoppers' re-enactment aired in three days.

All Mike said to Evan was, "We'll manage. The Analysis Division is predicting they won't hit again for at least a week, maybe longer, and if the Crime Stoppers' video brings in leads we'll get more manpower to help us check them out."

Mike glanced at Evan. He seemed edgy. Of course catching this armed robbery crew was his priority. He was probably worried the case would lose momentum in light of a high-profile murder and he was probably right. Still they had a job to do and the faster they gathered evidence against Dorrien the sooner they could concentrate on the robberies.

"How did the interview with Mr. Domke go?" Mike asked.

"He's sharp, but he arrived too late to help us. What about Ms. McKinney, does she know anything?"

"Lisette was alive when Beth McKinney found her."

"And," Evan prompted.

"The McKinney woman claims Lisette spoke before she died, said 'Fun time Howard'. I don't know what it means. She claims she doesn't either, but maybe Lisette knew the guy. The husband knew Lisette was an RCMP informant, so maybe he arranged for this Howard to kill her." Mike shrugged, his hands never leaving the steering wheel. "Or maybe he killed her himself and she was rambling. My money's on Hugh doing the job himself. That scene yelled of close-up, personal anger. A professional would have handled it differently."

Evan's eyebrows rose. "Can we get a warrant to arrest the husband? If your Mountie friend testifies to motive, Dorrien will probably plead guilty."

"Yeah, right. I doubt they'll let us blow their investigation before they get enough evidence to put Dorrien's boss, Karlek, away forever."

"But, this is a murder."

"That's our problem and we'll get him using solid evidence and correct procedure. Just don't count on help from our Mountie friends."

Mike agreed with Evan. The evidence was clear and he wanted to act as fast as he could. Hell, he understood the need for caution, but he hated delaying justice. Lisette had been a good kid, maybe she needed more backbone but he'd liked her and she'd played Jack's game. The least the Mounties could do was to help prosecute her killer.

Evan interrupted his thoughts. "Did Ms. McKinney give you anything else?"

Mike pulled himself taller in the driver's seat. "Apparently, when she approached the site she saw a movement in the bush. That's what drew her attention to the body."

"The assailant? Do you think she can identify him? If she picks the husband out of a line-up, we're almost guaranteed a conviction."

"I tried, no luck with Hugh's picture. Ms. McKinney was more than a hundred metres away and the trees provided cover so the chances of getting a positive ID were small."

"Should we keep an eye on her? After all, if she saw him he might have seen her and if he knows she and Lisette met regularly he might think she was Lisette's police contact."

"Damn, you're right. I was wondering what they talked about, hoping it would help our case, but I must be getting sloppy not to consider Hugh's reaction. If he's worried . . call Communications, get a car assigned to her house."

Evan finished the call just as another came over the radio. The Shotgun Gang had struck again. This time they'd hit the Guardian Trust Branch on the city's north side, so much for projections and analysis.

"I'll drop you at the trust company," Mike said, "then I'll talk to Dorrien, check back at the scene, and pick up the warrant. We can compare notes later."

*****

Hugh Dorrien's office filled the 20th floor of a brass and glass office tower on Jasper Avenue. The sign on the oak door read Cross-Canada Realty Management. Thick broadloom, modular workstations, and richly upholstered visitor seating testified to Dorrien's business success.

The young, front-line receptionist efficiently referred him to Dorrien's tight-lipped personal assistant, Tony Bendall. Bendall dressed in tailored clothes, wore his hair in a close-cropped cut, and manicured his nails. He wasn't as tall as Mike and was slimmer, but he was not a small man. He was someone a witness would describe as average everything, unless they got on the receiving end of his cold stare.

"It's important I talk to Mr. Dorrien immediately," Mike said.

"You don't have an appointment." Tony Bendall waved his hand, dismissing the badge Mike displayed. "He's got important meetings all day, maybe I can fit you in tomorrow morning." Then he peered at Mike through squinted eyes as though trying to read him. "Why should you get special treatment?"

Mike unclenched his jaw, refusing to let this fancy thug annoy him. He wasn't in the mood to put up with attitude; he had things to do and this was just a stop to say they'd notified the husband. He planned on playing this investigation strictly by the rules.

"This involves his wife."

Tony gave him an 'Oh Yeah' look, but punched the intercom button. "Mr. Dorrien, there's a Detective Ceretzke out here insisting he has to talk to you. He says it's about Mrs. Dorrien."

The expression on Tony's face turned sour as he listened then hung up the receiver. With cool disdain, Tony led the way to an ornate, double door. He knocked once before opening it to allow Mike entrance.

Hugh Dorrien advanced across a wheat-coloured carpet, his smile frozen in place. "What's this about Lisette?" He looked at his watch. "I have an important meeting in a few minutes."

"I've been told."

It was the first time Mike had seen Hugh Dorrien in person. He had grown a boxcar moustache and his broad face wore more wrinkles than the photos revealed. Of course, those pictures were publicity shots taken during his days in professional hockey.

"Please sit down, Mr. Dorrien. I'm afraid I have bad news."

"Look, what's the problem." Dorrien remained standing.

"Your wife has been hurt."

"What's happened?" He glared into Mike's eyes without blinking.

"Sir, I'm sorry to inform you that she was seriously injured earlier today."

"How? How bad?"

"She died as a result of her injuries."

Dorrien stumbled as he stepped backward, attempting to support himself against the edge of the mahogany desk that stood just out of his reach.

"How—was it a car accident?"

"No, sir. She was stabbed while jogging."

Hugh gripped the desktop, his knuckles turning white. "She was mugged? Do you have any idea who did it? Any witnesses?"

Mike noted his clenched teeth, the tremble in his voice. Dorrien was a good actor, though maybe a bit heavy on the shock. He pulled his notebook from his jacket pocket and flipped to an empty page as he cautioned himself not to jump to conclusions that might prejudice the case. He didn't want Dorrien falling through cracks created by sloppy police work or by ignoring common sense.

Hugh demanded, "How do you know the victim is Lisette?"

"We have a witness who knew her."

"Who?"

Mike pretended to refer to his notes while studying Dorrien. "A woman she often met in the park." Then he added silently, and a RCMP sergeant and me. We all knew her, maybe better than you did.

When Dorrien didn't volunteer a response, Mike resigned himself to digging. "What can you tell me about your wife's routine?"

A single knock echoed through the room as Tony opened the door. "Mr. Carruthers is waiting."

It wasn't subtle but then it wasn't supposed to be. Hugh continued gripping his desk. He seemed to have aged years in those brief moments.

Tony Bendall asked, "What's wrong?"

Hugh ran his large hand over his face and stroked his luxuriant moustache. "Lisette is dead."

The knuckles of Tony's hand tightened around the door handle. "Killed by some damn mugger on that damn run of hers."

Though still pale, Hugh turned toward Mike and cleared his throat before speaking. "Detective, I may sound callous but Mr. Carruthers is not a patient man and this appointment is too important for me to miss. Can you come by the house later?"

"We will be searching your house today."

"Why? What for?"

"Her desk calendar or a diary to see if there's any indication she planned to meet someone, or letters that might help us identify her killer." Mike studied Hugh's strained face then swept his gaze over his pinstriped suit, neatly knotted necktie, and polished shoes. Dorrien must have a pile of bloody clothes hidden somewhere.

"I thought you said she was mugged."

"We do have to check all possibilities, sir."

"Of course, Tony will supervise. He'll be available within the hour." Hugh Dorrien turned away, his hands clasped, his stare focused out the window.

Mike brushed past Tony and walked through the outer office, noting a corpulent middle-aged man, perhaps the impatient Mr. Carruthers, pacing. A second man, carrying a briefcase that looked like real leather and wearing the complacent expression of someone getting paid for every minute he waited, flanked him.

Mike acknowledged their presence and left the office. Then he ducked into the men's room to avoid meeting the camera crew that was rushing in the direction he'd just left.

The vultures were descending.

Dorrien's quick permission to search the house worried him. It probably meant he had left nothing for them to find. Of course, Dorrien knew his permission made no difference, because Mike could easily get a warrant. Before filling out the details on the warrant request, he would check back at the crime scene to see if Ident could suggest any additional items.

When he arrived at the park, the taped area was still surrounded by civilians interested in the workings of the investigation and media types looking for lurid details to colour their next release. Mike parked on a side street and cut across the grass, thus avoiding the reporters.

"Pete," Mike said, as he approached the crime scene investigator, a middle-aged man bent in a permanent stoop.

Pete Humphries was picking through leaves and bits of debris in the roped-off area. Eventually, he peered up at Mike and asked, "You in charge?"

"Yes. Have you found anything?"

"Nothing close to the body except the knife. A kitchen knife with a long, wide blade. It did lots of damage." He held up a plastic bag containing an eight-inch chef's knife.

Mike recognized the brand by its moulded black handle and the bright red dot located just above the blade.

"Took samples of the soil and vegetation but there's not much physical evidence. We've got the photos, measurements, and sketches. Shouldn't be much longer."

"It's possible the assailant used the hiking trail to approach the site. A witness saw some movement as she came around the bend. Do you mind if I check it out?"

Pete squinted at Mike, then shrugged. "On a walking trail it's unlikely you'll find anything usable, but yell if you do. They're forecasting snow by the weekend and we don't want to lose any evidence."

Mike's answering grin was more of a grimace. Pete would double-check the scene himself but Mike appreciated him not saying so. Anyway, he planned on being very thorough. Putting Hugh Dorrien away for Lisette's murder was the minimum that he owed her.

Standing on the asphalt path, Mike surveyed the scrub brush covering the slope leading to the river's edge. Poplar, larch, and pine grew in this stretch of parkland. The trees were spaced a couple of metres apart with chokecherry and wild rose bushes filling the gaps. Long grasses, dry with the arrival of fall and its nightly frosts, tangled the undergrowth. A covering of leaves also hampered his search.

Pete was right, he couldn't hope to find anything. Still Mike pushed through the undergrowth and downhill to the trail. It would have been easy for Hugh to hide in the thick shrubbery behind the lookout. When no one was in sight he could have darted out, covered Lisette's mouth, and stabbed her.

Mike wiped his hand across his face, but the image of Lisette's mutilated body did not vanish. Damn, if she was going to name someone, why not Hugh?

He scanned the packed soil of the path. Tracks showed the traffic of dogs, birds, and humans. Some prints were clear, others were scuffed, some were deep, and others barely visible. Near the edge of the trail he spotted the imprint of a smooth sole, no jogging shoe or hiking boot had made that print. Mike searched in both directions but found no other prints that matched. He trudged up the hill and over to the Ident man.

"Pete, I've found a print."

Pete looked up from his meticulous chore. "A dirt trail is full of them." His voice was heavy with sarcasm.

"The others are going somewhere. This is a single and it's clear; it's just off the main part of the trail in the loose dust and it's from a dress shoe, not one with tread."

Pete's face broke into a wide grin. "You're learning. I'll be right there."

Mike showed Pete the print and watched as the crew photographed the evidence and readied the mix to make a cast. Then he shoved his hands in his jacket pockets and started toward the street that was vacant except for the Ident van, a police car and, in the distance, his black truck.

He waited until he'd reached the privacy of his vehicle then punched a number into his cell phone. The phone rang twice before a bored voice said 'Royal Canadian Mounted Police' in English and French. Then Mike spent more minutes waiting for the switchboard operator to connect Sgt. Pierce.

"When are we going to talk about this case, Jack?"

"When you get concrete information to pass to the unit."

"Unless I find some hard evidence at her house, we'll need your informant's testimony to guarantee a conviction."

"You're searching the house?"

"As soon as I pick up the warrant. Maybe she left you a letter, one that incriminates Hugh."

Jack remained silent, ignoring his quip, or maybe taking his sarcasm as a serious possibility.

"We've got a shoe print, so I'm noting a pair of shoes on the warrant. Ident is hoping for a match on the weapon. Bloody clothes are too much to hope for, but I'll list them."

"Don't mess with anything that might affect my case and don't go picking through Dorrien's stuff. Call me when you're done."

The phone went dead in Mike's hand. He punched the disconnect button with his thumb and muttered a few words about bureaucrats as he pulled the truck away from the curb.

Mike picked up the search warrant with no fuss or delay, then detoured to collect Evan.

The Dorrien residence was situated on Peacefield Boulevard, in a district bordering the North Saskatchewan River. The area had been elegant about eighty years earlier, when Edmonton was new and expanding rapidly. Most of the original homes still stood and the area retained the indefinable atmosphere of old money.

The house was white with black shutters and one story taller than its neighbours. Doric columns supported a deck that ran the length of the second floor and stretched to the roof. Carvings decorated its façade and at one end of the yard, a gazebo added a touch of old world elegance.

Tony opened the lead-glass door, looked over the warrant Mike handed him, then stood back as the officers trooped into the house. The detectives separated. Mike headed upstairs to the bedrooms. Evan opted to stay on the main floor. Two constables climbed to the third.

Instead of the delicate pastels and feminine ruffles Mike figured would reflect Lisette's taste, her bedroom vibrated with raspberry red and forest green.

Moving to the armoire, Mike systematically searched through the untidy piles of silk underclothes, wool sweaters, and pastel scarves. He checked corners and felt under drawers for hidden paper.

"I thought you wanted her appointment book," Tony said.

Mike ignored his interruption. He checked each item of designer clothing, pulled spare change and odd bits of jewellery from pockets, then carefully replaced them when he found nothing of interest.

"Where are Mr. Dorrien's clothes?"

"They have separate rooms. Mr. Dorrien's is through there." He waved toward a closed door.

Mike nodded, then continued searching Lisette's room. A roll-top desk faced a floor-to-ceiling window. He walked toward it, noting the panoramic view of the river valley. He rummaged through desk drawers, hunting a diary or a calendar, but found nothing. Her purse contained an address book and folded inside its pages was a scrap of paper that read 'I've found it, let's meet. Usual time. Usual place. J.H.'.

Mike turned toward the hovering aide. "Do you know anyone with the initials J.H.?"

"No. Let me see that." The assistant grabbed at the note.

"Sorry," Mike said as he returned the note to the purse and flipped the pages of the address book to the H's. No J.H., no Howard, just a number listed for her hairdresser.

He started toward the cream door that led to the adjoining room. Tony stepped into his path.

"You've already searched her room. Why do you want to go in there?"

"Read the warrant."

Shouldering Tony aside, Mike opened the door. Bright sunlight, alive with tiny dust specks, streamed onto a draped easel in the centre of the room. He lifted the cover that concealed an unfinished portrait of a young girl. She laughed as her swing carried her high in the air. The child resembled Lisette. Mike let the cover fall. She must be Joelle, the daughter.

The tiny sitting room was sparsely furnished in white wicker with the red and green colour scheme carrying over from Lisette's bedroom. This must have been where she painted though the only canvas in sight was the one on the easel. When he opened a large closet Mike discovered built-in racks filled with the rest of her painting gear.

Tony hovered, checking the time and examining each item as Mike finished with it.

"Is that Dorrien's room?" Mike pointed to a door opposite the doorway to Lisette's room.

"You don't have to search it."

Mike opened the door and walked into the room. It was a clone of Lisette's, with the colour scheme reversed so that the dominating colour was forest green.

When he headed toward the walk-in closet, Tony protested. "Mr. Dorrien won't like you going through his clothes."

Mike checked the shoes for signs of blood. Smooth sole; size eleven and a half; gleaming as if recently polished. He bagged a pair. Each shoe went into a separate bag and Mike added it to the small collection of evidence he'd gathered.

He pushed the clothes aside. No neat pile of bloody clothing awaited discovery.

His search of the second floor complete, Mike headed toward the stairs to the third floor. A young woman sat on the top step, with a kid on either side of her. She was reading them a story. Why hadn't she taken them for a walk or at least kept them out of the way? She looked at him, her blue eyes bold and assessing. When she lowered her gaze to the picture book, he felt dismissed.

"That's the nursery. There's none of Lisette's things in there," Tony grumbled.

Mike stepped into the room. The officers searching the nursery looked up from their task, meeting his gaze with a shrug that indicated their lack of success. Admitting defeat, they started down the stairs. The kids bent their heads back, watching wide-eyed as the officers hugged the wall to get by them. Mike noted the grin that widened the nanny's lips.

Mike found Evan in the cavernous kitchen where late afternoon sunlight gleamed off white appliances. Tony trailed the group, anxiously cataloguing their findings.

A woman, who could be cast as a walking advertisement about the dangers of eating disorders, looked up from dicing onions with a wood-handled cleaver. Her eyes were red.

Mike stepped closer. Were her tears the result of grief or the onions? He couldn't be sure.

"That's an awkward knife for the job," he said, noting its similarity to the murder weapon.

"Someone took my best knife."

"What kind of knife is that?"

A heavy sigh escaped her thin lips. "Chef's knife."

"Is it the same brand as that?" he asked, motioning toward the cleaver in her hand.

"Yeah."

"Would you show me the others in the set?"

She froze for a moment, then put the cleaver down, wiped her hands on the towel that lay next to the cutting board, and reached for a knife block. Five of its seven slots held knives. The sixth held a pair of scissors. The largest slot was empty. All the knives' handles were moulded black plastic with a red dot just above the blade, just like the one they had found near Lisette's body.

Mike stifled a satisfied grin. At least he wasn't walking away empty handed; the murder weapon had come from the victim's house. Strike out random violence.

"When did you last see the knife?"

"Last evening."

"Who could have taken it?"

Caution filled her steady gaze. "Did someone use my knife to kill her?"

"The murder weapon appears to be the same brand."

Her shoulders sagged. "Anyone."

Taking notes and nodding, Mike asked if they could search the kitchen again.

"Whatever." She returned to her dicing.

"Mr. Bendall," Evan said while searching through drawers for the knife. "There's a locked room at the end of the hall. Would you unlock it?"

"That's Mr. Dorrien's office. He's the only one with a key so you'll have to talk to him."

Evan looked at Mike. Mike frowned; he had mixed feelings of how to proceed. Damn you, Jack. How was he supposed to do a thorough job when the most likely place to find that pile of bloody clothes was off limits?

He shook his head. That warrant wouldn't cover forcing the door of Dorrien's den, but forcing it would hurt the ongoing RCMP investigation.

After completing a fruitless search for the knife, they took another for comparison. Mike then asked Tony to arrange a return visit so he could interview his prime suspect, Hugh Dorrien.

CHAPTER 5

Beth's composure had returned to normal, though tears threatened and sudden shivers still took her by surprise. The short autumn day had faded into twilight. A comforting gloom surrounded her as she sipped coffee from an oversized mug and stared through the vertical blinds covering her living room window. She had felt chilled even after her prolonged shower, so she pulled on a heavy Aryan sweater and peppercorn, corduroy slacks.

Beth remembered the day she'd met Lisette, graceful even in her eighth month of pregnancy. Her hair a glossy auburn cascade, her makeup subtle and perfect as she sat with her face turned to absorb the sun's rays.

"I hope you have found a better place," Beth said, raising her mug in a salute as her tears again threatened to overflow.

That first day, nearly three years ago, Beth had felt outclassed knowing herself to be shorter, heavier, and ordinary when compared with Lisette's museum quality beauty. The awkwardness of those first moments had been banished by Lisette's radiant smile and words of encouragement.

Soon after that meeting Lisette's daughter Joelle had been born. Two weeks later, Lisette had resumed her daily run and they'd continued meeting ever since. Running kept their bodies in shape, but the daily therapy of conversation kept their mental and emotional well being in tune.

Beth had shared Lisette's pride in her children. Lisette had glowed the day Joelle first smiled and bragged about her strength when she mastered sitting up. When her son, Jarrett, who was two years older than Joelle started riding a tricycle, Lisette had proclaimed him a natural athlete just like his father. Her bitter tone had hinted at the mixed blessing. She had also shared her worries of childhood illnesses, playground accidents, and bilingual early education.

Lisette had also confided darker moments.

Beth firmly pushed those thoughts away, choosing to bring forward only the easy memories. Lisette had been free with her advice, with her sympathy and with her humour. She had helped Beth through some bad times. Her persistence had made Beth's decision to break off with Richard easier and her patient counselling had kept the break-up permanent. Lisette's calm acceptance of fate's cruelty had kept Beth from killing Richard after he'd destroyed her parent's business by broadcasting lies. Whether he knew it or not, Richard owed Lisette his—well maybe not his life—but definitely his unmarred face. If she'd got him in her grasp before Lisette had calmed her down she would have left twin claw marks down his cheeks.

It was difficult for Beth to believe three years of summers had gone by in fifteen-minute intervals. They had never once met away from the trail, never met each other's families, never spoke on the phone. Such a strange friendship, but one that suited them both.

As Beth stared vacantly out of the window with her memory picture show running through her mind, a police car pulled to a stop in front of the narrow strip of parkland separating her home from those of her neighbours. However, it was only some moments later, when no one had emerged from the car, that her curiosity began growing. Then a Channel Six news van pulled behind the patrol car and Richard Tanner emerged.

Beth stepped away from the window hoping he hadn't seen her. Of all the reporters to send. Why hadn't Richard passed the story to someone else? He should know she would never talk to him. As he stepped from the van, the street light highlighted his sandy-blonde hair and his wide crooked smile. She felt a familiar tingle run through her. God, he was attractive, but she had grown too strong to let him weasel his way into an interview just because they'd shared a bit of the past.

Beth watched as he approached the police car and spoke briefly to the driver. He was probably playing the good old boy, pretending to be every cop's best friend. With a pat on the car roof, he turned toward her door. Chuck, his faithful cameraman, lagged behind.

They'd had fun together, the three of them. For more than a year, she had helped them with in-depth research about weird and wonderful topics. They had searched out people and their secrets, tracked down shady business ventures, and delved into the history of local characters. At least while she'd been an unofficial part of their team, Richard hadn't destroyed any innocent reputations. That was over, she reminded herself through her growing anger. She didn't need his kind of reporting again. She had learned first-hand how it hurt people.

Beth watched him study her home. He was undoubtedly comparing it to the one they had dreamed of owning together and she knew it stood up to the comparison. She had bought it a year after they'd parted ways, thanks to a risky but lucrative stock deal. The kind of deal Richard had always scorned.

She watched as he prowled, searching the windows for signs of life. He carelessly tromped through the flowerbeds edging the sidewalk. Fortunately, she had stripped the beds of their annual flowers leaving only mulched perennials and trimmed bushes for him to trample. He stood back and peered at the full height of the twelve-foot cedar guarding the nook where the garage joined the main house. Then his gaze drifted to the security camera mounted above the front door.

The angled, vertical blinds and the dark house hid her from his view. She ignored the ringing doorbell and his insistent pounding. He called her name into the intercom and stared soulfully at the security camera but she remained motionless.

The phone rang and reflex made her pick it up. She cursed under her breath when she saw Chuck's gaze focus on her movement.

He nodded his head in greeting but didn't alert Richard to her presence. Chuck was too good to be stuck with Richard. She had often told him he should find another reporter to work with but you had to admit the man was loyal.

Beth stepped further into the shadowy room. She wasn't really hiding from Richard. Him, she could tell to drop dead, preferably in a den of man-eating lions so that no fragment of him would be left to pollute the earth, but if he knew she was inside so would the other reporters and then she would never find peace.

Detective Ceretzke's deep, melodic voice flowed from the telephone, dispelling her rationalizations. "Miss McKinney, Detective Ceretzke here. I have assigned a car to watch your house. It's just a precaution, so don't be alarmed by their presence."

"They're already here, so is a Channel Six news van. I know the reporters are just doing their jobs, but I wish they would stay away."

"Others will be there before long and it may be a while before they give up. Lisette's husband, Hugh, is famous enough for them to turn this into headline news."

Beth's stomach tightened. Reporters needed only a drop in the way of facts to turn a story into a front-page splash and even the tiniest of ripples endangered innocent bystanders.

"Is it okay if I stop by now? I want to ask you a couple more questions."

"If you must."

"Just a suggestion—don't talk to the reporters until I get there."

"I don't intend to talk to them at all."

"Good. I'll be around in a few minutes."

Two more news vans pulled to a stop in front of the house. Beth watched as Richard glanced at the street and shrugged in resignation. Her breathing tightened when he motioned to Chuck and started speaking into his microphone. Eventually, he signalled Chuck to stop shooting and turned to meet the competition.

Beth shivered. Maybe she was wrong, maybe she should have talked to him and made sure he got the facts right this time. Still, she had thought he had the facts right two years earlier.

*****

Mike pulled his truck to the curb across from the patrol car and stepped out. Reporters had taken over the lawn, some presenting facts to their cameramen, others talking amongst themselves. When they saw him, they rushed his vehicle scavenging for details to spread during their next broadcast.

He crossed the road to speak to the Hilda Carstairs, the constable assigned to watch Beth McKinney. She was a ten-year veteran he had worked with for a short stretch just before making detective.

Hilda rested her arm on the hood of the car, relaxed but alert. She looked tired; he'd heard she was recently divorced and that her kids were in their teens, a combination designed as an endurance test for any parent.

The constable nodded toward the media flocking in their direction. "Are they who I'm protecting her from? They're the only company she's had since I got here and she won't let them in."

"Glad to see you, Hilda. You're working this turf now?"

"For the past three months. Community policing is a pleasant change because I get to know the people in the area, not just cops and bad guys. What's this about? Is there any danger to her?"

"It could turn into a situation so don't be shy about calling for backup." He wasn't worried she would do otherwise because she was a level headed, cautious cop, the kind with lots of reasons to stay healthy. He stepped away from the car.

"I'm going to talk to Ms. McKinney, if I can get through these reporters." He stepped toward the microphones, camera lenses, and demanding voices.

"Do you have any leads?" . . "Did Ms. McKinney see the assailant?" . . "How did Mr. Dorrien take the news?"

"The department will issue a statement in its own time. You people know that so stop hassling Ms. McKinney. Give her a break."

"Detective, just one thing."

Something in the voice made Mike stop and look over his shoulder. Tanner's tooth-plus smile greeted him.

"Tanner, I didn't figure you'd be circling this story. Do you think it's big enough to help you up the ladder or do you just need a change from taking pot-shots at me about the Shotgun Gang?"

Richard took Mike's arm in an attempt to lead him away from the other reporters.

Mike refused to budge. Tanner lowered his voice and asked, "Off the record, is there any truth to the rumour that the RCMP is involved in this case?"

Mike, unable to keep his face expressionless, turned his shock into a lopsided grin and shook his head. He hoped Tanner would think he was amused but his mind was whirling. How the hell did he find that out! Tanner always knew too much and long before anyone else. Speculation around the department was that he had an inside source.

"Where do you people get this kind of information?" he asked. Then he stalked away with the news people dogging him to the house.

Beth stood behind the door as she opened it. Mike figured she was hoping the shadows would help her avoid the photographers. He knew it wouldn't work because those guys could take pictures at any angle and by candlelight.

As she shut the door, she asked, "How long do you think they'll be outside?"

"They want to get something new for tonight's broadcast. If you don't talk to them, they'll have to try someone else. Have they been bothering you on the phone too?"

"I turned the ringer off after you called."

Her flustered look made him realize he was leaning toward her, memorizing every detail of her face, trying to get behind her public mask to see what made her tick. He pulled back, shaken by his own intensity. "You seem to be an old hand at handling reporters," he said, searching for the words to put her at ease.

"I've learned that what you tell the media and what they report is the difference between fiction and non-fiction. I try not to talk to them anymore."

He waited, expecting her to elaborate instead she motioned him toward the living room. An oversized, sectional sofa and complimenting chairs in mauve and blue crowded between oak tables. Massive ceramic lamps and colourfully painted clay plant pots filled the room with warmth. A blue-grey carpet spread across the floor. A fieldstone fireplace filled the length of one wall; the other was covered with textured wallpaper. Blue window coverings completed the homey space.

His imagination conjured quiet nights listening to music and snuggling in front of the fireplace. The room reflected her air of efficiency, quality, and solid character. Mike ran his hand over the sofa back. Who shared this room with her? A feline body rubbed against his leg in answer to his thought.

"Can I offer you a cup of coffee?" Her question pulled his attention back to the case.

"Sure can," he said, bending to stroke the cat's black, furry head.

He followed her through the foyer and down a short hall to the kitchen. She flipped on the hall light. Mike used the opportunity to check out the rooms they passed. The cat walked beside him, pausing whenever he did. Down the hall from the living room she had an office, complete with an oak desk and a high-tech computer set-up. One wall was covered in shelving that was filled with books whose titles contained the words 'programming', 'investment', and 'money market'. Flanking the desk was a closed cabinet.

Poking his head into the doorway, Mike commented, "That looks like some set-up, just like one I saw in a magazine last week."

"It's my latest toy. The best on the market when I bought it six months ago and it's already dated."

Mike's knowledge of computers was limited to the basics needed to write up his reports and the phone number to call if things didn't go well, but he muttered encouragement to keep her talking. He wanted to know more about her.

"You must really be into computers to justify that kind of cash layout." He noted the extensive hardware, custom-outfitted desk, and the ergonomic chair. What kind of money did librarians make?

Mike saw the muscles in her neck tighten and her shoulders rise and wasn't surprised when she turned and asked, "What do my spending habits have to do with Lisette's murder?"

Her back remained rigid as she continued down the short hall to her kitchen. The room wore the intimate atmosphere that semi-darkness provided, until she flipped on the overhead light and lemon yellow and white flashed from every polished surface.

She glared at him over her shoulder as she opened the white-laminate cupboard and reached for a mug. "You said you wanted to ask more questions?"

Mike closed the blinds on the door leading to the deck, blocking out inquisitive cameras. His comment must have hit a nerve. He would have to watch her touchiness, as there was no point in alienating witnesses, especially good-looking ones.

"Tell me what Lisette, Mrs. Dorrien, told you. Don't worry about whether it relates to her death or whether you think it's important. What did she say about her family, her friends, and her husband's friends? I need details."

"Why?" Her hand shook as she poured his coffee.

"Maybe she said something that can lead us to her killer." Mike took the cup from her. It wasn't a lie, just not the entire truth.

Beth's shoulders sagged and she chewed her bottom lip. "I doubt I can be of much help, but I'll try. We met in the park in running weather. In winter I cross-country ski on the trails, but Lisette runs on an indoor track and spends every January in the south cruising and enjoying health spas. She was fanatical about keeping her body firm. Lisette didn't have an ounce of fat on her. I told her she was perfect, but . . . "

Beth blew her nose, then pointed him in the direction of the breakfast nook. Mike pulled out a chair, startling a grey feline. It leapt to the table, over a chair back and down the hall, surprising the larger black and white cat into similar action.

Ignoring their boisterous game of tag, Beth brushed her hand across her eyes and turned to look toward the window. Mike let his gaze take in the spotless kitchen counters, empty except for a pot of herbs growing among a clutter of small appliances.

The room reflected quality and that translated, in Mike's mind, to a high price tag.

"Why would anyone hurt Lisette?" Beth asked. "There's so much violence in the world, too few good people."

"Was Lisette one of the good people?"

"She tried to be, that's all any of us can do. Her life wasn't easy. Her dad died when she was a kid and her mother collected new boyfriends every other week. When Hugh Dorrien came along, a famous hockey player, ex-player by that time, he offered her an escape."

Running his hand through his hair, Mike asked, "Did she ever mention anyone who might want to hurt her? Family, business associates, anyone?"

"No."

Beth stopped speaking for another long minute, then as Mike was about to ask another question, she added, "Her mother is dead. She has a sister, Odile, who lives in Paris. But Odile hasn't visited since Hugh was transferred here about three years ago." Looking intently into her coffee, Beth murmured, "Lisette has two kids, Jarrett and Joelle, what are they going to do now?"

Mike sipped the coffee. It was strong with a dark, bold flavour, just the way he liked it. He took a second sip knowing he couldn't let himself think about those kids, yet. Once Hugh was locked up, he'd figure out some way to help them. Right now, he had other concerns.

"Did she mention if her husband was upset lately even about small things? Her friends? The classes she took? Her painting?"

"You know a lot about her."

Mike took time to savour another swallow of coffee while he weighed what he could legitimately claim to know about Lisette from today's investigation. "She has an easel at her house. Did I assume incorrectly?"

"No, you're right."

Everything about Beth's face tightened with distrust. The lines at her eyes and mouth deepened, her lips puckered. Her schoolteacher-look reappeared. Why was she suspicious that he knew details of Lisette's life? This was a murder investigation, he was supposed to know everything about the victim.

After a long pause, she said, "Lisette did take painting classes. Her husband didn't want her having a career so she found other ways to fill her time, but mostly she kept to herself. She wasn't happy about much in her life except her kids. She lit up from the inside when she talked about them. I never met them. She promised to bring them to the park one day, but she never did."

Beth sipped her coffee. The multi-coloured cat sprang to the counter, to the fridge top, and to the top of her cupboards. After a triumphant look in their direction, it began its grooming ritual.

When the pause in conversation dragged on for too long, Mike prompted her. "What else did you talk about?"

"We talked about problems, sometimes offering suggestions, sometimes just listening. I work in a library, the financial reference section, so sometimes the topic was my day at work."

"Were there other men in her life?"

"Lisette was married. They weren't happy one hundred percent of the time, but she swore they were okay. He is a lot older than her."

The cat stretched, then peered down at him as if judging its chances of landing on his shoulder. Mike tried to ignore it. Why was she evading his questions? She wasn't giving him anything he didn't already know. He had to push harder.

"Is that all? What about a boyfriend or business associates of Hugh's or relatives? Anyone named Howard or with the initials J.H.?"

Beth seemed deep in thought as she stared into the depths of her coffee mug, finally she raised her head, and met his stare.

"This wasn't a random mugging was it? You think her husband wanted to harm her."

"Maybe."

"She said Howard, not Hugh, so you're looking in the wrong direction."

"Are you sure you heard correctly?"

"Yes. Her words were very clear." Beth paused again, looked away then finally raised her gaze to meet his, and added, "Still, if it was someone she knew, it might be her boyfriend."

Mike felt some of the tension drain from his shoulders. Finally. Mike waited for her to continue. When she didn't he asked, "What can you tell me about him?"

"The first time he came up in conversation was last spring. We were at the lookout when she made some comment about meeting him for lunch. She never mentioned him by name, so his name could be Howard. And she wouldn't give me details, just said if she disappeared it was because she'd run away with him."

"That's all? No hints about what he looked like or where he lived or worked?" Mike squeezed his shoulder muscles, trying to release the tension that had returned double-strength. Lisette shouldn't have even revealed that much! Jack should warn his informants to forego giving their friends hints. He looked into Beth's eyes. Had she told Hugh about Lisette's planned escape?

"She said nothing else about him. Look, I've told you what I know, maybe more than I should have." She pushed her chair away from the table.

Mike didn't follow her example. She might want the interview to be over, but he felt certain she knew more and he planned on finding out what it was. Still, he sensed the more he pushed her, the less she would tell. Maybe if he tried another tact?

"You can help us by not telling anyone what she said before she died or about the boyfriend. Those are details I want kept out of the news."

He waited for her nod of agreement and then asked, "Would you come back to the lookout with me so that we can ascertain exactly what you saw, try to establish where the person you saw stood, and how clearly you saw him? Tomorrow morning would be best. I could pick you up around ten."

She shivered, then said, "Of course I'll help, Lisette died in my arms. But I have commitments until ten-thirty, eleven will be better for me."

Mike headed for the door. The black and white cat followed. A thud alerted him to the descent of the multi-hued grey before it appeared beside them at the front entrance.

"I'll see you tomorrow. Try to get some rest." He looked at her ashen face and added, "Look, this could be a random assault, but I'll be checking anyone she knew named Howard and searching for possible motives."

He pulled a business card from his notebook and handed it to her. "Call if you have any concerns or if you remember anything more. A car will be outside all night."

"My security system is reliable, but thanks for the thought."

She closed the door behind him.

He stopped and looked at the security camera mounted above the door. If the system was like everything else in that house it was top of the line and expensive. How did she manage to live so well on a librarian's salary?

*****

"I should never have introduced Lisette to them. I got her killed," Mary said giving her suffering and anger full rein. "You promised they could keep her safe. I asked you to watch over her, but you swore they would do it better. You said they were the experts."

Mike raised his hands as if warding off a physical blow. "I'm sorry. Believe me, Mary, you can't be feeling any worse than I am."

"You're sorry, but she's dead." Mary turned her face away and dabbed at her eyes with her lace-trimmed handkerchief. Her tears were none of his business.

Mike reached out and pulled her close, his hand barely touching her thinning white hair through its invisible barrier of hair spray.

She pulled away, straightening her thin shoulders. She couldn't put all the blame on Mike. Jack Pierce had warned Lisette she'd be risking her husband's wrath if she worked for him. But Lisette had seen only the carrot, not the danger. She knew what her friend was risking and had tried convincing Lisette to fight for the kids in the courts, but Lisette had been adamant that the only way she could win was if Hugh was in jail. "Was it her husband? Did he find out she was informing and kill her?"

"We don't know yet. There wasn't much evidence at the scene so it could be an unrelated incident."

"And I'm Mary Queen of Scots!"

"We have to check every lead."

"But it was probably Hugh?"

Mike rubbed his neck. "The Mounties heard she was in danger so the odds of her being killed by someone else are slim."

"They knew about this and did nothing. Wait until I talk to Robert. Chief of police or not, he should have kept track of what was going on."

"Mary, the Chief only knew what was in my reports and I didn't know until it was too late."

"I told her she could trust you." Mary bit her knuckle in an attempt to keep her tears at bay. She looked at a picture on her mantle, the picture of a WWII soldier. "I'm glad Patrick didn't live to see me let a friend down so badly."

"They were ready to get her out and then pick up the kids. Jack's source claimed we had a grace period of a couple of days. It was just bad luck they acted so fast."

"Bad luck," Mary said, glaring at him. Young people didn't understand that bad luck was just stupidity compounded. "You always have put too much faith in bureaucrats. I knew that the first day I met you, when you were hanging on every word that detective uttered. If I hadn't taken you under my wing and educated you right, you'd still be in uniform."

"It was my first day on the job. What was I supposed to think, a secretary telling a senior detective he wouldn't know how to think logically if his life depended on it?"

"That detective was wrong and he was smart enough to listen to me. Smart enough not to trust the system all the time and look what happened to him."

It was an old story, one that Mary tried to mention infrequently because she rarely saw a point to boring people with her reminiscences. Mike knew this story, he knew the punch line was that the detective was now Police Chief Horban and that he still sought Mary's advice on cold cases.

"You should have learned to trust only those who proved worthy. Maybe Lisette would be alive if you hadn't convinced me the Mounties could protect her." Mary stopped the flow of condemning words. Assigning blame wasn't going to change anything.

She pointed to a watercolour of two children playing on a bank overlooking the North Saskatchewan River. "Those are Lisette's kids. She gave me that picture last Christmas and said she hoped her next Christmas would see them all free from Hugh's influence.

Mike followed her into the tiny sitting room. Mary lowered herself into her decrepit chair, then rested her chin on her knuckles, her elbow sinking into the worn brown fabric of the chair's arm. She watched as the aged sofa sagged under Mike's weight. He rested his elbows on his knees and clenched his hands.

"After so many years of being close to crime, forty-seven years with the Edmonton Police Service and the ten since as a consultant, you would think I'd listen to my own hunches. Maybe they were right to force me to retire at sixty-five. Maybe these last years were nothing more than Robert being kind to his old mentor."

Mary felt tears fighting for release, but she couldn't give way until she knew the tears were for Lisette and her children and not a sign of an old woman's self-pity.

"Mary, you've always been an asset to the force. The detectives know it. You're the best at analyzing tough files."

"That's changing, the new guys don't know me. They think I'm senile and ten years out of date and maybe they're right."

She rubbed at her eyes, letting her handkerchief absorb the dampness leaking from them. "When the Mounties asked me to contact Lisette, I should have refused to do it. But no, I was flattered by the attention and bargained away my doubts by insisting that the city police in the person of Detective Mike Ceretzke be brought into the case.

"I put the responsibility for her safety on you. That wasn't right. A person can't dodge responsibility, even when they're old."

"You trusted me to watch over her. I failed."

Mike looked concerned. He was a good friend and had tried to break the news of Lisette's death gently, now he was trying to take the blame onto himself. She felt weary and old, something she would never have admitted feeling before he came to her door. People shouldn't die when they had as much to live for as Lisette had.

Mike leaned across the ancient coffee table and reached out to take her hands. "I'm going to call your son."

She pulled away from his grasp and stood up, energy sweeping through her at his threat. "You'll do no such thing. Just because I'm not seventy anymore doesn't mean bad news will kill me. I've handled more bad news . . ."

"OK . . but I think . . ."

"No, don't think." She paced, impatient with her previous silliness. "Just let me be involved in this, let me help put Lisette to rest. Tell me about your leads, maybe you're right and this crime had nothing to do with Hugh. Maybe we can both be absolved of blame."

Mary read the relief spreading across Mike's brow. He took his responsibilities so very seriously, but she just now realized that he included her on his list of concerns. She wasn't sure she liked being anyone's responsibility.

"Well, starting with the least likely hypothesis, the woman who found her could have stabbed her and when Hendrick Domke arrived she could have pretended to have just found her. Maybe they weren't such good friends. Her home is high-priced and located in an expensive neighbourhood."

"That's not a crime."

"No, but I don't think librarians earn the kind of money that place is worth. Maybe she's tied-in with something illegal, maybe even Hugh's organization in some way. It would be a shame if she's involved because she seems like a nice person."

"Were there witnesses to her finding Lisette?"

"Not yet. Her story is that she passed a couple of women shortly before arriving at the scene. Canvassing of the regular park users will continue for the next few days, especially between eleven-thirty and twelve and if necessary, we'll be back again next Monday to catch any weekly users. We're using the media to ask anyone who was in the area to come forward.

"Did they have a personal relationship, Lisette and this woman?"

"Ms. McKinney claims they did. We'll try to verify that. Did Lisette ever mention a Beth McKinney to you?"

"Yes, she said she was one of the very few friends she had. Lisette respected her."

"Okay, that corroborates part of her story."

"Second scenario?"

"It could be random. Crime on the park trails is low, but it does happen. Of course, most assailants don't carry butcher knives that match ones missing from the victim's kitchen. That points right at Hugh."

"You're sure it's from the Dorrien house?"

"They have a set just like it, with the right knife missing. Pete's checking it out but we all know we're just going through the motions. Hugh either hired someone to kill her or did it himself. We just have to find the evidence to prove it."

Mike walked toward her current painting project propped on a sloped easel near the window. The painting portrayed the vine-covered house across the street, though the late afternoon sunbeam that emphasized the vivid colours was one of her best creations.

"I suppose her husband has an alibi?"

"He was too busy to talk to me this afternoon. I'll interview him tomorrow."

"Too busy! He must be a cold . . poor Lisette." Then Mary cleared her throat and in a louder voice asked, "The injuries." She felt a tear escape down her cheek but otherwise maintained her professional detachment.

"Multiple wounds to the chest, neck, and back and lots of defence wounds."

Mary couldn't hold her anger back any longer. The image of her beautiful Lisette marred, fighting for her life, probably terrified, was more than her self-control could take. "Damn the rules, you know he did it. Go arrest him."

"I want to, but this one needs to be played by the book. We don't want him freed on a technicality and you know he'll hire experienced lawyers."

"You're right. Unfortunately."

"When did you last see Lisette?"

"We had lunch at the Kozy Kitchen a couple of weeks ago. She seemed upset but wouldn't confide in me. She missed her art class last Thursday but that wasn't unusual."

"You didn't hear from her on the weekend?"

"She didn't leave a message if she tried reaching me. I was in Banff attending a workshop, the air bus from Calgary didn't get me back here until noon today."

Mike noted the information. "Apparently she spoke to Ms. McKinney, said something like 'Fun Time Howard'. Does that make sense to you?"

"Howard, not Hugh?"

"She was definite about that. Look, Mary, for the sake of nailing this in the courts I want to cover every angle not just Hugh. Did Lisette mention anyone named Howard to you? Maybe someone in your art class?"

"Howard Toomby is in her class. She chatted with him all the time, but he's ninety and in a wheelchair, so I don't think he counts as a suspect."

"What about someone with the initials J.H.?"

She paused to think. "Jay Howardson helps me with my larger

evening classes. I think, no I'm sure, he was involved with Lisette's class last spring and he taught that class for me during my vacation in May. But he's married and has three daughters."

"She had a note signed J.H. in her purse. It asked her to meet him."

Mary shook her head. Both Jay and Lisette were her friends. The idea of them betraying their families was inconceivable.

Then Mike asked, "Anything else you think we should check?"

"She was taking self-defence instruction at the Alberta Karate School. Perhaps your Howard is in that class."

Mike walked toward Mary and hugged her again. "Let me have Howardson's address."

"He'll be at my class tomorrow evening. Why don't you talk to him there? Get there before six-thirty, that way you won't upset his family if it's nothing." Jay had enough to worry about with all his financial problems and his wife's nagging him to finish his CPA courses. He didn't need the grief of being hauled to the station and badgered into a frustrated lump of jelly.

She knew Mike misinterpreted her concern when he said, "And you'll be there to protect him and to hear firsthand whatever he might know. Mary, you know I value your help. I'm not going to cut you out of the loop."

"I know, but I need to be involved this time. Whatever I do, it still won't be enough to atone, so call me if you need anything. Anything." Her voice remained firm as she showed him to the door.

Mike was a good detective. The best on the force in her opinion, even better than Robert Horban had been. She knew if anyone could make a solid case against Hugh Dorrien, Mike could.

*****

Mike returned to the station to check what Ident had gathered and to plot out the next day's tasks. After he talked to Dorrien, he would go after statements from the staff and any alibi witnesses

Hugh named. Mike initiated computer checks on Dorrien and his business associates. He also requested background on Beth McKinney and Hendrick Domke. Then he phoned a couple of his counterparts in nearby cities on the off chance they had similar crimes. They were routine steps but until the lab results arrived, little remained to do but talk to people and collect paper.

It was late. His day was over. It was time to recharge his batteries with a hot meal and a cold drink.

His cell phone started ringing as he walked through the door of his apartment. Pushing the door shut, Mike answered the buzz.

Without preamble Sgt. Jack Pierce said, "I discussed the problem with my boss. He says our informant is off-limits to you. We can't risk blowing our investigation of Karlek just to convict Dorrien, but we'll give you other info concerning Dorrien, just ask. In return, we expect you to find out if Lisette mentioned Hugh's business to anyone."

Mike wandered into his galley kitchen and opened the fridge. A pizza box looked out at him from an otherwise empty shelf.

"You'll give us what you have on Hugh?" Mike asked as he lifted the lid and sniffed at the pizza. Then he slid the box onto the counter. If the Mounties wouldn't let him have their informant, why would they help with information about Hugh?

"Marvin will tell you in person tomorrow morning at the meeting he scheduled with your group. He told me that if it relates to Lisette's murder we won't hold back unless it puts our source or our investigation in jeopardy."

Mike closed the fridge door hard enough to rattle the box of empty beer cans sitting on top. "What does your wonderful source say about getting her killed? 'Oops, I got the timing wrong?'"

"Waiting was my call, Mike. I made the final decision."

"You could've . . ."

"Got myself into a lot of trouble with a lot of important people, wrecked our case, alerted Dorrien to the existence of another informant, and probably have got that person killed too. I understand that Lisette's your priority, but remember why she signed on with us. It wasn't to keep crime down, kids off the street, and the world drug free. It was strictly to get herself and her kids out of a bad situation with our help and financial backing. She knew what Hugh was doing and the risk she was taking, so cut the guilt and pass the pieces around."

"You're not being fair to her."

"Of course I'm not. She was a great kid and didn't deserve to die like that, but all we can do is finish this for her. So go prove Hugh killed her and get the kids away from his influence. I'll keep using my informant to get evidence until I can arrest Hugh and Neil Karlek, and clean up a big part of the major crime in this country. Now tell me how you're going to get him."

"We've started interviewing witnesses." Mike remembered the Mounties' comprehensive databases. "Can you run a check on Ms. Beth McKinney, especially a financial check? She's living beyond her salary." He plucked a slice of three-day-old pepperoni from the pizza top. She probably wasn't stuck with toxic pizza for supper either.

"Do you think she might be linked to Hugh?"

"I doubt it but check your sources anyway. I've already started the search on our end. I'll be meeting with her at the scene tomorrow morning. How much do I tell her about the investigation?"

"The more she knows the better chance she'll slip up and say something that puts her in danger, if she's not one of them. If she is, we don't want them knowing about our case. Tell her only what's absolutely necessary. Better yet, I'll meet you and field her questions."

"That's not necessary. I can handle it."

"Sure you can Mike, but I want to help. I liked Lisette too."

"Then why didn't you save her?" he asked, as he disconnected the call without giving Pierce a chance to reply. Mike looked at the rock-hard pizza topped with suspicious meat slices, wilted peppers, and shrivelled anchovies. He closed the lid, folded the box in half, and dumped the whole thing in the garbage. A burger sounded better. A beer, better yet.

Maybe some food would help him figure out how he was supposed to convict Dorrien if the Mounties wouldn't co-operate by confirming the motive.

CHAPTER 6

"Hey Beth, wake up."

The voice seemed to come from a long distance away. But slowly as Beth focused she realized the words came from her answering machine.

"Beth, it's Jim. Are you awake?"

Peering at the glowing numbers on her clock radio, she mumbled, "Yes, I'm awake." Then she lifted the receiver of her bedside phone. "It's four-thirty in the morning. Why are you calling?"

What catastrophe would cause her younger brother to phone so early? Had some disaster occurred? Beth opened her eyes wide, her heart pounding with a sudden rush of fear.

"It's six-thirty here and I've got an early class. Besides your phone was either busy or not accepting messages last night. You made the national news and I thought I should hear the gory details before I talk to the parents on Saturday. It's my week for the call."

Lisette. Beth felt a hot rush of tears fill her eyes. How had she forgotten for even a moment?

"What did they say?"

"They reported that you're an eyewitness to a murder."

Tears of anger mixed with those of grief.

"That damn Richard! I didn't see anything but a blur."

"What's Tanner got to do with this?"

"He's a reporter and a bunch of them hung around my house all last evening, just like the vultures they are. I didn't talk to any of them."

"But there was a murder?"

"Lisette . . ." She fought through her tears as she filled him in on the details.

"And that miserable Richard Tanner had the nerve to come to you for a story?"

"Reporters have short memories and thick skins."

"Well I don't. Don't talk to him. Damn, I could kill him."

Beth heard the tightness in Jim's voice and felt her throat close.

"If it hadn't been for him and his so-called mistake, Mom and Dad would still have their fitness club and their house."

She heard condemnation in his voice. So he still blamed her for letting Richard into her life. She knew he was right. If she had never met Richard, if they had not ended up living together, and if she hadn't kicked him out, things might have unfolded differently.

Two months after they broke up he decided to do an exposé on a fitness club that had recently opened. He reported fraud and irregularities in billings. Then Richard, who prided himself on the accuracy of his facts, got the club name wrong. He'd named her parent's club instead of the offending firm. A slip he claimed, but it cost her parents their dream when customers cancelled contracts and new memberships dropped to nil.

The station issued a retraction, hidden at the end of a newscast, and paid a settlement that was too small to save the club. It was closed less than six months after it opened. Her parents sold their house to cover the remaining debts. The shattering of her lifelong dream had left Beth's mother bitter, unable to face returning to work for someone else. Her father negotiated an early retirement package with his security and alarm system company and they were now travelling, getting by on his reduced pension.

"Are you all right? Do you want one of us to come and stay with you for a few days?" Jim asked, interrupting her thoughts.

"You little brother, are about to start midterms. Margaret is busy teaching. And Myrna is far too busy raising our nieces to think of leaving. Besides, I have Splatter and Magpie for company."

"Hey, seriously, if you need anything, no problem. So, what do you want me to tell the parents?"

"Hopefully the police will have arrested the murderer by then. I think they're focusing on Lisette's husband and I told them about someone she was seeing. If they haven't arrested anyone by the time you talk to Mom and Dad, and especially if it turns out to be a random attack, please downplay the whole thing. I don't want them worrying about my safety. Now, tell me the rest of the gossip."

They reviewed school and family news until Jim had to leave for his eight o'clock class.

Beth replaced the receiver wondering why she had refused his offer of company. Maybe it was a big sister thing. The six years between her and Margaret, the next in line, had always forced her into the protector and leader role. Leaning on them now when they all had their own busy lives didn't seem right.

Sleep wouldn't return after Jim's call, so Beth dressed in her sweats and prepared to work off some of her tension. Having a personal trainer for a mother had been a plus while growing up, but her busy schedule at graduate school and then a demanding career had allowed her to rationalize getting out of shape.

When her parents closed their gym, she had bought some of their equipment knowing she would feel like a traitor if she patronized another club. If her stock market windfall had arrived in time to save the gym, she would have insisted they let her buy into their business. As it was the sale of some equipment had helped her parents without hurting their pride and today the equipment gave her a chance to exercise without running through the park. She would face that tomorrow.

Instead of lowering her aggravation level, the blaring lies broadcast during the morning news program raised it. The reporters speculated about the murder, they related public details of Lisette's life and Beth knew they would get to the gossip later. Beth added another set of repetitions to her weight training and a step-routine to her workout in a futile attempt to banish her anger.

Hugh was an important person in Edmonton's economic realm and the news reports devoted more airtime to him than they did to Lisette. One program covered every business deal and hockey goal he'd ever made. Not being a hockey fan Beth was unfamiliar with his reputation as a fighter.

Station Six showed pictures of her house and of her opening the door. Worse yet, Jim was right, Richard had reported that she'd witnessed the entire assault and hinted that she could identify Lisette's assailant. If he ever came within reach, she would strangle him. Making a sideshow of Lisette's murder was deplorable, but to tell outright lies . . She'd thought he still had some ethics. Obviously, she was wrong.

She used ten minutes of yoga deep breathing to calm herself, then switched her answering machine to a no-ring, no-message mode, showered, and dressed. Over breakfast of a bagel, an orange, and two cups of black coffee, she phoned her sisters and assured them it was all a mix-up.

She took her third cup of coffee to the computer planning to use the time before her lesson constructively. If she stopped to think, grief might catch up with her.

*****

"Jay," Sheila Howardson said, as she scanned a section of the newspaper that lay scattered across the kitchen table.

"Lisette Dorrien was killed—that real estate guy's wife—wasn't she in that art class you taught last spring?"

Jay's mug of blueberry tea slipped from his grasp. He jumped up, knocking his chair over while frantically pulling the scalding spots away from his skin. A blue stain ran across the pale, grey tabletop sinking into the sports page and dripping onto the lime green chair cushion.

Sheila grabbed a towel from beside the sink, thrust it at him, and then turned to grab a roll of paper towels.

"What's the matter with you?" She dabbed at the blue liquid. "How am I going to get these stains out of the chair?"

He held his clothes away from his body, allowing the spilled tea to cool. The damp spots clung to his thin chest. He pulled the paper across the table onto the soggy pile he'd been reading. The headline read 'Murder in Capital Park'. Beneath it was a picture of Lisette and Hugh Dorrien at a charity ball.

"Take your clothes off here. I don't want you putting them in the hamper." Sheila looked away from the mess and at her husband's pale face, then she remembered Lisette. "Is she the same person?"

He nodded and righted the chair. He unbuttoned his shirt, pulled his arms from the sleeves, and prepared to wad it into a ball. Sheila touched the gauze pad on his forearm and looked at him with a question in her eyes.

"I scraped it on the stucco when I got home last night. Just tripped and fell right against the wall. It's nothing. Lisette—dead."

"What was she like? From the picture she was beautiful."

"Yes, she was and nice too. She was very nice. Look at the time. I've got to get changed. I'll take this stuff to the cleaners. Oh, I'll be home for supper after all."

Sheila sat at the table and stared at the stains. Jay hadn't reacted that violently when his own father died suddenly.

*****

Mike Ceretzke and Evan Collins faced Sergeant Jack Pierce and Inspector Marvin Brown of the RCMP, across a metal table. Associate Superintendent Samantha Weisman sat at the head of the table, her back to the display board.

Mike looked around the room at the participants of the information-sharing meeting. So far, the sharing was one-sided. He shared; they listened. Evan had a glazed look in his eyes; his son must have kept him up half the night again. Still Mike would prefer putting his life in his partner's hands than in those of either of the RCMP officers. Evan was young and eager and he managed a daily workout. Jack Pierce looked as if he hadn't been inside a gym in years and Marvin Brown's paunch screamed desk jockey.

Sam Weisman kept herself fit. She was one of the first women Supers on the force, a sign of change that some older officers still couldn't accept. They figured her undergraduate Arts degree should have led her into social work or teaching, not police work.

Since the Mounties added nothing to Mike's information, their brainstorming session fizzled without providing new scenarios or leads. A silence that felt like failure permeated the room. The failure to co-operate freely, regardless of Jack's promise the previous night. The failure to wind-up the case quickly and the failure to put Hugh Dorrien behind bars forever.

Marvin Brown's only contribution was to tell them he wanted Hugh on his payroll, not in prison. Super Sam had scowled at his edict. Mike hoped he could trust her to quash the Mounties influence.

He felt the Super studying them, testing her options before speaking. How much co-operation was she going to offer them?

"Evan, I want you to stay with the robbery task force. That's your priority."

Mike felt a pang of regret shoot through him. Evan didn't look upset though Mike knew he wanted to work the case. Still the robberies were his baby though Mike believed they could delay the robbery investigation for a day or two.

"Mike, you and Sgt. Pierce work on the Dorrien case. Does anyone have a problem with that?"

Usually Mike respected Sam's decisions, today was the exception. He wanted Evan on the case not some over-the-hill cop. One look at Sam's closed face told Mike to forget appealing to her sense of fair play. He would just have to put aside his feelings and learn to work with Pierce.

CHAPTER 7

When the doorbell rang at ten o'clock, Beth debated answering fearing the reporters had returned for a second onslaught. After the TV reports she'd seen, she did not intend to speak to them, ever. She swivelled her chair, opened the tall cabinet beside her desk, and pressed a button to activate the front door camera. Detective Ceretzke, dressed casually in a fisherman-knit pullover and slacks was looking around her yard.

She bit her lip. Why this early arrival? Was it some tactic or had he learned something about Lisette? Maybe they had caught the guy.

Hoping she was right, Beth spoke into the microphone. "I'll be right there." Then she turned her attention to the keyboard and typed a brief message. She activated the screen-saver, dislodged Splatter from her lap, brushed at her jeans and sweatshirt in a half-hearted attempt to rid them of cat hairs, and jogged to the door.

"Detective, do you have news? Have you caught someone?"

Holding his hands up to fend off her rapid-fire questions, the detective shook his head. "Sorry, no news yet. Just thought I would drop by and pick you up so you wouldn't have to drive to the park."

"That was not necessary." Beth held back a sigh. Did all men think they could steer her life and monopolize her time? Maybe they were all like Richard. She studied Ceretzke. Something had him antsy and preoccupied. Why was he here so early? Didn't he trust her to meet him at the park? "I told you I wouldn't be available until eleven."

"When I brought Hilda coffee and donuts," he motioned in the direction of the patrol car, "she said you hadn't gone out all morning. I thought you might have cancelled your plans. Did you know your answering machine isn't taking messages?"

He bent to greet Splatter and Magpie, rubbing Magpie's head. "I recognize you from yesterday." Magpie flicked his black tail at the detective's attentions and rubbed against Beth's leg. "And you look familiar," he said turning his attention to Splatter. Always fickle, Splatter caught the scent of donuts and pawed at his fingers. She sniffed critically. When he pulled his hand back, tiny claws held it tight. He squatted and rubbed her head with his free hand. "A donut connoisseur! What's your name?" He looked up at Beth with an inquiring grin.

She stood back, allowing him access. "Meet Splatter and Magpie. Go pour yourself a coffee. I have to finish something before we can go." She waved vaguely toward her den. "I'll be only a few minutes."

Back at her computer she checked her calendar and typed, 'Sorry Janice, something came up. Can we continue tomorrow, 8:00?'

The screen typed back, 'I work tomorrow a.m. Just send the documentation and we can continue Thursday at our regular session. There's no rush on this one.'

'Will do, talk to you then.' She sent the needed information, closed the file, and exited the program. Only when the screen went black and she pushed her chair back did she notice Detective Ceretzke leaning against the doorframe, coffee mug in hand.

"I'm impressed. You really know what you're doing with that set-up."

Biting back her first retort, Beth said, "I'm finished now. Let's get this over with."

She headed out of the den and down the hall to the front door, grabbing a denim jacket from the hall closet on her way. When he looked hesitantly at his half-finished coffee, she reached for the mug.

He gulped another swallow then surrendered it and watched as she set it on the hall table in front of her collection of soapstone carvings of seals and whales.

"That's good coffee but what if the cats knock the cup over and it damages your shiny hardwood floor? I'll return the cup to the kitchen while you put on your shoes."

He was a neat freak, damn, and a good-looking one. Richard had been a neat freak and good-looking too. He had also thought a woman should look pretty, keep an immaculate house, be a perfect wife, and earn enough to allow for all the 'extra luxuries' he could ever want. What a jerk!

When the detective returned from the kitchen, she hurried him from the house. The morning air was crisp with the temperature hovering around zero degrees. Feathery, fair-weather clouds broke the blue of the sky and promised a warm afternoon. Gusts of wind ripped at the remaining leaves stripping the branches bare and readying them for their spring look. Could winter be far away?

Sunlight reflected off the shiny black truck parked behind the patrol car. It had a newly washed and polished look that reminded Beth she would have to clean her own car soon.

The detective held the door for her and said, "A car will continue patrolling the area, but someone will be back here in time to accompany you to work."

"How long do I rate this kind of attention?"

"We'll cut it to a regular drive-by patrol in a couple of days, but until then I want someone escorting you whenever you leave the house."

"I can't see why I'm in any danger."

"It doesn't hurt to take precautions, especially after those news reports aired claiming you could identify the murderer. How did the reporters get that idea anyway?"

Beth pulled the door of the big truck closed. So he thought she'd talked to a reporter. Let him. It was none of his business whether she did or not, just as long as he realized she wasn't holding anything back from him. She stared out of the vehicle's front window.

He didn't push her to answer and they drove in silence for a few blocks. From the corner of her eye, Beth studied the man beside her. He handled the vehicle well, shifting gears smoothly and keeping his concentration on the road. Even when a teenager cut them off, he responded with only quick reflexes and a show of professional skill.

"Do I pass?" he asked.

"Pardon, pass what?"

"I haven't had my driving analyzed this carefully since I got my license."

"I'm admiring your expertise."

"Driving has always been a passion of mine. It's one time I can be in total control."

"Not like in the real life of a cop? I suppose you feel adrift sometimes."

"If the case doesn't develop the way you want or the evidence for a conviction doesn't materialize, you can think no one's controlling the play. Still, when a clue falls into place and brings everything into focus it's a great feeling."

"You solve the puzzle and move onto the next one." Beth turned away from him. His answer reminded her of Richard's attitude, finish this story and onto the next. Don't think about the people whose lives are wrecked. Ceretzke was thinking about his win-lose record, not about Lisette. And she thought he cared.

"Hey, the job is more important than you make it sound, for good or bad we help shape people's futures." His tone was sharp. His words clipped.

Beth felt his rebuff had merit. She was acting as if he was Richard's clone and though there were similarities, she knew nothing about the detective. She knew she should apologize if only for her thoughts but remained silent. He turned his attention to a group of elderly walkers energetically pumping their arms as they crossed the road. He seemed to have forgotten she was in the vehicle.

They drove through Edmonton's quiet residential streets in silence until the Capital City Park came into view. It lay about halfway between two major traffic arteries with a residential street running parallel to the bike trail that ran its length. They pulled to a stop directly across from the lookout.

To break the growing silence, Beth asked, "Any luck finding a real witness?"

"Canvassing has been fruitless. Not many people are home during the day in this neighbourhood and even when someone is home the chance of them remembering a strange vehicle is slim. A lot of people park along the street and walk to the lookout to view the North Saskatchewan River. It's a favourite spot for photographers too."

Beth watched the ever larger homes flow past. Students of all types used the park's resources. She'd seen artists, photographers, and sun-tanning scholars while on her daily run. Even Lisette said she used the panoramic view of the river valley, the downtown skyline, and the river itself, as inspiration for her landscapes and as background for her portraits.

Beth noticed two uniformed officers stopping people walking through the park. "Are they canvassing for witnesses?"

"Yes. We'll keep it up for a few more days. Do you remember anything about the women you passed? Something that could help us identify them?"

"They weren't regulars, at least I don't recall seeing them before." Then after a momentary pause, she said, "They might have been photography students."

"Why?"

"There's often groups of them around and those women were carrying bags—maybe camera bags. They usually gather at the parking lot because it has a clear view to the river, but they could have hiked to the toboggan hill to get a different background for their pictures." Beth's voice faded, as her memories overwhelmed her. "Do you think they saw something?"

"They were walking toward you, away from the lookout and toward the parking lot?"

She nodded.

"That narrows the time of the assault considerably. Can you

estimate how long it would take them to get from the lookout to where you met them?"

"Five minutes at most."

"I'll have the photography classes canvassed as well." Detective Ceretzke unfastened his seat belt and opened his door.

Beth remained in the vehicle, frozen, staring across the park to where crime scene tape encircled the lookout. The police had trampled the grass and this late in the year its recovery would be slow. She closed her eyes trying to remember how the park had looked before but she only succeeded in visualizing Lisette's body sprawled on the grass.

"I know it's tough but we really do need your help." He opened her door and extended his hand.

His voice was low and held a gentleness that made her feel he understood her trepidation.

"Will the horror ever go away?"

"Catching the murderer will help."

A jolt of energy shot through Beth's arm as he took her hand and helped her from the vehicle. She straightened her shoulders, inhaled an extra deep breath, and walked across the short grass. As they approached the lookout, her breathing grew rapid. She took another deep breath and held it.

She fought against the image invading her mind. Who could have hated Lisette?

A man wearing an overcoat and fedora walked around the taped perimeter of the crime scene. He waved at them and the detective said to Beth, "Sgt. Pierce of the RCMP asked to meet us here. He may have a few questions for you."

Beth caught the resentment in his voice, though he managed to keep a welcoming smile pasted to his lips. She nodded toward the Mountie but wondered if their problems with each other were professional or personal?

Sgt. Pierce was plump, not yet fat but on his way. He peered at Beth through thick bifocals that rested midway down his large beak of a nose then extended his hand toward her.

She noted the enlarged knuckles, the cracked cuticles, and the ragged nails. Accepting his hand, she asked, "Sergeant, why are the Mounties interested in this case?"

"I'm adding it to our national crime database. It holds information on violent crimes committed all across Canada and allows us to match up outstanding cases."

"You think the attack is part of a series, that someone is prowling for victims? Are our parks turning into danger zones?"

"We'll try our best to stop it right here. Now Ms. McKinney, what can you tell us about Lisette's routine?"

Sgt. Pierce took the initiative in the questioning while Detective Ceretzke hung back, a resigned look cloaked his feelings. Beth wondered at the sudden role reversal. Just who was in charge?

The answer wasn't important to her though the spitting contest she was witnessing said the men thought otherwise. All she had to do was answer their questions and let them sort out jurisdiction.

"Lisette started her run on the north side of the river and crossed it using the freeway's pedestrian bridge," Beth said. "She liked to get the smoggy part of her run over early then run full-out through the park. There's a steep grade up from the river that gave her a challenge and got her heart pumping before the longer, flatter part of the route."

Beth felt certain they knew the park's layout and were allowing her to ramble simply to hear any details the free flow of thoughts might add to her story.

"She stopped at the lookout to stretch, then ran through the picnic area to the bike bridge and over the bridge to the north side of the river without stopping. She never went farther through the park because of the playground and pool. It was too populated to maintain her speed. Besides, dodging strollers and kids breaks your stride and concentration."

Beth grew quiet as they crossed into the cordoned-off area and walked toward the lookout. The spot where she had found Lisette jumped into sharp focus as the background blurred into shapes and colours.

She forced her mind's eye away from the memory, concentrating instead on the lookout, seeing and recording every detail of the wooden structure. The initials 'ME + SR' carved into the sturdy, cedar rail; a gouge in the pentagon shaped floor; the shiny, sweat polished railing overlooking the river valley; the three, worn steps leading down the hill to the hiking trail.

A memory flashed. That was where the man had stood.

Beth crossed the plank floor to the side facing the river valley. Gripping the rail, she rocked back and forth. The forest spread before her contained millions of tiny yellow and red flame-like leaves flickering in the breeze amid stationary spires of evergreen.

She looked straight across the river, then eastward away from the freeway and the downtown high-rises, past the golf course, to Peacefield Boulevard. That was where Lisette had lived and where her husband now controlled their children's destiny. Beth couldn't see the house from here but Lisette had once pointed out where it stood. Lisette had loved that stately mansion. Ironically, Hugh had insisted they buy it to enhance his public image.

"I think he was involved in something not quite legal—her husband, I mean."

"Why?" Sgt. Pierce asked.

"Lisette said Hugh was adamant that his public image remain beyond reproach, above suspicion was what she meant. Other times she seemed scared."

"Of her husband?"

"Yes. And of other things."

"Did she talk about him often?"

"Not often and she always seemed to regret having said anything after she did."

"What did she say about him?"

Beth released her grip on the railing and turned to sit on the wooden bench. She clasped her hands together tightly and drew them into her lap. The police officers leaned forward, notebooks in hand.

"They met in Montreal. He was an ex-hockey player and the

answer to her dreams. She was a model who was stuck in 'catalogue hell'. Those were her words. The way she put it was if you hadn't made it big by the time you were twenty-three you were over the hill in the modelling field. She met Hugh on her twenty-fourth birthday.

"Her mother pushed her and her younger sister, Odile, into modelling when they were kids. She was sure they would break into the big time. Of course, Mama just knew they would meet a rich guy who would look after them. She was partially right. Lisette got the guy and Odile the modelling career.

"After Lisette's dad died, she pushed even harder. Lisette told me that her Mother started dating again and that her dates usually had connections to the modelling business. Odile is still a model. She moved to France just before Lisette and Hugh were married. After the wedding, Lisette spent a year playing lady of the manor, spending her days in salons, lunching with friends, and shopping. Jarrett was born just before Hugh was transferred to Edmonton. Until they moved west, I think things were working in their marriage. Even when we first met they seemed okay, then she began sending signals that she was afraid."

"Did she say what she was afraid of?"

"Once we were talking about our greatest fears. She said hers was Hugh taking their children away. She seemed convinced that he hired their latest nanny to keep her away from her kids. I don't know if that was true but she never seemed to take them anywhere on her own. She always had Hugh or the nanny along."

"Was he abusive?" The Sergeant's voice took on a harsh quality.

Beth knew she hesitated too long before answering but she needed to find a middle ground between the truth, as she believed it to be, and what Lisette had told her.

"She never spoke of abuse but I wondered. In the photos I've seen he looks massive and the media said that when he played hockey he was always in the penalty box for fighting. Lisette was tall but very thin. He might have been physically threatening even without meaning to be."

Sergeant Pierce changed the topic. "Did she mention other

people, anyone she didn't get along with? Someone who might have wished her harm?"

"Not that she mentioned. No, I'd have picked up on that. She said Tony, Hugh's secretary, was a sneaky weasel who spied on her. Of course, Melissa, the nanny, was another person she couldn't tolerate. But no one who would harm her."

"Anyone else?"

"Sometimes she talked about Hugh's business associates, but as irritants, not as people she felt were threatening. They seemed to call day and night, always wanting to meet with him outside of office hours. Eventually, he had an outside entrance built so his callers wouldn't disturb her and the kids."

Beth caught the look that passed between the officers. It was the first sign of rapport they had shown.

"Did she talk about any people she might have planned to meet yesterday?"

"She only ever mentioned one friend to me, Mary Carpenter, her painting instructor. She is someone you should talk to. I think they spent lots of time together."

Then leaning against the rail, she said, "Of course there was her mystery friend but she never really talked about him." The detective's face remained expressionless but Sgt. Pierce perked up.

"Tell me about him."

"As I told Detective Ceretzke yesterday, she didn't say much. I think she met him last spring. Since then, she has made comments about being rushed and having to meet someone at lunch. She'd never had luncheon dates before."

Sergeant Pierce nodded his head solemnly and glanced at the detective with eyebrows raised.

Beth looked from one man to the other. The Mountie's reaction had been identical to the detective's. Excitement, politeness, and then diversion. Did they know something about the guy?

They worked as a team after that, hurrying her through the details of where she had stood and what she'd seen. Always demanding more impressions. Eventually they convinced her to try visualizing the scene in an attempt to coax even a single detail of the man's appearance from her.

Sgt. Pierce said, "Close your eyes. You're approaching the corner. What were your thoughts?"

"I was pushing myself but I felt good. The day was cool with a breeze, perfect for a run."

"OK. You're turning the corner. What do you see?"

Beth remembered the blue sky, the fallen leaves, the bare trees encircling the lookout.

"The rest stop but no one's there. No one's in sight at all."

"Where did you see the person?"

She wrinkled her brow in concentration. "To the right, that would be east, of the lookout."

"Let your mind take over. See the scene as clearly as you can."

"There wasn't much to see, just a flutter of colour and movement."

"How far from the lookout?"

"Maybe a metre."

"How far above the ground?"

"Above the height of the bushes and the railing, maybe a half metre above."

"Is it a jacket or a hat?"

She recalled a triangle of sunlight where the arm met the shoulder. "A jacket."

"What colour."

"It blends with the trees. Brown I think."

"Now open your eyes and see if we have it right."

Beth spotted a shape standing in the trees. Her breath caught. The detective looked familiar, far too familiar.

"Ms. McKinney, do we have the location right?" the sergeant demanded.

Beth chewed her bottom lip while debating her answer. Could she say the detective could be the man she'd seen? Somehow that seemed a bad idea but she planned on watching him closely. Very closely.

"He should move farther left. The height seems about right, so does his stance."

Two hours had passed before Sgt. Pierce left them at the vehicle and drove away.

CHAPTER 8

Beth knew the police took no pleasure in torturing her with her memories of finding Lisette, still, they had dredged deeply to find the details they needed. The detective didn't attempt to hide his scrutiny of her as they walked back to the vehicles.

When they reached the truck, he asked, "How about I buy you lunch as a thanks and an apology for the pain we've inflicted."

He must have read refusal in her expression because he added, "Hey you have to eat and having company for lunch beats a lonely sandwich at home with morbid thoughts."

Beth found herself grinning for a brief second, then she remembered Lisette. "Don't you think you should be finding the person who did this?" She waved vaguely toward the park.

"Not during lunch."

He held the door open, then circled the vehicle, and climbed in beside her. "Where would you like to go?"

A shiver ran up her back. Maybe lunch wasn't a bad idea. She could use the time and informal atmosphere to learn why he and the sergeant had reacted indifferently to the idea of Lisette meeting a mystery man. "I think I would enjoy a bowl of soup at the Kozy Kitchen," she said.

The neighbourhood restaurant specialized in homemade soup and gourmet sandwiches. The enterprising couple who owned it showed a willingness to cater to their clientele's particular tastes, a trait that was making them competitive against the encircling franchise operations.

Looking at her watch, Beth calculated the time before she was due at work. "Make it Dutch Treat." She didn't want to owe him even a lunch. "I have to be home by one-thirty so I can be ready to leave for work at two."

"I thought you worked evenings."

"Sometimes. Sometimes I work afternoons."

"Do you think you're ready to go back to work?"

"I'm ready."

The drive to the restaurant took only minutes along tree-lined streets. Forty-five years earlier, the restaurant had been a farmhouse and the subdivision had been prime agricultural land. Now the downstairs of the house held an open dining area, the upstairs a neighbourhood pub.

Simon, owner and dessert chef extraordinaire, greeted them personally. Beth often stopped at the restaurant for a quick lunch before a long shift.

Simon blinked his eyelids rapidly and smiled broadly. "I didn't know you two knew each other."

Beth couldn't think of an appropriate response. Telling him they were taking a break from investigating Lisette's murder didn't seem appropriate.

They followed him to a window table overlooking the backyard with its high fence, barbecue pit, and picnic tables. Two men sat among the falling leaves playing chess, their beer mugs and basket of pretzels within easy reach.

As Simon seated them, he said, "I was sorry to hear about your friend. Her death was a real shame."

Beth mumbled her agreement. Simon's puzzled expression seemed strange but before she could say anything, he turned to greet another customer and the waitress arrived to pour coffee.

She turned to Detective Ceretzke, prepared to comment on Simon's behaviour but he was already speaking.

"Tell me about yourself," he said, leaning toward her. He propped his chin on his fist and looked as if he was captivated at the possibility of her response.

Beth answered abruptly. "I'm just a hard-working librarian who likes to run for exercise and who buys expensive computer equipment." Her mind was only half on her reply, the other part was wondering at Simon's unusually abrupt behaviour. Maybe he was uncomfortable about death, or perhaps she was being super sensitive, or maybe there was a crisis in the kitchen and he was distracted.

"You're more than that from what I've seen."

Beth shook off her mood. Simon wasn't her problem. She was here to learn something about Detective Ceretzke and spitting and growling answers wasn't going to make conducting a probing conversation easy. His expression remained inquisitive, as if he was too interested in her answers to react to her irritability.

"Can I make some guesses about your life?"

"You're the detective." She shrugged then concentrated on unfolding her serviette. The waitress stopped long enough to take their orders and place a basket brimming with steaming breadsticks and a tray of flavoured butters, on their table.

"I would say you have a real talent for decorating."

"Wrong." She reached across the table to take a meltingly hot breadstick and slather it with garlic butter. "I hire a good decorator, ensure she knows what I want, and that what she recommends fits my lifestyle."

"Which includes furniture that can survive the occasional romp by two cats?" His voice held a hint of laughter.

"That too." She bit into the herb-flavoured breadstick. "Next guess."

"You're one great money manager."

She thought for a long moment before answering. Was there any point in fighting this invasion of her privacy? Too many databases held personal information and were easily accessible to law enforcement for her to bother delaying the inevitable. "Yes, I am. I also dabble in the stock market, successfully, and I have a business advising people on the basics of on-line investing and financial planning."

"That's what you were doing this morning?"

"Right again. The information is available but people need to learn how to access it. I also research companies and track market trends for clients."

She felt herself forgetting why she was there and paused to gauge his reaction to her comments. She knew one person's passion could bore a disinterested listener. The detective was of course a professional listener and displayed every sign of rapt attention.

"All this because you're a reference librarian?"

Beth wiped the sheen of garlic butter from her fingers. Not even a professional listener always asked diplomatic questions. She should have settled for a sandwich at home. With a pained smile, she debated flipping the questions to those pertaining to him. After all, what man could resist his favourite topic?

She decided to answer this last question, first. "No. I have a Masters in Business Administration and I am a Certified Financial Planner." She shrugged as he raised his eyebrows. "I didn't like corporate life. Now I do what I want for myself but the library job keeps me in touch with people and brings me a regular salary in the event I make a big mistake in the stock market."

"Does that happen often?"

"To me, not yet. A few small ones but I rarely gamble and I watch my stocks closely. Making money on the stock market is more hard work than luck. You have to pay attention to details like company policy and products and be aware of marketplace trends."

The waitress placed a bowl of steaming potato soup and a sandwich platter in front of each of them.

After taking a tentative taste of the soup, Ceretzke sighed as if at peace with himself and reached for a breadstick. They ate in silence for a few minutes.

" Winning with stocks is easier said than done," Ceretzke said as he buttered another breadstick.

"Did you get burned with an investment?"

"An agony of buying high and selling in panic when the prices dropped."

She nodded, recognizing the familiar pattern. "People ignore common sense when it comes to money. They forget all their planning and react at a gut level."

"Tell me about your family," he said, moving the conversation to a more personal level.

Beth decided to refuse to answer, claiming a need for privacy, but his engaging smile made her relent. "I have two sisters and a brother. Jim's at McMaster University majoring in business administration. Margaret teaches in Yellowknife and Myrna is one of that vanishing breed, a stay-at-home mom."

"Your parents?"

She wanted to scream at him to stop, but knew from experience that kind of response would only excite his curiosity. From long practice, she shortened her answer to only current, pertinent details.

"They spend the winter in Arizona."

"Do they live here in the summer?"

"They sold their house two years ago."

"Is that why you have such a big place? Is it home base for everyone?"

A home base, that sounded good, but financial security and investment potential were also valid considerations. Again, she censored her reply. "Once university ends in the spring the house fills with people. My Dad looks after the yard and Jim has a standing summer job with my old investment firm. Mom visits her friends and during school vacation my sisters come and stay awhile."

Their conversation lagged as they finished their lunches. Sitting back with refilled coffee cups, they watched the waitress bring their calorie laden, double-chocolate cheesecake dessert. Silently calculating the damage in the number of kilometres that she would have to run to wear the lunch off, Beth savoured a mouthful while the detective quickly devoured his.

"Are you a native Edmontonian, Detective?" she asked. After all, questioning him was the reason she had agreed to this lunch.

"The name's Mike. I'm a Saskatchewan farm boy who, as the story goes, left the farm for the bright lights. I taught for a few years in Saskatoon then decided that the classroom wasn't for me. I thought police work might have more action and less paperwork." He ran his hand through his hair and grinned. "I may have been wrong about that but I wasn't wrong to make the jump to police work."

"Surely there was more to the decision than that? Why not go into another field? Why police work?"

"It's a long story," he mumbled. "Maybe I'll tell you about it someday."

So, she wasn't the only one hiding facts. Why was he evading the question? She took pity on him and didn't press.

"Have you been with the Edmonton force a long time?"

"Since 1980. In 1988, I started moving through other areas of the service and in '92 I made detective. I've been in Homicide since the spring of '96."

"You like the work?"

"Parts of it. I don't like the need for it, but how did we get onto my credentials?"

"You've asked me a lot of questions today, I thought I'd return the favour."

"But my questions are necessary to the case."

"Not all of them. What do you do in your spare time?"

"I belong to some teams, basketball in winter, baseball in summer. I hit the gym whenever I can, usually about the time most people roll over for another hour of sleep. And in my non-existent spare time I help coach a kid's basketball team." He turned his palms upward, cocked his head, and smiled broadly. "Also I have no pets or houseplants. Is there anything else you would like to know?"

"You haven't mentioned your family. Do your parents still farm?"

"My brother John and his son, do most of the actual work now. In her last letter, my Mother wrote that Dad's health was failing and being closer to the doctor would be better for him. Unfortunately, they can't afford to buy a place in town unless John buys the farm and he can't get a mortgage because a couple of bad years have already pushed his credit to the limit. Dad might have to sell to someone else. It's not a great option."

Beth pondered the wisdom of giving an opinion. Financial planning might be her area of expertise but volunteering advice on family or finance was as dangerous as discussing religion or politics. Beth finished her coffee then checked her watch. "It's time I got going."

She placed her share of the bill on the table and watched with interest as he struggled to let her pay her own way. He finally accepted gracefully, earning a few positive points in her evaluation. Richard would have insisted on paying and would have pouted if she hadn't relented.

On the drive back to her house, the memory of Simon's strange condolences and hesitant greeting pushed into her consciousness.

They pulled to a stop in front of her house and the detective followed her to the door. "Let me check that everything's okay before I leave."

Beth felt uneasy. She and Lisette had never dined together at the Kozy Kitchen. Had Simon known of their friendship in some other way? She couldn't remember seeing him in the park. She followed her thoughts to the conclusion that Simon's condolences might have been for Detective Ceretzke, but that meant he had known Lisette. Why pretend they were strangers? Beth remembered how guilty he had looked when he explained away his knowledge of Lisette's painting. It was almost as if she had caught him in a lie. Until she found out what was going on she best be careful in her dealings with Detective Mike Ceretzke.

Beth stepped inside. "When the security system is operating no one gets in without triggering the alarm. Checking the house isn't necessary, but thank you for the offer."

"Still, it doesn't hurt to be careful."

"Detective." She barred his way by extending her arm to the opposite wall. "I have no intention of letting you search my house."

Reading annoyance and frustration in his tightening lips and in the lines creasing the corners of his eyes, Beth started closing the door.

"Just be careful until we arrest Lisette's murderer. I don't like those news reports saying you can ID the perpetrator."

"Good-bye, Detective." She closed the door feeling relief at being alone again, then headed for her den where she opened the cabinet by her desk and switched on the internal monitoring system. She activated the cameras in each room, looking for possible security breeches or signs of tampering.

When she was certain everything was secure, she wandered into the kitchen, wondering if Hendrick also had a police car patrolling his neighbourhood. She pulled on the fridge door, a sound that brought Magpie running. He rubbed his body against her leg. Splatter jumped onto the countertop. She took every opportunity to reach for the heights.

"OK guys, time you were fed." She petted Splatter and put her back onto the floor then praised Magpie for not jumping up.

They made a strange couple but they were her friends. Her parents had presented them to her after she refused their offer of a large dog. Dogs were great but she wasn't home enough to provide the company one needed.

As a compromise, her father had installed a fully equipped security system, the best his company sold—with a few modifications of his own—then gave her the kittens for company. She appreciated that gesture though she knew it was one they could barely afford.

CHAPTER 9

"What do you mean, you want to get rid of her? That wasn't part of our plan."

"You killed Lisette and that reporter said she saw you do it."

"We can't just go around killing people. This is getting out of control."

"Me and Jerry, we don't feel comfortable knowing someone can spot you. Shane Murphy was your man once but he's on our side now. He knows we have to protect ourselves."

"That's ridiculous. We're in this together."

"Jerry said if you got caught you might work a deal with the cops, a deal that includes us and we don't like that threat hanging around."

"The police will be watching her; I can't risk getting close."

Nick Fortain's gaze darted from side to side, checking each of the food kiosks in the shopping centre courtyard. Students from the neighbouring high school surged in, talking in loud voices, their words lost in the general uproar. Office workers scanned the packed tables, shook their heads at the lack of space, and ordered their lunches to go.

"Don't worry. We already took steps." Nick shrugged his massive shoulders and tugged on the beak of his baseball cap. "Maybe we'll just scare her or maybe we'll make an accident happen." He snickered certain he was close to perfecting the laugh that would fill an enemy with terror. "She works until closing, doesn't she? Things can happen to a woman when she leaves work late and alone."

"You fools are asking for cop trouble."

"We ain't fools. Besides, if the cops catch us maybe we can work a deal that includes you."

"Remember it was your stupidity that started all this and don't even think about blabbing to the cops about me."

Nick leaned back, hands raised. He wasn't scared of the skinny psychopath sitting across from him but why tick off the boss? "Just kidding. The Fortains don't talk to cops. Trust me, we'll settle this witness thing, then get back to business. Yesterday's job went without a glitch. Just in and out. No heroes. We're getting so good maybe it's time we gave ourselves a raise, after all we're taking the risks, you're just hanging around looking pretty."

"Don't forget where you get your information. Without me, you wouldn't know the security set-up or what was worth taking. My cut stays at sixty percent."

Nick hunched over the table. "I'm out of here before someone spots me, but don't think you're going to keep working us for nothing. We're talking again after we deal with Miss Nosy Witness."

He walked toward the mall exit, leaving a coffee cup and an empty chip container, but taking the remainder of his burger.

*****

Mike Ceretzke met Jack Pierce at the gate of the Dorrien house. Mike had been pondering the reason for Beth McKinney's sudden coldness when the Mountie caught up with him. He asked if he could sit in on his questioning of Hugh Dorrien saying he wanted to watch the subject of his long-time investigation up close.

Mike would have preferred conducting the interviews himself and reporting his findings to the unit; however, the Super had ordered him to co-operate, not to like doing it. He could understand her reasoning for burdening him with the Mountie, because Jack did know Dorrien's background better than the rest of them and keeping the RCMP happy was good corporate politics.

Tony Bendall met them at the door and guided them to the sitting room where Hugh lounged on a fragile-looking sofa. His assistant didn't enter the room but closed the glass doors behind them. The doorway through which they entered fed off a hall that started at the front entrance and ran to the back of the house and Dorrien's office. A second set of doors led into the dining room.

Mahogany pillars stood guard at each entrance. The flooring visible around the oriental carpet was mahogany, as were the wood mouldings that emphasized the blue walls. An upright piano stood along one wall. Elaborately framed needlework flowers covered another. Figurines of slender men and women lined the mantel and were clustered on the piano.

Mike was sure he hadn't seen a tatted doily since his grandmother died but they covered the furniture in this room. The room's Victorian feel contrasted with the bold bedrooms that he had searched the previous day.

"Mr. Dorrien, thank you for talking with us. You haven't met Sergeant Pierce who will be assisting with the investigation."

Hugh ignored the introduction as he reached for a silver tea service centred on the intricately carved, mahogany coffee table that separated him from the police officers. "Please sit," he said, pointing at two museum quality chairs. "Can I offer you something to drink, coffee, tea?"

Mike refused the offer of refreshments. He studied Hugh noting his pinched lips, slow speech, and distracted attitude. Were they the result of shock over his wife's death, worry for his future, or maybe good acting?

Any amateur would know to establish an alibi for the time of Lisette's death and Hugh was not amateur. He wouldn't overlook the need for a solid alibi, but Mike asked where he'd been anyway.

Hugh leaned forward, his elbows pushing into his thighs, his fingers forming a triangle. He rubbed his fingers up and down his lined forehead. "I had nothing to do with Lisette's death. She was the mother of my children, my wife."

Mike waited for him to continue.

Hugh covered his face with his hands. After a moment, he looked up and said, "I was the guest speaker at the Businessman's Club from noon until one. A roomful of people can verify my presence."

"And before that?"

"I was at the dentist's office until about eleven-thirty. A new crown was bothering me."

"Your dentist's name?"

"Dr. Peterson, in Riverway Centre."

"Did you and your wife have marital problems?"

"No more than anyone else. The move West was hard on her. She hated being two thousand miles from her friends and had trouble cultivating new ones, but she was adapting."

"What about her family?"

"Just her sister Odile, is left. She lives in Paris but she'll be attending the funeral."

"Do you suspect anyone of wanting to hurt your wife?"

"Lisette didn't have enemies. Her friends and associates were the people I work with and my clients. Of course, I don't know those other people, the ones the news reporters claimed were her friends."

Hugh shifted his lower jaw forward, reminding Mike of a bulldog. "Detective, I think you should be out arresting known criminals. This was a case of some junkie wanting cash. I told her not to run through the park, that place is full of strange people. There are robberies all over the city; young punks are getting out of hand. The news has been full of reports of home invasions, gas station robberies, heck even the banks aren't safe. Didn't some guy get killed during one of those robberies? Lisette was another a victim of senseless violence."

"Did your wife carry anything worth stealing when she ran?"

"A wrist pouch designed to hold her keys and some cash. I bought it for her last Christmas. It's metallic and slips on like a bracelet. Was it missing? If it's missing that proves it was a robbery."

Refusing to give Hugh the comfort of an answer, Mike asked, "Did she have close friends, maybe men friends? Someone she took a course with or an old family friend?"

"What do you know about him?" Hugh's voice rose as he loomed toward the officers.

"Was she involved with someone, sir?"

Hugh visibly pulled himself together. He lowered his voice to a whisper. "She claimed she had an art class every Thursday and self-defence lessons Tuesday, but I didn't believe her. Her running too, who knows who she met in that park? Maybe that skinny karate teacher."

He dropped his head into his hands, then as quickly looked up at the officers. "Men were always after her. She was so beautiful. Once, a couple of years ago, I found her with a guy, at his place. She said they were just friends having coffee but she'd taken Joelle with her. After that, I made sure we had a nanny I could trust to keep an eye on the kids. If Lisette wanted to sleep around, well maybe I could handle that, but she wasn't going to take my kids with her."

"Where can we find him?"

"The cemetery. Don't look at me like that, he died of cancer three months after I caught them together."

"Why didn't you divorce her?"

Hugh paced the room, like a bear who couldn't sit still. He clenched and unclenched his hands.

"Our prenuptial agreement gave her fifty percent of everything if we divorced. Even that wouldn't have mattered if I could guarantee winning custody of my kids, but with these bleeding heart courts who can guarantee anything. No, she was my wife and the mother of my children. I wasn't going to lose that again."

"Did you lose a family before?" Mike asked, trying to appear innocent of his knowledge of Hugh's background.

Hugh sniffed. Mike assumed it was his way of expressing disbelief.

"As if you don't know already."

Neither Mike nor Jack responded and after uttering a long sigh, Hugh said, "I was married before, when I was in the National Hockey League. She couldn't take me being on the road half the year and walked out while I was out of town. What a homecoming that was."

Hugh sat back on the sofa, his emotions again under control, his voice close to normal. "What about the woman who found her? I thought she saw the whole thing and could identify the guy. Get her to look through your books of mug-shots, or draw a sketch, or whatever you do."

"She arrived at the scene after the attack and didn't get a clear look at your wife's assailant."

"That's not what that snoopy reporter said," Hugh muttered.

"Reporters don't always have their facts right."

Deciding he had got all he needed to verify or destroy Dorrien's alibi, Mike vacated the fragile chair and motioned Jack to follow his lead.

"That's all for today, Mr. Dorrien. We'll be back tomorrow morning to question your staff. Here's my card. You can contact me anytime whether it's to get an update or because you remember something relevant."

Bendall ushered them into the fragrant autumn air. Jack remained silent until Mike slid behind the wheel of his truck.

"Do you believe that bit about Lisette having an affair?" Jack asked.

Mike frowned. "I doubt she'd take her kid along, but his outbreak surprised me. Doesn't seem in character to react so strongly."

"Maybe he thinks it will make him look innocent?"

"If we need a motive to take to court that prenuptial agreement will be a good one. Money and jealousy are a hard combination to beat when it comes to murder."

"He can't claim jealousy if he's lived with promiscuous behaviour for years." Jack fiddled with a loose button until he pulled the wrong thread and the plastic trinket fell into his hand.

"Maybe he finally snapped. That knife suggests the murderer had access to their house, now we have a motive, with your informant's testimony it might be all we need."

Jack ignored the comment and asked, "Why didn't you interview the staff today?"

"This is my case, I'll decide how to run it." Mike ran his fingers through his hair. When the Mountie didn't respond to his outburst, he explained, "I want to keep him off balance. Besides if we can destroy his alibi, we'll just have to ask them a different set of questions."

"What do you want me to do?"

"Check the third party angle to see if Hugh imported someone to do the job. Check his assistant for a history of violence, somehow I doubt his only talent is keyboarding. Dorrien's alibi sounds good, so it will probably stick. If that's the case, we have to prove he ordered the hit."

Jack shoved the loose button into his suit pocket. "Don't worry, the Mounties always get their man, besides this is a Joint Forces Operation so we have information coming from several agencies. Our analysts are sorting through relevant material and will pass on their interpretations. Meanwhile don't press Dorrien too hard. We don't want you arousing suspicions that there's still an ongoing undercover investigation. That would only endanger our remaining source."

"It's a poor informant who sends a warning too late to be of help. Is he, she, or it, continuing to be useful? Maybe he's provided the name of Lisette's murderer."

Jack fiddled with his buttonhole. "Nothing on the killer yet, but it's early."

"Are you sure you can trust your person? What kind of people betray friends and co-workers anyway?"

"Usually criminals trying to save their skins. Lisette was the exception."

"Can you tell me who your source is?" This was treacherous ground but Mike felt he had to ask.

"Sorry, this one's a deep cover source who will be of use to me for as long as it takes to convict Neil Karlek. I'm not handing you that ace. Besides, if you make a case against Dorrien that'll stick, we can apply pressure to have him testify against the rest of the organization. You'd be a hero."

"When we make our case, we'll use it to convict him of murder. He's not going to deal his way out of jail."

"Yeah, well let's talk about that later." Jack stepped back from the truck window, stuffed his hands into his overcoat pockets, and concentrated on kicking imaginary dirt off the vehicle's tire.

"Mike, don't try laying a guilt trip on me. I'm justified in trying to recruit Hugh and in protecting my source. You know once we ID the big players we've got to keep on them, get every bit of evidence against them we can. Lisette's information helped but she can't testify for us now."

Mike rested his elbows on the steering wheel and cupped his chin in the palm of one hand. He stared across the road to the riverbank and across the North Saskatchewan River toward the lookout where Lisette had died.

"Tell me again, Jack. Why does the distant hope of bringing down the head of a gang of criminals outweigh getting a murderer off the street?"

Jack leaned into the window and touched Mike's shoulder. "I don't deal in moral issues." Then backing away, he added, "I have to get back to headquarters, what are you doing next?"

"Trying to get him in spite of you."

Looking across at the Mountie, Mike breathed deeply. What the hell, the guy was a cop following orders, just like him. "I'll get to the dentist and the Businessman's Club to check his alibi, maybe we're giving him too much credit and there's a gap in the timing we can use. Then I have to attend the autopsy. Look, I'll meet you for breakfast at the Kozy Kitchen tomorrow morning. We can talk to Dorrien's staff after that, if you still want to sit in on the questioning."

Mike begrudged the invitation but maybe Pierce wasn't such a bad guy, except for his plan to make a deal with Dorrien.

Mike turned his truck around in the street and headed toward the freeway and the south side of the river. It was 3:07 p.m. He checked his watch again when he arrived at Riverway Centre, a strip mall located less than a kilometre from the lookout where

Hugh had killed Lisette. It had taken him eight minutes to drive from the Dorrien house to Dr. Petersen's office.

A grocery store and a hair salon hemmed in the dental office and the smell of fresh baking and perm solution duelled for dominance as Mike strode toward the entrance.

Dr. Petersen's receptionist, a voluptuous blond sporting stuck-on nails and wearing casual attire, continued detailing her plans for the upcoming weekend to someone at the distant end of a phone line. Mike waited until she changed the topic to the prowess of her latest boyfriend, then he reached over the counter took the receiver from her hand and hung it up. Her surly look made him regret giving way to the impulse, but only for a second.

"Did you want something?" she asked.

Did she have him pegged as a salesman who would forgive bad manners? Mike sent her his best official business look.

"Detective Ceretzke, city police. Sorry to interrupt your call, Felicity," he said, reading her nametag, "I'd like to speak to Dr. Petersen."

With obvious satisfaction, she smirked as she answered. "The doctor is busy with a patient. He doesn't like me disturbing him."

"Please, disturb him."

Before the clash of wills worsened a pale but relieved patient entered the waiting room from the back office.

"Well, that's it for another year. For sure I'm going to floss daily, these cleanings are a nuisance."

He smiled encouragingly at Mike as if to say 'No problem, dentists are really painless'. Mike returned the smile as he watched the middle-aged man rush to the street. He turned to stare at the receptionist until she grudgingly vacated her chair and strolled toward the inner sanctum. Mike followed.

"Stay here. I'll tell him you're waiting," she said.

He ignored her and continued down the hall until he encountered a portly, balding man making notes on an index card.

"Dr. Peterson, this man wants to talk to you. He's from the police."

"Thank you, Felicity." The doctor waited for her to wiggle back to her desk, obviously enjoying every step she took. Once she was seated, he turned toward Mike. "How can I help you?"

"Detective Ceretzke." Mike extended his hand. "I have a few questions to ask about Hugh Dorrien. Did he have an appointment on Monday?"

"Hugh? No, not an appointment. He just called and asked to be squeezed in because a new crown was causing him some pain. He arrived sometime around eleven and I ground it down."

"And he left at what time?"

"It only takes a few minutes to adjust the bite. Let me think. It was after Vern Staples left and before Ursula Hoogenberg, she was scheduled for 11:30, but always arrives early. My guess would be 11:15 to 11:20, but you have to check with Felicity for an exact time. "But surely you don't think Hugh was involved in his wife's death? He's a good fellow."

"It's routine procedure to check everything thoroughly. Was Mrs. Dorrien also your patient?"

"Sure, they'd been coming to me for two or three years. Why?"

"Just information for the files. Thanks for your time."

The smug look on Felicity's face told Mike she had overheard their conversation. Swallowing his impulse to be rude a second time, he looked straight at her and asked, "Can you tell me what time Hugh Dorrien left this office Monday?"

She savoured her power, making him wait as she carefully flipped pages in her appointment book then ran her long claw down the entries, pausing at each name.

Tired of her tactics Mike said, "An exact time would help with the investigation of his wife's murder. Your information could be key in convicting him."

Maybe it was the force of his personality or an image of being on a witness stand with the entire case hinging on her testimony, but she moved immediately to the correct entry. "He arrived at 11:10 and left at 11:30. I keep exact records."

"I'm sure you do. What did you think of Mr. and Mrs. Dorrien?"

Felicity darted a glance toward the back office. "He's a sleaze, always making suggestive comments as if I'd have anything to do with a fat old geezer who reminds me of my pervert of a grandfather."

Mike winced at the description.

"Lisette was all right, I was sorry about what happened to her. We used to talk whenever she was waiting for Dr. Petersen. You know, the park's so close I spent my lunch hour sun tanning there all summer but I guess it won't be safe doing that anymore."

"The park's still safe. You can't let one random act of violence keep you from enjoying its benefits."

"I don't want to get killed. Maybe I'll go to a tanning parlour."

Mike knew one-track minds were hard to change, so he thanked her politely and left her to her preconceptions.

He climbed into his truck and stared at the clinic entrance. Hugh could have left the dentist's office at 11:30, drove to the lookout, and been the man Beth had seen at eleven fifty-five. But could he then drive downtown for a noon hour luncheon?

No, the timing didn't work unless Lisette was stabbed earlier or Hugh was late for the luncheon. Mike returned to his truck and drove downtown to the Businessman's Club.

The traffic was sparse but it still took fifteen minutes to make the run into the downtown core, find a parking space, and walk the half block to the Businessman's Club.

He waited ten minutes in a brown room with patched leather chairs and threadbare carpeting. The floors creaked and moisture stained the ceiling. Dishes of dried potpourris sat on scarred end tables, someone's attempt at disguising the scent of mildew.

Eventually, a harried middle-aged man ushered him into the office of the club manager, Ms. Hawrick. She reminded Mike of a midget heron, all neck and legs, as she perched awkwardly on the edge of her desk, surrounded by a mound of multi-hued papers.

"Which colour do you like best?" she asked, peering at him over Ben Franklin glasses.

As he stepped closer, Mike noted the sheets were promotional material for the club's speaker series.

"Pink always grabs people's attention."

"No, too many men still think it's a feminine colour. I think the lime green will work better. You're a police officer right? What did you want?" She continued studying various sheets of paper as she spoke.

"I need to confirm that Mr. Dorrien was here Monday noon."

"Of course he was, he was the guest speaker. Damn, look at this. They misspelled 'retrofit' in the title of the talk."

She grabbed a blue pencil, rummaged around the desk top until she found the original copy of the circular and underscored the offending word. Her pencil approached her open lips as she looked up at him again, but she jerked it away before biting it.

"What time did he arrive?"

"A few minutes before twelve, maybe five or ten minutes before. We start promptly because it's a lunch session and most people want to be back at their offices by one."

"You're sure that it wasn't a few minutes after twelve? It's hard to be accurate to the minute."

"It's not hard when you know up to a hundred-fifty hungry people are going to be expecting the program to start on time. I watch very closely what time the speakers arrive. If they're late, we don't ask them again. What about the saffron? Do you like that better than the lime?"

CHAPTER 10

Hugh paced from the front of his desk to the tall narrow window that looked into his backyard with its forest of mature trees. Then he prowled behind his computer desk and peered into the disc drive, pushed the eject button, and rested his hands on the back of his ergonomically designed chair. Restless, he walked toward the bookcase-lined wall and ran his hands over the leather bound volumes of classics that felt velvety to his touch.

Scowling, he turned away and resumed his pacing. He passed his desk and stopped in front of a watercolour of his kids playing in the summerhouse. Lisette had painted it the previous year.

"Bitch," he muttered as he swung the painting to one side, revealing a wall safe. He mumbled the combination as he concentrated on turning the dial. The door opened on the first try revealing a pile of papers, file folders, and stacks of cash.

He reached inside and felt around. He removed the money and separated the other items. Next, he lifted each file folder and placed it on a new pile. After staring into the empty safe he shoved everything back, closed the door, and spun the dial.

He turned his attention to the desk, examining every stack of paper on its tidy surface and every computer manual that lined an attached shelf. Then he opened and emptied the centre drawer. From the locked side drawer came a handgun that he placed on the desktop until he completed his search. He replaced the desk's contents and slumped into his chair.

He was a dead man. It was inevitable that one of his enemies would pounce now, when he couldn't protect himself.

His gaze jumped to each corner of the room. Where could it be? He lifted the edge of the desk calendar, first feeling underneath then spilling pens and paper sideways as he lifted it high enough to see the desktop.

He pounded his thighs with his fists. He had returned it to the safe, hadn't he?

He tapped his finger on the telephone receiver and finally picked up the phone and looked underneath.

A knock at the door brought him upright in his chair. He straightened his tie, buttoned his suit jacket, and forced the lines of fear from his face.

"Come," he called in a voice pitched a little higher than normal, but that tiny betrayal of fear wasn't bad, considering.

Tony opened the door and scanned the room. "Did you need me anymore today?"

Hugh grasped at a slim possibility. "Tony, did you take a computer disc out of here?"

"Mr. Dorrien, you know I would never take anything from your office."

"Well, have you seen it?"

"How was it labelled?"

"It wasn't."

"Maybe you reused it by mistake?"

"I didn't."

"It's not in your disc holder? Did you back the file up on the hard drive?" Tony approached the desk, ready to start searching.

Hugh thought a minute then looked up and waved his assistant away. "Did that detective find a disc?"

"No. They didn't come in here. I locked the door and told them you were the only one with a key."

"Did they take a disc from anywhere else in the house?"

"I could only follow the one cop, but I checked everything they took away. There was no disc."

"Was my wife in here yesterday?"

Tony rubbed the back of his neck. A diamond and ruby ring flashed on his little finger, his sleeve pulled back to reveal a chunky, gold watchband. "Well, I know you don't want anyone in here alone, but yeah, I saw her closing this door yesterday morning before she dressed to go running. I thought you were in here so I didn't say anything."

"She took it." Hitting his right fist into the palm of his left hand, Hugh glared at the watercolour. "If she wasn't already dead, I'd kill her."

Remembering that Tony was staring at him with his gambler's face, Hugh waved his hand in dismissal. "She probably left it upstairs in her desk. Forget I mentioned it. It's nothing important." He cleared his throat and forced himself to focus on Tony. "Are the funeral arrangements complete?"

"They promised to release her body tomorrow so I set the funeral for Thursday afternoon."

"What about Odile? When does her flight arrive?"

"Thursday morning. I'll pick her up at the airport."

"Then you might as well take off."

Hugh held his pose until the door closed, then lowered his head to the desktop. Think you idiot. You thought you were being so smart keeping records as insurance in case you needed to bargain for your life or your freedom. Now the records are missing. Ten years worth of names and places, enough to get you jailed or killed or both. Where could she have put it?

The disc had been in the safe Sunday night, he knew that much because he had updated it with information about Saturday's Fifth Street meeting. He must have put back. But it wasn't there now. She must have taken it Monday morning.

The police hadn't found it on her body or they would have asked about it. The same applied to the Mounties. If they had it, they'd be trying to deal with him.

If the cops hadn't found it while searching yesterday, she must have hidden it, but why would she take it? Could she hate him so much she was going to give it to Mr. Karlek? Or was it just another of her schemes to make him angry?

Knowing the odds of finding the disc were against him, he climbed the polished mahogany stairway to the master suite. One reason they had bought this monster of a house was the large suite that included two bedrooms and baths, joined by a small sitting room. Growing up in rural Quebec, he had shared a room with three brothers. During the glorious years with the NHL, he had shared locker rooms and hotel rooms. He had earned the right to his privacy.

Not that Lisette had minded. She had made him promise before they were married that she would always have a space of her own. Her years of modelling had taught her the value of privacy.

He searched without real hope of finding the disc, even suffering Helen's bitter silence and her scowl while he disturbed the order of her spotless kitchen to search for it. Perhaps he would get rid of her too. He should have got rid of her long ago, when the others left. Why hadn't he? He couldn't remember now. She had always sided with Lisette, probably wouldn't tell him if Lisette had given her the disc. No, Lisette wouldn't give it to Helen. She barely communicated with Helen. Said the woman gave her the creeps the way she constantly watched her.

Hugh pounded the handrail as he ascended the staircase. He remembered now that he'd kept Helen on because she made Lisette nervous.

The last place he searched was the third floor nursery. Lisette had renovated it to include a large, bright play area, a room for each child, and a separate suite for the nanny.

Melissa, the nanny sent to them by an agency in Montreal, leaned against the doorway of the children's room with her hands crossed over her chest and her eyes closed. She looked as young as Jarrett. Hugh felt her gaze focused on him as he threw toys from the cupboard onto the floor. He knew he was losing control and probably looked like a fool, but couldn't help himself. If he had any chance of finding that disc, he had to take it.

His son was a solid child who was large for five, just like he had been. Jarrett watched for a few minutes then approached timidly. He hugged a stuffed tiger in the crook of one arm and his sister's delicate fingers in his square paw. Hugh didn't want his kid scared of him. Maybe the boy would toughen up now that Lisette wasn't around to baby him.

"Daddy, can we play too?" Jarrett's whimper grated on Hugh's nerves.

Hugh bent down, grabbed him, and hugged him so tight he squirmed. "Jarrett did Mommy give you a computer disc to keep for her?"

When the child remained silent Hugh caressed his hair, ending the caress with a gentle tug that made the boy stiffen. He had to learn to respect his elders. Hugh knew he was still coddling the boy. His father would have strapped him until he got an answer but that was a different world. These days if you hit your kid someone would sue you. "Son, it's very important. Did Mommy give you anything to keep for her?"

When the boy shook his head, Hugh gave him a final squeeze and released him. He should have known Lisette wouldn't have put her little boy in the path of his anger. Jarrett backed away, pulling at Joelle to follow.

"Melissa, take the kids out of here. I'll be finished before long."

"Come, little ones. Let Daddy alone. Perhaps Helen can find a treat for you."

"I want Mommy not you," Joelle demanded, rubbing her delicate little fist across her runny nose.

"Hush my baby. Your Mommy can't be here."

Hugh listened as the whimpering receded into the hall and down the stairs. What was he going to do with those kids now? Jarrett was almost old enough for boarding school, but Joelle was still a baby.

He clutched the door jam. If he didn't find that disc, the problem wouldn't be his to solve. She must have taken the disc out of the house; maybe she even gave it to someone for safekeeping. Someone like one of her new pals.

Hugh dragged himself back to the sitting room that Lisette had used for her painting and slumped into a wicker chair. He stared at the nearly completed portrait of Joelle. Lisette had captured the air of fragile unhappiness Joelle habitually wore.

He jumped as soft fingers glided across the back of his neck. Reaching over his shoulder, he grasped the slim hand and pulled Melissa into his arms.

"Where are the kids?" His voice was low and husky.

"Helen is stuffing them with cookies. What's so important about that disc? You seem frantic."

He nuzzled her thick, curly hair. "It's nothing I can't fix."

He pulled her closer, immersing himself in the lemony fragrance of her hair.

"Now that she's gone, we don't have to be secretive. She can't divorce you and take the kids away," Melissa said, rubbing her hand over his chest.

Hugh heard a triumphant undertone in her voice.

"We're free to do whatever we want. We could even get married."

"Let's be careful, little one. The police might get ideas if they suspect there's anything between us." Hugh nibbled at her neck. She was a pretty distraction and a convenience, but she would have to go. He didn't intend to be tied to any woman in the future.

She jumped off his lap and tugged at his arm, pulling him in the direction of Lisette's room. "Let's celebrate our freedom."

"I said we had to be careful! Go tend to the kids. We've time for that later."

He pushed her out the door. He still had to locate that damned disc before one of his enemies made use of it. Could anyone trace it back to him? He'd coded the information but how easily could they decipher his code?

*****

Responding to a slight nod, Jack approached the person lounging against the glass wall. When near enough to speak without being overheard, Jack eased his waistband and studied the scene before him. A field of eight was running, not a bad turnout. The sulky drivers pulled on the reins, calming the horses.

Jack concentrated on the track as he spoke, using his folded program to cover the movement of his lips. Noise from the crowd and the people clustered around closed circuit televisions, ensured their privacy.

"What's so important you can't talk over the phone?"

"I'm worried Dorrien's cracking and I want out. He was panicking today about some disc."

"A disc?" Jack turned toward the voice, then forced his attention back to the racetrack. "What do you know about it?"

"It's important, it's missing, and Dorrien's freaking. Get me out."

Noting the building hysteria, Jack spoke sharply, "You know you're too valuable to us right now. We'll get you out when the time is right." Then in a more persuasive tone he added, "Once we secure Dorrien you can take a break."

"Are you going to get him for Lisette's murder?"

"Sure, with the knife and his motive—you never told me that he suspected she was having an affair."

"It didn't matter. Nothing matters if you get him and let me out of this cloak-and-dagger game. Why haven't the cops arrested him if they have a witness?"

"She's co-operating with the locals and when they make their case, we'll step in. Just hang in there, it won't be much longer." Hoping that his reassurance was convincing, Jack turned the questions back to his informant's role in the current fiasco.

"Why did you tell us to wait to get Lisette out? Are you trying to play both sides in this game? Don't risk losing our patronage."

"What? You think I did it on purpose? It wasn't my fault, I just told you what I heard. Don't you trust me?"

Jack didn't like the look of sullen hatred he saw in his informant's face. "You make sure your information is accurate and we'll trust you, otherwise we'll throw you to Karlek." Jack studied the race as he considered his hollow threat. He worked on the assumption that even if your dog doesn't love you, it can still be taught to fear you.

"How should I act when you question the staff?"

"Like you don't know me. I don't want anyone guessing who you are."

"Yeah, right! No one knows about me except half the RCMP."

Jack glanced at the people on either side of them. He didn't think they'd noticed the loud outbreak. Maybe he better give some reassurance since the timing was too critical to risk an attack of hysteria. "You're a code number at headquarters. I'm the only one who can link your name to that number and I won't do it unless you fail to be an asset."

"Yeah, what about that homicide cop, the one who's investigating Lisette's murder. I bet he knows."

"Your identity is safe. I didn't tell Lisette you work for us and I don't plan to tell Detective Ceretzke either. Go home, relax."

Jack drifted into the crowd, separating himself from his source. It was true that currently he was the only one who knew his informant's identity. It had been true since last month when his partner died of a burst appendix. The poor guy figured it was an ulcer and waited to have it checked. He didn't make it through the emergency surgery.

Now Inspector Brown wanted to assign him a girl as a partner. Women were all right as informants, but as a partner? Maybe it was time he retired? He had enough years in to qualify for full pension, but what would he do if he retired? Start travelling? He hated travelling. Something always went wrong when he packed a suitcase. The airline lost it, or the plane was delayed, or the weather was lousy.

It would be different if Marnie was still alive or if the kids lived closer. What did people do when they retired? They all claimed to be so damned busy, but every one of them gained weight and looked bored.

*****

Mike returned to the station after his fruitless check of Dorrien's alibi. He headed for the staff lunchroom hoping to find something edible left over from someone's lunch.

He found Evan Collins pouring himself a cup of coffee. Evan leaned against the counter and flashed a weak smile when Mike walked in.

Mike was glad to see him, knowing they could compare notes and maybe brainstorm a bit. "Evan, anything more on the Shotgun Gang?"

"The Analysis Section took a closer look after that last TV interview where Tanner claimed some homeowner spotted people carrying shotguns into his neighbour's house. Now Analysis is making noises about similarities between the Shotgun Gang and that string of residential B&Es."

Mike examined the inch of black sludge in the coffeepot. No wonder Evan looked glum. If the crimes were linked, the task force's workload would multiply and public pressure would skyrocket. Robbing banks was impersonal. Homes were not. "Why did they come up with that lame-brained theory?"

"They say the weapons are the same type and a common element, so they passed on word that the same people could be responsible for both."

"What happened to their theory that it was kids?"

"Analysis Section says the thieves needed detailed knowledge of the security systems to manage those break-ins. Also, the items they've been taking aren't the usual cash and electronics that kids go for, but valuable jewellery and collections of coins and stamps. That kind of merchandise sells in specialized markets. CAS suggests we consider the house B&Es the work of professionals, specifically the Shotgun Gang, at least until we prove otherwise."

"They're hallucinating. No way the same guys are pulling off both kinds of crimes. But I suppose it won't matter what I think of their report, Super Sam will be on our necks for those and the trust companies."

Evan stirred two sugars and a heaping teaspoon of creamer into his cup, then sucked his stir-stick clean.

"Are you working on the robberies at all or sticking with the murder until you put Dorrien away?"

Mike poured the dregs of coffee into his cup and shook his head. "You heard Super Sam, I won't be much help to you until Dorrien is behind bars. That could take longer than I figured because the case isn't going smoothly. Hugh has an alibi that seems to stick so we can assume he hired the hit. The Mounties are checking that angle. But don't worry, the way the Shotgun Gang operates your task force will be chugging away long after Hugh Dorrien is convicted."

Mike knew catching the gang would involve time and luck. The witnesses' descriptions varied, but the consensus was that they were Caucasians, one 6'3" about 200 lbs., the other about 6'1" and slimmer. They wore gloves and Balaclavas and carried shotguns. The surprise wasn't that they had killed people during their robberies, but that they hadn't killed more.

Mike opened the fridge. It was empty except for a bowl of apples and a container of cream. He grabbed an apple, remembering it was Super Sam's latest idea for keeping the troops healthy. Damn CAS for linking the gang to those B&Es. Now Tanner had all the ammo he needed to increase the pressure on the task force.

Evan tasted his coffee, then added another teaspoon of sugar. "Super Sam figures we have something special here because we would have caught normal thieves by now. It's not as if criminals are very smart as a group, but these guys know what they're doing and how to blend between jobs. I hoped publishing those surveillance photos would bring in a few tips, but we haven't had any useful calls."

Mike swallowed a mouthful of coffee and grimaced. "They have to be hiding somewhere. The surveillance picture made the front page of half the papers in the province, so eventually someone will recognize them."

"Maybe their friends don't read newspapers?"

"Or watch TV? Our Crime Stoppers segment airs Thursday and that last video is clear enough to smoke them out of hiding."

"The legwork on this case is killing me. Are you sure you can't spare some time?"

"No way. Tomorrow we're talking to the staff; I'm on my way to the autopsy now."

He took another sip from his cup, then dumped the remainder in the sink. The Medical Examiner's office made better coffee. He would get a cup there while he waited for the preliminaries to be completed. He pulled the apple from his pocket and bit into it.

The tail end of rush hour slowed his progress. The Ninth Street Bridge was blocked by a fender bender, but the tie-up lasted only until the pressure of blaring horns forced the drivers off the bridge to a side street to exchange insurance information.

The university area and Fourteenth Street were no slower than usual, which meant traffic crawled at a steady twenty kilometres per hour. An overabundance of empty parking spaces surrounding the provincial government buildings testified to the lateness of the hour. The Medical Examiner's office staff had disappeared for the day, but they had kindly left the coffeepot full and ready for the night crew.

Mike grabbed a cup, sighing in relief as its strong, bitter blackness washed away the frustration of the drive. He circled the plants in the building's atrium, thankful they absorbed the smell death.

Mike pushed open the door to the autopsy area. They had started without him, but the number of official witnesses made his presence redundant.

Edmonton's M.E., Dr. Elizabeth Smythe, had received her training in Miami, a city recognized for turning out top forensics experts. She was good at her job but had the personality of an ornery porcupine. Now, with her attention focused completely on the procedure she didn't acknowledge his presence. "Bruising to the neck," she droned into her microphone then paused and examined the eyelids.

When she reached the first stab wound, her only comment was "a cut located two centimetres left of the carotid artery."

Mike let his attention wander as the M.E. continued describing wounds made by a wide blade, sharp on one edge, thrust into the body to varying depths. He watched as she examined and cleaned

Lisette's fingernails. Eventually, she looked up and acknowledged his presence.

"Skin under her nails. We'll send it for DNA testing but we're looking at two months maybe even longer for results, because the lab's swamped. You might want to check your suspects for scratches on the left forearm because the knife wounds suggest a right-handed assailant."

She finished examining the chest cavity and was about to open the skull when Mike asked, "How long did she take to die?"

"Up to fifteen—twenty minutes. None of the wounds caused immediate death."

Maybe her verdict would destroy Hugh's alibi. "The witness said she died about 11:55, so the attack took place sometime after 11:35? Could she have lasted longer?"

"Doubtful. I make twenty minutes the outside estimate, but it was probably closer to ten."

"Can you tell me anything else?"

"In my opinion, the assailant grabbed her from behind with his left arm and used his right to stab her. From the bruising, I would say she put up a fight and he choked her to subdue her. It'll all be in my report."

She turned back to the body and started cutting through the skull. Mike looked away.

He left the lab, mentally calculating the sequence of events. If the M.E.'s calculation was right, Hugh could have stabbed her as early as 11:35, so he would have had time to retrieve his car and get downtown for his twelve o'clock luncheon. Maybe they didn't need to look for a third party?

Still, if Hugh had stabbed Lisette and she'd been lying there from 11:35 until 11:55 when Beth McKinney found her, why wouldn't an earlier passer-by have seen her? And, if Hugh had stabbed her that early, who had Beth seen in the bushes at 11:55?

He was glad to exit the M.E.'s building and inhale the cool, starlit air. Instead of heading home, he returned to his desk and pulled the case file from his active basket. He flipped through the computer-generated drawings and photos of the crime scene. The photographer had shot sequences approaching the lookout from both directions and then labelled them with detailed information, including the distance of each shot from the body.

Mike cleared his desk and placed the photos in order. Moving from west to east the body wouldn't have been visible unless you turned and looked into the bush. However, from east to west, the direction Beth McKinney had taken, an observant person would have spotted the turquoise suit at twenty metres. Seeing her at a hundred metres was nearly impossible.

From the lookout itself, the underbrush partially shielded the body. Mike hoped the canvassing officers were asking the park users which direction they had been travelling on Monday. Finding the last person to pass Lisette alive and the last one to approach the site from the east without seeing her body, could pinpoint the time of the attack. When the women Ms. McKinney claimed to have passed were located, he wanted to ask them if they had lingered at the lookout. If they surveyed the area looking for a good picture, they should have noticed Lisette's body.

Had something really drawn Beth's attention to the site at 11:55, or was the assailant long gone by then and they were hunting a phantom? He better push Jack to complete the research into her source of income. In addition, he planned to double-check the blood-splatter analyses of Beth's clothes to see if the lab results verified her story or raised any questions.

*****

Mike arrived at Mary's watercolour class half an hour before the evening class was scheduled to start. The downtown classroom resembled one where he'd been taught high school art many years earlier. Tables were clustered at one end, sinks for washing-up abutted the wall, and a cleared area provided room for the students' easels.

Mary was alone in the classroom arranging a battered, leather-bound book, a crystal vase, and a figurine of a shepherdess on a table. She wore a mauve smock over a heavy, rose sweater and red wool slacks.

She seemed to be weathering the shock of Lisette's death though her tissue-paper skin was pale and her usual cheerfulness was missing.

"Is that tonight's project?" Mike asked, announcing his presence from the doorway.

"Hi Mike." She stood and dusted her hands as she stepped back and appraised the arrangement. "Jay will be right back. He's bringing in some supplies." She looked over his shoulder. "Here he is now."

Mike turned and faced a scrawny man juggling two boxes and an easel. His pink scalp was visible through his wispy and light brown hair. His washed-out eyes hid behind thick glasses and he stood no more than 5'6", weighing in at maybe 140 lbs., soaking wet. Mike crossed him off his list of suspects. Lisette could have taken the guy even without self-defence training.

"Put the supplies on the counter, Jay." Mary motioned to the back of the room where storage cupboards lined the wall. He took his time setting down the supplies before starting to remove his windbreaker, then he hesitated and left it zipped up.

"Detective Ceretzke wants to talk to you about Lisette Dorrien. Did you know she was killed?"

"I read about it in the paper this morning."

"Mr. Howardson, did you know the victim well?" Mike asked.

The little man made a show of thinking about the question. Then he looked at Mary as if for confirmation. "Last spring's class was when we met, wasn't it?"

Mary inclined her head slightly.

"Can you explain this note to me?" Mike pulled a copy of the note he had found in Lisette's purse from his notebook and displayed it to Jay, who examined it carefully. Mike caught Jay's furtive glance in Mary's direction.

"That is your handwriting, Jay," Mary said, destroying his chance of denying knowledge of the note.

"Look, you won't tell my wife will you? It's over. That's what the note was about, a final windup meeting."

Mike stuffed the copy into his notebook. Why were they always concerned about their families after they were caught? Why not think of them before they started prowling around looking for love, or romance, or adventure, or whatever the hell it was that they hunted.

"How long did the affair last?" Mike asked.

"Affair?" Jay looked up, his glasses sliding down to rest on the tip of his nose, his eyes widening in panic. "No, not that. I was tutoring her, private lessons in Portuguese. She was getting quite good at speaking it."

Mike had to admit his story made more sense than imagining Lisette cavorting with this skinny little guy. Had she been preparing to escape from Hugh's grasp totally? What country had she planned to run to?

"Why don't you want your wife knowing about the tutoring?"

"Sheila thinks I'm taking courses to become a CPA. It's her dream that I become an accountant and get a better job. Do you know what a bookkeeper makes? Not enough to raise three daughters. The money I got tutoring Lisette helped a lot. So does my pay for assisting Mary with this class, but Sheila would have hated knowing I was working every evening and not spending them studying like she thought.

"Sheila kept nagging me to finish the program. I put her off for almost a year. Then she found out they offered the last course I need on Wednesdays and insisted I sign up. Wednesday was the only night Lisette could take her Portuguese lesson. Apparently, her husband is busy that night and she wanted to surprise him after she became fluent in the language. I saw her at church last Sunday and slipped her the note. I wanted to see her again to pass on the name of a tutor she could contact."

Mike noted the agony in the little man's eyes and thought he could guess his motive for seeing Lisette just once more. She had been a woman that men dreamed of dying for.

"I couldn't believe she'd been killed."

Jay turned to Mary and patted her shoulder. "I still can't believe it. She was such a strong person."

Tears welled in Mary's eyes and she raised her hand to brush them away. "Yes, she was strong and loyal and she loved her children."

"I wish I could help catch whoever hurt her."

"We all want to help but Detective Ceretzke is a fine detective. He will apprehend the guilty party just as soon as he stops worrying about losing the case in court."

Mike flinched at her underlying message. She should realize that he had to be cautious. With all the law enforcement restrictions and the numerous rights criminals basked in these days, he couldn't just arrest Hugh because he was guilty. He had to weave every loose end into the case or the defence would unravel the entire tapestry and Hugh would go free.

"You didn't hear about the murder on last night's news?" Mike asked, getting his interview back on course. "It was all over the radio and TV."

"I wasn't home. I was working another part-time job, doing the books for a woodcarver on the south side. In fact, I slipped and scratched my arm when I fell against his rack of chisels."

He took off his jacket revealing a gauze pad on his left forearm. "Sheila doesn't know about that job either."

"Would you take the dressing off, Mr. Howardson."

Jay peeled off the strips of tape, flinching as he pulled hairs out of his arm. One look at the scratches told Mike that fingernails hadn't made them.

Students drifted into the room and set up their work areas. They waved at Mary but gave the group the privacy they so obviously wanted.

Jay gripped the corner of the desk. "You won't tell Sheila, will you?"

"Not a word Mr. Howardson, but tell me, what do you do with the extra money from your jobs? Doesn't your wife notice you're spending more than you earn?"

Jay's eyes lit up, reminding Mike of sunshine on stonewashed jeans. "I have three daughters. I'm investing it for their weddings. If there's anything left after the last one's married, Sheila and I will take a second honeymoon."

Mike caught the twinkle in Mary's eye as she winked at him and smiled. As usual, he could have trusted her assessment of Jay Howardson and spent his time elsewhere.

*****

Simon's strange behaviour at the Kozy Kitchen replayed through Beth's mind, preventing her from concentrating on the book catalogue lying on her desk. Browsing through publishers' promos for the latest business and legal books was the least fascinating part of her job and eventually she pushed he catalogue aside, gave in to her nagging worry, and phoned the restaurant.

After cursory greetings, she got to the point. "When you offered condolences about Lisette being killed, you weren't speaking to me were you?"

"Beth, I wasn't aware you knew Mike, much less Mrs. Dorrien."

"So they visited your restaurant?"

"They met here a few times, that's all. The first time was last spring; an older lady and another guy were with them. After that, the other man and Mrs. Dorrien were usually alone, though sometimes Mike joined them."

"Are you sure it was Lisette Dorrien?"

"She wasn't the kind of woman you forget. I know the older woman too. Her name is Mary Carpenter."

He paused and then before Beth could reply he said, "But you know, I don't think they were social lunches."

"What do you mean, not social?"

"Well, they were always so heads-together serious. They would stop talking when the staff approached them. Whatever it was they were discussing they sure didn't want anyone to overhear."

"Thanks Simon." She prepared to hang up then nudged by

intuition, asked, "The other guy, was he chubby, with glasses and a big nose?"

"Could be. I remember he wore a hat, not a baseball cap, a real hat."

"A fedora?"

"Yeah, that's what they're called. You don't see many people still wearing that kind of hat. I hope this doesn't mess you up with Mike, he seems like a great guy."

"Nothing to mess up. He's just a cop investigating the murder of a friend. Anyway, thanks again for the clarification."

She hung up wondering how one clarified detail could distort so many others. However, it was time for her shift on the general reference desk so working out the meaning of this subterfuge would have to wait.

An hour into her shift, a voice that she recognized too well broke her concentration. "Beth?"

Keeping her finger on the line of the book that told her the botanical name for a pineapple was Ananas comosus, she glanced up and met Richard Tanner's earnest expression.

"Sorry to track you down here but you don't return my calls."

Damn his nerve. An unsuspecting person could believe those sad eyes belonged to an admirable human being. She knew better.

"Do you have a reference question?"

"Look, if you don't want to be sociable that's fine, but give me some details about Lisette Dorrien's murder."

"I have nothing to say to you and even if I did you'd probably misquote me." She grabbed a pen ready to note the Latin term and its source on the reference request.

"Can't you forget the past? It was years ago and you were the one who ended it. If anyone should be mad, it's me."

"You should be angry? You destroyed my mother's dream." Beth looked into his gorgeous eyes. He was still a child, a laughing, malicious, hurtful child who insisted life be played according to his script. Why did he have to confront her here? She glanced sideways, wondering if her outbreak had drawn unwanted attention.

"Hey, mistakes happen."

She slammed the card and pen into the book. "Here's a quote for you. I didn't see anyone clearly enough to identify. Now get out."

She pulled the card out of the book and put it in the callback file. Then she turned to the person approaching the reference desk. Great, it was Mr. Howe. She pasted on her best smile and asked, "What can I help you with tonight?"

Beth hid her grin when Richard quickly sidestepped the ripe street person who pushed forward in his desire to have his question answered.

Mr. Howe regularly spent cool evenings at a library table researching obscure points of Canadian history. He was just the type of demanding patron she needed right now.

From the corner of her eye, Beth watched Richard leave with a last look over his shoulder. She knew that look well. He was planning his next assault tactic. He hadn't changed, he still refused to admit the word 'no' could apply to him.

*****

Richard decided to walk back to the television studio. It was only four blocks and he liked the quiet darkness of the downtown core. The night was cool, the breeze gentle, and the streets nearly deserted. Only a few weeks earlier the summer festival season had been in full swing and the area had been crowded with people and noise. Street performers and jazz musicians had taken turns with local restaurants and rickshaw runners to sell their wares and talents to a clientele anxious to enjoy the warm summer evenings. Now, with the onset of fall, shoppers headed for the enclosed downtown malls and the network of tunnels and walkways that served to shut people away from the severity of Edmonton's winter. Richard enjoyed the outdoors, even in extreme weather.

Tonight he couldn't let his mind wander to such trivia; he needed to analyze what had gone wrong with his approach to Beth.

He rarely failed to get his way with people. Direct contact, with his best puppy dog eyes, boyish charm, and classic good looks usually won over hardened hearts. Ah well, he'd learned two years earlier that Beth was immune to his charms.

He walked faster, trying to shake his anger and guilt. Beth had been so righteous about getting him out of her life, claiming she didn't want to live with someone who couldn't think about other people's feelings. Obviously, she was doing just fine without him. Look at that house. Her family couldn't have been hurt too badly by his slip-up if she could afford to buy at the high end of the market. Her parents must have helped her finance the place with the money the station paid them.

He pushed his fists into his jacket pocket and walked faster. The wind had shifted and the weather was turning nasty. Why was Beth being so sanctimonious? She refused to believe his error was just that, an error. They'd done a retraction. He'd been stupid to do the story, because it had reminded him of Beth and their final argument.

If he hadn't been thinking about that—about her—but that was history—a valuable lesson about letting personal matters infringe on business. He had learned never to do that again. During one of their fights, Beth had claimed he was like a diamond, hard and shiny and with a superlative cutting edge, but only good for decoration. She'd meant it as an insult, but he liked the comparison. It made him feel like a shining star.

If Beth really looked at him now she'd see that the fallout from that little mistake had hurt him too. If he hadn't been such an asset to the station, they would have fired him. They were still holding it over his head and with his contract up for renewal in the spring, he couldn't afford to have another black mark on his record. As it was, he hadn't got the breaks that should have come his way.

Well, this series of robberies was helping and with his inside source he could keep ahead of the official releases but eventually, the bumblers on the police force would stumble over the gang. He needed another scoop to solidify his reputation.

Richard brushed by a couple who were sauntering along, holding hands. That used to be him and Beth. Why had Beth claimed she wasn't able to identify the killer? If the station brass discovered that he had reported the wrong information again—but the other stations had picked it up. He had only been the first and his source had told him that Beth saw the murder take place. Could Beth be lying, trying to ruin his career? Maybe she was hoping the station would fire him. How badly did she want revenge? How could he stop her from talking to his boss?

CHAPTER 11

During her shift on the reference desk, Beth responded to numerous requests for back issues of newspapers and magazines. Five clients required explanations of how to load the microfilm reader. She located information on paternity rights under Canadian law and reciprocal maintenance agreements between provinces.

An elderly woman searched for the address of the Fraud Division in London, England, positive she was the victim of a crime but refusing to go to the local police, as she felt Scotland Yard to be a superior organization. A grade twelve student wanted a course calendar for the University of Southern Florida. He figured their beaches would be the best of any campus in the States. Sandra Horton wanted to check Who's Who for a choreographer named Lester Horton, hoping he might be her father. Unfortunately, he had died fifteen years before she was born.

Exhausted from grief, a sleepless night, and a confusing day, Beth was glad to see the evening shift end. She was on her way to the elevator and the parking garage with a group of co-workers when Carla Wright, a librarian recently returned from England, called her name. Carla was in charge of the library's latest moneymaking effort—a service that provided in-depth computer research for a fee.

"Please Beth, can you give me just a moment. I've a real stickler of a client with a dilly of a question. It's a rush and right up your alley. Won't take but a moment."

Beth felt fatigue weighing her down, but Carla rarely asked for help and the service was important to the library's future. "It can't wait until tomorrow?"

"Nah. Client's paying for speed and he's yelling bloody hell as it is. I don't mind the overtime, but I think you can speed the process."

With a feeble wave to her departing co-workers and the image of a hot bath and soft bed disappearing, Beth followed Carla to a terminal. Half an hour of effort later they faxed a ream of documentation and a bill. Beth had mixed feelings about charging for a service she was conditioned to provide for free, but the user-pay policy made sense in an age when public facilities were expected to earn their keep.

She stifled a yawn.

"Sorry about waylaying you, but it would have taken me half the night to get what you pulled up so quickly. Maybe you should put in for full-time with this little service of mine. I'd love to have you. You've got the skills."

Beth cringed, sensing the increasing pressure to climb onto a corporate tightrope.

"I'm happy with the status quo."

"You shouldn't be. You could be running the whole show in five years if you put your mind to it."

Beth stifled another yawn. "Let's get out of here or I'll be too tired to drive home."

"Whatever. But I think you're wasting your talent."

They waved to the security guard and headed for the elevator that connected the library to the underground parking garage. Beth paused before stepping inside, wondering if she should have alerted her police guardian that she was leaving, but she was too tired to wait for a car to arrive. Besides, she had nothing to fear. She was just driving home.

The underground parkade serviced two hotels, a major theatre, the art gallery, and the library. As part of Edmonton's downtown pedway system, it linked several civic government services including city hall and police headquarters.

"Why don't students start researching their papers long before they're due?" Carla asked. She loved grumbling about the patrons. Of course, she was forever complaining about management and other employees too. Even her friends, especially her men friends, weren't exempt from Carla's caustic remarks.

"It's a month before the final papers are due. Hold your complaints for three more weeks when the last minute crowd really gets out of hand."

"Forget the students, was that Richard Tanner I saw you brushing off?"

"He was looking for an interview."

"You shouldn't go around offending media types, especially ones as good looking as him. Send him to me if he comes round again, I'll talk to him."

"You wouldn't want him; he's a lower life form. Besides, don't you already have a guy?"

"So, does that mean I shouldn't check out new models?"

Beth shook her head at her friend's comment, uncertain whether to take her seriously. Better to change the topic. "Did you manage to help the guy researching the history of the computer industry? What was it, ten thousand words due tomorrow?"

The elevator opened into a brightly-lit foyer with doors leading to the stairwell and the parkade. The metal parkade door thumped closed, firmly locking out stray visitors to the main library complex.

The underground parkade reminded Beth of a dungeon. The disadvantage of working the evening shift was never finding a parking spot close to the elevator. Well, she wasn't alone in that and staff had learned to travel through its echoing emptiness in groups of at least two.

Still, underground parking was heated and her car remained clear of snow. Both were advantages in the winter and in the summer, it eliminated feeding metres. It was a fair trade-off.

Tonight the lot was lightly sprinkled with cars, but the majority of them were clustered close to the elevators leading to the theatre. The fall plays were drawing large crowds and rave reviews.

"He was lucky, a recent article . . ." Carla's words froze to a stop. A van hurtled toward them out of the dark concrete cave.

"Damn, stupid drivers!" Carla yelled.

Beth jumped backward, colliding with the locked door. The vehicle sped toward them. Beth swirled to safety beside a parked car, dragging Carla, who was still shaking her fist and yelling, behind her.

The van raced by, careened off the fender of a car, then slammed to a sudden stop. A glance assured Beth that their path to the door and the elevator beyond it was clear. She plucked her keys from her coat pocket and dragged Carla, still yelling abuse at the driver, toward the door.

Beth wasted precious seconds fumbling with the key. She pulled the door open. A loud crack sounded and pieces of concrete flew from the wall, missing her head by inches.

Carla stopped yelling, ducked her head, hunched her body, and rushed through the open door, pushing Beth before her.

Beth pushed the door closed while Carla pressed the elevator button. The groan of metal giving under stress filled the hall.

"Oh, God. Hurry up. They're forcing the door. Who are they?"

"Does it matter? We've got to get to a phone and get help."

The elevator doors slid open. Beth followed Carla inside and pushed the button for the main floor. Were the elevator doors usually so slow to close?

The parkade door burst open. Through the closing elevator doors, Beth saw the sleeve of a navy jacket, a gloved hand, and reaching fingers.

Carla shook her hands as she danced from one foot to the other. "Who are they? Why are they after us?"

"Press all the buttons so it'll take a while to get back down here. They'll have to wait or take the stairs."

Carla grabbed the elevator's emergency telephone. "No one's answering."

She left it dangling when they reached the main floor.

The doors leading from the stairwell into the library were locked from the inside so with the elevator still ascending, they should have a few minutes before the men could reach them.

The main floor was dark. Hans, the security guard, must have turned off the overhead lights once they left. Dim light from the street lamps and the glow of the nearly full moon created glowing stripes between the stacks. Beth searched for a hiding place.

"We've got to get to the office and phone for help. Then we have to hide until the police arrive."

The distance wasn't great and a few bookracks offered cover, so with more speed than caution they raced across the children's story area toward the head librarian's office. Once they were safely inside, Beth closed and locked the door.

The entire floor seemed empty so the security officer must be patrolling the upper levels. Had he heard the gun shot?

Beth crouched between the desk and a bookcase sitting under the glassed portion of the inside office walls. She pulled the phone to the floor and dialled 911.

"There are intruders here with guns. We're hiding in the Public Library, main branch, librarian's office."

"May I have your name, please?"

"Just get help here."

The door to the stairwell slammed open. Two figures crept into a band of light.

Carla gasped and clutched at Beth's arm.

Beth spoke softly into the receiver. "They're on the main floor of the library."

"Can you describe them?"

"They have guns—some kind of rifle or shotgun or maybe a long pistol. There are two of them. They're wearing heavy jackets. One jacket is dark blue; I can't tell about the other, it could be brown or maybe black. They're both wearing jeans. One has a beard. I think they're Caucasian, light-skinned anyway. It's hard to tell. They're looking around, trying to spot us."

Carla tugged at Beth's sleeve and pointed toward the elevator. The number five winked off and four lit up.

"The elevator's moving. It could be the security guard. How long until someone gets here?"

"They're on their way Miss, . . what is your name?"

"Beth McKinney, I'm a librarian. They're coming this way."

Beth held her breath. The sound of Carla's rapid breathing filled the room, but didn't cover the pulse pounding through her veins. She watched the men approach. A couple more steps and they would be able to see her head. She ducked and pulled Carla down beside her.

"Oh God, oh God," Carla whispered.

Beth put her hand over her co-worker's mouth and shook her head.

The door handle rattled.

"Over here," a baritone voice called out.

Carla drew closer to the desk.

The door crashed open, bouncing as it hit the wall. Beth flinched as Carla squeezed her hand.

Where were the police?

A flashlight played above their heads but the desk hid them. Carla stiffened. From under the desk, Beth watched the man step nearer.

"Are you all right?" The emergency operator's voice broke the silence.

Beth dropped the receiver and grabbed a heavy book of cataloguing rules from the bookcase. She spun out of her crouch and stood facing the man who loomed dark and threatening in the light filtering through the windows. A Balaclava left only his eyes, nose, and mouth visible.

She threw the book at him, hitting him on the right shoulder. His left arm pulled upward at the impact. The gun barrel flew toward the ceiling and a shot shattered the glass wall above Carla's head.

Picking up another book, Beth threw it at the man's head. This time he successfully dodged it.

Carla picked up a crystal pyramid paperweight and heaved it at the looming man. The heavy triangle glanced off his temple. He staggered, then turned, and stumbled from the room.

Beth crouched, looking around. Now what? Books and paperweights might work as a surprise tactic but he could easily return with his friend and shoot them.

Carla pulled items from the desk and stacked them on the floor between them. She had a stapler, a coffee cup, and a letter opener.

"Are you all right? Was that a gun shot?" The voice coming through the receiver sounded frantic.

"Where are the police? These people are trying to kill us."

"You're okay?"

"No, we're not! Get us some help!"

"The police are on their way."

In the distance, Beth heard the faint throb of sirens. She peeked through the shattered glass clinging to the wooden frame above her head. The men huddled in a dark corner. The injured one was talking and looking at the office. He tried raising his gun, but his arm didn't work; the other man took the weapon from him.

Beth pushed Carla down, wondering how they could escape. A long minute dragged by before she heard the stairwell door sigh closed. Beth felt limp as the pulsing tension left her body, as quickly as it had flooded her veins.

Again, Beth peeked over the window ledge. The elevator doors opened and the night security guard stepped into the library.

Beth spoke into the phone.

"They left. They went down the stairs to the parking garage."

"Do you know what kind of vehicle they were driving?"

Looking at Carla, Beth whispered, "Did you see what colour of van they had?"

"It was dark, black maybe, or blue."

"We only know that it was a van, dark in colour."

"Is it safe for you to leave the phone to let the officers into the library?"

"Yes. They're gone now." Beth stood, holding the edge of the desk for support, then lurched out of the office door, her legs nearly collapsing under her.

A raspy male voice called from behind a pamphlet display rack. "Hold it right there."

She stood immobile in the beam of a flashlight.

Slowly she turned toward the voice. "Hans, it's Beth McKinney, I was going to unlock the front door for the police."

"Oh, sorry to scare you, but I thought you and Miss Wright left a while ago."

"We had a problem in the parking garage. Would you please unlock the front door, I want to make sure Carla is okay."

After that things faded into a blur of activity. Too many people asking the same questions. Their voices demanding that she think clearly. Carla preened under their attention and Beth let her tell the tale, increasing the number and variety of details with each repetition.

By the time she spotted Detective Ceretzke, most of the action was over and the investigation was focused on the logistics of the attack in the parking garage.

He strode through the open door and with a single pause to sweep the area with his sharp gaze, he continued to where she huddled in the back seat of a police car.

"Where's Constable Carstairs? She was supposed to protect you."

Beth felt annoyance sweep across her face. She fought her anger for control. "I told her I would call when I was ready to leave and I didn't. It didn't seem real that anyone would want to hurt me."

"You should have stayed home, away from this kind of danger."

Beth closed her eyes against the guilt she felt. She was a person who preached the wisdom of listening to professionals. The professionals had told her there could be danger not only in their words but also in their ongoing patrols. She opened her eyes, forcing her tears to remain unshed. "Go ahead and tell me I'm stupid, that I not only risked my own life but that I put Carla in danger too."

His tone softened as he asked, "Where is Constable Carstairs now?"

"I asked her to take Carla home. Carla isn't involved in this, is she? Does this have to do with Lisette's death?"

"We don't know anything yet. Right now we should get you home."

"I told the constable I would wait here until she got back. As you can see, I'm well protected."

Beth waved her hand at the police officers checking for fingerprints and examining the marks on the metal stairwell door. She'd already shown them the car that the van had hit and watched as they scraped flakes of paint from its fender to put in their ever-present evidence bags.

"I'm personally seeing you home," the detective said as he took her by the elbow. "We'll take your car. Mine is still at the station."

Shrugging his hand away, Beth turned to face him. "You're also going to tell me why people are trying to kill me."

"Let's get you home first."

The only cars left close to the library entrance were a white sports car and a rusted station wagon. She walked toward her sports car.

"You do like expensive toys," he said in an awed whisper.

The day had been long and emotional, the preceding night nearly sleepless, and someone had just tried to kill her. Beth gritted her teeth, she counted to ten, but the words escaped anyway. "It's leased. I lease a new car every three years. I own computer equipment that helps me earn my living. Tomorrow I'm buying a cell phone so I have a better chance of staying alive. Now can we drop the topic of my decadent lifestyle?"

He took the key from her shaking hand, helped her into the leather passenger seat, and slid behind the steering wheel. She felt him sneaking covert looks in her direction, but he said nothing on the drive to her house. When they reached her home he didn't ask permission, but thoroughly inspected the house while Magpie followed at his heels.

Beth slumped into a kitchen chair with Splatter, impatiently waiting for him to reappear and comment on her professionally equipped exercise room, or her atrium complete with an eight-person hot tub, or her partially enclosed sundeck.

Instead he pulled the plug on the screaming kettle and poured water over the tea bag. "I've arranged for a guard to be outside your house all night, but perhaps you want to call a friend to stay with you?"

She didn't answer, but stroked Splatter until the cat tired of the attention and jumped onto the top of the fridge, settling there to watch the unfolding events.

"You've been through an ordeal. You should call someone to stay with you."

She shook her head. "There's no one I would ask."

"Can't your parents come to stay for a while?"

"I don't want them involved." Magpie jumped onto her lap and she felt the vibration of his purring. Her parents had their own worries to deal with; she couldn't force hers on them too.

"How about I hang around for a while. Just until you feel okay about being alone?"

He stood close, his hand on her shoulder. It was a friendly hand with a warm, reassuring touch. She fought the urge to clutch it and pull his arms tightly around her. She wanted to lean on someone.

"I can't ask that."

"You didn't. I offered."

Beth felt calmer as she inhaled the faint hint of his cologne as it mingled with soap and a trace of sweat. Tranquillity flowed through her and with it came an overwhelming fatigue. "I want to know who those men are."

"We'll go over your descriptions again tomorrow, but now you should try to rest. I'll stay until the surveillance car gets here."

"No." With all the security built into her home, Beth felt safe but she didn't want to be alone. "I won't be able to sleep yet. Maybe you could stay a while. We could talk, just until I calm down."

CHAPTER 12

The bureaucratic pressure to resolve the case, so that the investigation of Hugh Dorrien's serious criminal activities could continue, had Jack sweating. He wasn't sure what rated as more serious than murder but then his job was to expedite the process not agree with it.

He pulled the brim of his hat forward, attempting to cover his receding hairline. He tugged his overcoat closed. The dry cleaner must have shrunk it. It had fit fine in the spring, now it barely buttoned.

Minutes later he watched Mike Ceretzke pull his truck into a spot beside his own dark blue sedan. Ceretzke wore his grey suit with the jacket open, no need to camouflage his waistline. His hair was damp. Jack uttered a disparaging obscenity as he stepped out of his car, ignoring Mike's puzzled expression.

Jack refused to give him the satisfaction of knowing how much he envied his forest of hair. His few strands were dry before he stepped out of the shower. He tugged on his hat brim again, no point advertising that he was getting a bit thin on top.

They found a booth by the front window. Mike smiled at the hovering waitress and her ever-ready pot of fresh coffee.

"The egg and sausage special, Irene, and keep the coffee coming."

Then he turned back to Jack, who was silently debating the merit of starting yet another diet.

"Aren't you eating?" Mike asked.

"Just toast," Jack mumbled in the direction of the waitress as she filled his cup.

"Someone tried to kill Beth McKinney. I was up half the night with her, just got out of the shower ten minutes ago."

The raised eyebrow elicited a tired chuckle.

"Get your mind out of the gutter. She's a good person who needed a shoulder. That's it."

Putting on his business expression, Jack said, "Give me the details."

"Couple of men waited in the library parkade and tried to run her and another librarian down; they followed the women upstairs with a shotgun. Lots of property damage, but they weren't hurt."

"So those media reports spooked someone. Can she identify them?"

"She gave a description. It's vague, but we're sure neither was Dorrien."

"Too bad." Jack sneered at the toast the waitress placed in front of him, then rifled the jam caddie for the peanut butter. Spreading a container on each piece of toast, he said, "I have some better news for you. The Park Patrol found a bag in the bushes near the crime scene. Animals had spread the contents around, but we've got shoes that look like a match to your cast, bloodstained coveralls, and a toque."

"Why didn't we find it earlier?"

"The temperature plummeted last night, looks like some animal pulled it out of a burrow to make room to crawl inside. A dog, or maybe a fox or coyote tore up the contents but we still have enough for analysis."

Mike sat back, staring at his perfectly browned sausages. "It was a lucky find wasn't it?"

"Hey, don't scorn good luck."

"I'm not, just being suspicious. You would think the blood would have attracted an animal Monday night, not twenty-four hours and a big temperature drop later."

"There's no mystery, Mike. A country boy like you knows that most animals hide in the bush until they start looking for a burrow to hibernate in. It's logical that they'll clear the hole out first. Look, it's good evidence and maybe it'll even convict Dorrien."

"It does help with the timeline. I was wondering what Dorrien did with his clothes. Taking a change of shoes with him and wearing coveralls could cut his time considerably, but why not toss the bag in the river? That was a dumb mistake."

"Maybe he figured he could get back to ditch it before we found the stuff."

"The shoes match the print?"

"They're a size 11-1/2, just like the cast."

"You talked to Ident yet?"

"Not yet, but it's going to be a match. I'll bet on it."

Mike finished his last bite of sausage and wiped up the remaining egg yoke with his toast.

Downing a mouthful of coffee, Jack added, "My source contacted me."

"What now?"

"Hugh's looking for a disc; tore the house apart yesterday trying to find it. Hugh wouldn't say what was on it, but it must be important."

"We'll have to ask him."

"We can't do that. I don't want him suspicious of his staff. If we keep poking around we'll discover its contents ourselves."

*****

Tony opened the door and directed them to the sitting room where the two officers took the same delicate seats they had occupied the previous day. Hugh watched them enter, but sat silently, waiting for them to initiate conversation. Tony stood close to his boss with his arms folded across his chest, acting like the bodyguard Mike figured him to be.

Hugh didn't offer coffee or pleasantries.

Mike followed his lead and asked his first question. "Where were you last evening around nine o'clock?"

"Home. Why, what do you want to blame on me now?" Dorrien said, his wrinkles deepening into a scowl. He clenched his fists as if ready to take on the world. His powerful jaw jutted in their direction. "I'm not stupid; I know you're trying to tie me into Lisette's murder."

Mike remembered watching him play hockey; he had been a bruiser. "Can anyone vouch for your presence?"

"Melissa was out for the evening. Tony and Helen had gone home earlier."

"Did you receive any phone calls or visitors?"

"Lots of calls, everyone wanted to offer condolences. You want a list so you can harass my friends or will you take my word for it?"

"A list would be helpful. Have it available when we're ready to leave."

Hugh's expression darkened, but he remained silent.

Mike wondered who Hugh had lined up to do his dirty work at the library. He glanced at Tony but knew the bodyguard didn't fit the women's descriptions. Checking Hugh's callers would be a waste of time, but necessary. His next question was more important and might help hang Hugh.

"What kind of shoes were you wearing Monday morning?"

Hugh looked at his feet, as if waiting for them to supply the answer. "I don't remember. Why?"

"Where do you buy your shoes?"

"Is this relevant?"

"I wouldn't ask if it wasn't."

Colour flushed into Hugh's cheeks giving them an uneven coating of splotches. Hugh glared, but finally named an exclusive shoe store. "I get all my shoes there."

"So they will have records of what you've bought?"

"They know what I buy."

Mike added the store to his list of interviews.

"Could we speak to your staff now?"

"She wasn't killed here, so why do you have to talk to them?" Hugh asked, as he leaned toward them across the empty coffee table.

Mike fought an impulse to pull him across the table by his shirt collar and demand answers. Instead, he held his ground wondering if Hugh was trying to intimidate them. Hugh drew back.

"We need to clarify Lisette's movements on Monday morning," Mike answered. "We hope to find out if she mentioned a meeting, or if she phoned anyone, or was worried about something. Just routine questions that will help us fill in the details of her movements prior to her death."

Mike watched Hugh closely, hoping for a reaction that would lead him in questioning the staff.

"Let's see. Your staff consists of your assistant, the children's nanny, and who else?"

"The cook, Helen."

"Any cleaning help?"

"What would a cleaning woman know? This is ridiculous."

Mike repeated the question.

"Yes, we have a cleaning woman. Helen can give you her telephone number."

"No one else?"

"We hire firms to look after the yard and sometimes we bring in people to handle the heavier cleaning and of course there are caterers for parties. Tony will provide the names of those firms if you need them, but we haven't used any of them in the past week."

"Thank you sir, now if you would excuse us, we will begin our questioning with Tony."

The officers watched Hugh leave the room and then Mike turned to Tony who maintained his belligerent stance. He resembled a shark in his grey tailored suit and black tie. The tie was covered in a subdued repetitive pattern resembling a Picassos painting. His shoes were glossy leather slip-ons, maybe a size nine, too small to fit the crime scene cast.

"Mr. Bendall, when did you last see Mrs. Dorrien alive?"

"Monday before she went running."

"Where did you see her?"

"In the hall in front of Mr. Dorrien's office." He pointed vaguely toward the back of the house.

"Was she alone?"

"Yes."

"What was she doing?"

He looked toward the closed door and clenched his neatly manicured hands. "I think she was coming out of Mr. Dorrien's office. I thought Mr. Dorrien was inside so I went in but he wasn't there."

His body language screamed stress. Taking advantage of his mood, Mike continued his line of questioning.

"Why were you surprised that he wasn't there?"

"He didn't like anyone messing around in his office. Even the cleaner, Rosa, isn't allowed in there on her own. Lisette knew that she shouldn't have been there without Mr. Dorrien being present."

"Were there other places in the house he considered that private?"

"No, just his office."

"I wouldn't have thought real estate management was such a sensitive business."

"Most of the time it isn't. Most of the work is done downtown by the office staff."

Abruptly, Tony stopped talking and clenched his fists at his side. "What does this have to do with Lisette's death?"

Mike ignored Tony's question, but filed the knowledge that Hugh's assistant and Lisette were on a first name basis, though in an age of casual employee-employer relationships was that significant? Still he did call Hugh, Mr. Dorrien.

"What work did he do at home?" Mike asked.

Tony unclenched his fists, looked from one man to the other, twisted his ring, and then checked his cuticles. He gnawed at his thumbnail, destroying the perfection of his manicure before answering the question. "Sometimes he met clients outside office hours. Being available to help clients night or day is the best way to make them happy."

In a defensive tone, he added, "His business was prospering because people knew they could count on him when they needed him."

"What type of service does his company provide?"

Tony drew himself to attention and spoke as if reciting a commercial. "Cross-Canada Realty Management provides a comprehensive range of services to both residential and commercial customers. We handle mostly commercial space, some residential property too, but only for a select clientele. We find renters, show suites, collect rents, and arrange for maintenance and repairs when they're needed."

"What kind of maintenance?"

"Mostly we arrange for tradesmen. Some of our most prestigious homes are nearly a hundred years old and require constant attention. If a home is designated an historical building, the owner can't even do a proper renovation. Besides, not all owners want to invest in major renovations on rental properties so they just keep patching them up. That's one reason we stick mainly to commercial properties where we rarely encounter major maintenance problems."

"What services did Mr. Dorrien provide from his home after hours?"

"Someone might get in town late or be tied up in meetings all day. He was often asked to show office space at night. Mr. Dorrien supplied information about sites and took a few special clients to see available space."

"I'm surprised his staff doesn't do that."

"These are very important clients."

Catching Jack's glare, Mike decided not to push. Besides, he already knew Hugh's business included arranging meeting locations for drug sales and the storage and fencing of stolen goods. Was he also providing a convenient hideout for criminals lying low, criminals like the Shotgun Gang? Mike shelved the thought, planning to share it with Evan at their next meeting.

Hugh's criminal activities were Jack's business, not his. Mike moved the questioning back to the subject of Lisette.

"How was Mrs. Dorrien dressed when you saw her?"

"Navy slacks with a white and navy sweater, a matching bracelet and earrings. She always looked classy in that outfit."

Mike caught himself before he nodded his agreement. Lovely

Lisette would have considered it important to be beautiful and well-groomed even in the morning.

"Not dressed for her run?"

"She was on her way upstairs to change, so I figured she was heading out pretty quick."

"About what time was that?"

"Between ten and ten-fifteen. I was on my way to tell Mr. Dorrien we had rented the McConnell Building space, so it was early. Melissa had just returned from taking Jarrett to school. Yes, it was around ten."

"Wasn't that early if she didn't get to the park until noon?"

"You're right." He looked as though he was surprised he hadn't thought of the time difference before. "She didn't usually leave until about eleven-thirty." Tony pursed his lips and shrugged. "She must have planned on doing something else until then."

"Did she mention any plans?"

"No, but then she didn't report to me."

"Did she seem upset or excited?"

"No. Well, maybe she was nervous but that was because I caught her in the office."

"What about Mr. Dorrien, where was he at that time?"

"Like I said, I thought he was in his office."

Mike felt his patience evaporating. "If you were going to guess where he was, where would it be?"

"He could have gone anywhere. An outside door leads from his office to the street. His jaw hurt, so maybe he went for a walk. I don't know." Tony straightened the crease in his slacks.

Mike tried another tactic. "What was his schedule for the day?"

"Let me check." Pulling a small notebook from his jacket pocket, Tony flipped the pages backward. He looked up. "I like to keep a duplicate calendar of appointments, so I can check it when I'm away from my desk." He stopped at an entry and read it aloud. "Work out at the gym, eight-thirty to nine-thirty." He looked up and added, "Mr. Dorrien has been going to the gym every morning since the beginning of September."

He looked back at the notebook. "Meeting re McConnell Building, ten o'clock, but that was cancelled. Luncheon at the Businessman's Club twelve to one. He was the guest speaker. Then at the downtown office from one-thirty to four-thirty, to deal with paperwork and meetings."

Tony swallowed hard. "They were supposed to go out for dinner that evening and then to the opera. That didn't happen."

"What about the dental appointment?"

Tony looked at his notebook. "Dentist? I don't have a dentist listed here."

"He stopped on his way to the luncheon meeting."

"Oh well, of it was a last minute appointment maybe he noted it in the calendar on my desk. We use that as a master record. Does it matter, if he was at the dentist I mean?"

"Just checking details. Did you hear Mrs. Dorrien mention any friends she might have planned visiting?"

"No, she rarely went out and then it was just lunch with some woman."

"How do you know it was with a woman?"

"She said so. I had no reason to doubt her."

"So she never mentioned a man, maybe an instructor?"

"Arthur Howarth runs her self-defence class and Mary Carpenter was her watercolour instructor. Do you mean them?"

"Perhaps. How was your relationship with Mrs. Dorrien?"

Tony's eyes widened, then he paused digesting the meaning of the question. "She was a lovely lady but a very lonely person. Her paintings are beautiful but she missed Montreal as much as I do. I guess you could say we were soul mates."

"Where were you between eleven and twelve Monday?"

"Probably working here. I went to meet Mr. Dorrien at the office at one-thirty."

"Were you or weren't you working here?"

"Sure I was."

"Did you see any of the other staff?"

"No, I'm hidden away when I'm in my office. It's at the end of the hall next to Mr. Dorrien's. No one has reason to go there."

"Did you receive or make any phone calls?"

"Not that I remember but I'll check my records."

"How did Mrs. Dorrien get along with the other staff?"

"She was sort of okay with Helen the cook, but Melissa was a sore spot with her."

Mike pounced on that, recalling Beth's mention of discord. "What was the problem?"

"Melissa always hovered over the kids, not letting Lisette be alone with them for a minute. Lisette got upset and blamed Melissa for stealing the kids' affection. The kids like Melissa and that made for more jealousy."

Mike recalled the pretty girl he'd glimpsed when they searched the house and how she had met his inquiring look with a bold, sexy challenge. "Was the jealousy only because of the kids or was there something between Melissa and Mr. Dorrien?"

"Well, you'd think he would have sense enough to keep anything extra out of his home but Melissa isn't shy about flaunting herself. Lisette could have had cause to worry."

"Why didn't Lisette dismiss Melissa if she was jealous of her?"

"Mr. Dorrien's orders. Only he could fire the staff and we knew it would only happen if we countered his specific instructions."

"Which were?"

"Well, one was about going into his office and poking about."

"The others?"

"Just one other. He told us he would fire us immediately if we allowed Lisette unsupervised control of the kids."

"Why was that?" Mike asked.

"He's paranoid. I think it's because his first wife left him and took their kids. He didn't see them again until they were in their teens and he swore it wouldn't happen again. Swore he'd kill anyone who tried to take his kids away."

Mike digested the implications of the information. Would Hugh murder to prevent Lisette from taking the kids?

"Do you think he's capable of murder?"

"Well, he has a violent temper. They argued a lot but killing her like that seems too cold for him. Though, if they were fighting when it happened I'm sure he could have done it."

"Did Mrs. Dorrien have affairs?"

"You mean a guy on the side?" Tony stood straighter, but his body language screamed for action.

Mike tapped his pen on the notebook. Did Tony see himself as a knight ready to defend his lady?

"No way. If anyone fooled around it was Mr. Dorrien."

"And Melissa was just following orders when she kept Mrs. Dorrien from being alone with the children?"

"Yeah, that's right. We all follow the same rules."

"How long have you been employed by Mr. Dorrien?"

"About two and a half years. He recruited me out of the head office in Montreal."

Mike turned the conversation over in his mind, had he overlooked any questions? "Do you live in this house Mr. Bendall?"

"No, I rent an apartment a few blocks away. I'm close if he needs me, but I like having my own place."

"Do you know if Mr. Dorrien has enemies who might use his wife to get at him?"

"No one makes enemies in real estate management. Not likely."

"Where were you last night, about nine o'clock?"

"Why?"

"Just answer."

"I was at the home of a friend. I can give you her name; she'll vouch for me."

"If you would and the address as well."

Tony tore a sheet from the back of his notebook and scribbled a name, phone number, and address.

He handed it to Mike who asked, "Is there anything else you want to tell us?"

The young man shook his head.

"Then, thank you for your time. We may need to talk with you again, but keep my card in case you remember something."

Mike passed him a business card.

"Please ask Melissa to come in next."

As the door shut, Jack turned toward Mike. "Hugh's motive is firming up."

"We still need evidence to take to court and your informant's testimony would help."

"My informant is off-limits; I've told you that before."

A knock on the door interrupted their staring match. A light, flowery scent followed Melissa into the room. She wore her blonde hair in a knot on the top of her head, creating a cascade of unruly curls. Her healthy copper-brown skin spoke of hours of outdoor play. Patched jeans covered firm, muscular limbs. Dress her up and even elegant Lisette would have reason to worry.

"Melissa, we're here to ask you a few questions."

"Sure, anything I can do." She bounced lightly across the room and sat primly to the sofa. After a moment of squirming, she curled into a corner and pulled her tiny feet up after her.

"How did you come to work for Mrs. Dorrien?"

"Well, I was born in Montreal, but my parents are English. My Dad is a doctor; Mom is an accountant. They wanted me to go to university. Boring! I signed onto a placement firm for nannies right after high school. It's an easy way to see the country and I plan on going overseas if I take another assignment."

She pulled her sandal-clad feet further under her and leaned toward the officers.

"Anyway, Mr. Dorrien wanted someone fluent in both English and French. I jumped at the chance because all my friends were leaving the province, too. Anyway, that was when Joelle was just a baby, so sweet, and Jarrett, he's a doll."

Mike cut into the flood of words. "How do you get along with Mr. and Mrs. Dorrien and the other staff?"

"Hugh's fun. He is sort of old, but he's getting into shape. When he dresses up in his tux—wow. He's tough but lets you know the rules. Mrs. D. didn't like me. Always upset because I wasn't supposed to leave her alone with the kids. Hugh has a thing about it but I guess I can understand his point of view. I mean she was the one who threatened to take the kids away. Anyway, she behaved like it was my fault so we didn't get along so well. I guess being that rigid is an age thing."

She leaned back and smiled a Cheshire cat smile.

"Did you get along with the other staff, Tony and Helen?"

"Tony's gorgeous and he knows it. But basically he's a pain. I think the only reason they hired him was because he follows rules like a fanatic. He never seems to have much to do. Spends," she hesitated and rephrased her response. "Spent more time hanging around Mrs. D. like a lost puppy, than he did working for Hugh."

"Did he ever make advances to you?"

"No, worse luck. I'd love to put him in his place, but he was really stuck on her."

"On Mrs. Dorrien?"

"Yes sir." She leaned toward Mike, her eyes bright with mischief. "You could see it from a mile away. She would be just polite, but you had to sort of wonder if she didn't like him. He is so handsome and you know how some older women go for young guys."

"Did you ever see them together, doing anything that was more than just being friendly?"

"Well now, maybe." She gnawed thoughtfully on the end of a loose curl.

"Melissa, do you remember something?" Mike leaned forward, his face nearly meeting hers across the coffee table.

"Once I caught them coming out of Mrs. D's room. They acted all surprised, but Tony looked awful guilty."

Mike leaned against the back of his chair while watching the girl for further reactions. Tony hadn't mentioned the episode, but his fascination with Lisette was obvious. The possibility that the attraction was mutual was a complication he hadn't expected. Could Hugh's jealousy and Beth's suspicions of Lisette having a lover have a basis in fact? Could Tony be the man? He let the idea settle and went on with his questions.

"What are Tony's duties?"

"Well, he's at the beck and call of them both, or he was." Melissa looked up, flustered by her slip. "It's hard to remember she's really dead. Anyway, Tony would drive them around. He arranged to have their parties catered and set up their appointments. Hugh wanted Tony to help with meetings. He wasn't in the office all the time, but he was on call in case they needed him."

"What can you tell us about the cook. Helen, is it?"

"Helen Grimswold, she's from around here. She hardly even talks to the rest of us." Then just as breathlessly Melissa added, "Not that she's stuck up, just real quiet. When she's not cooking, she's reading—classics if you can believe it—like Shakespeare and Faulkner. I like historical romance myself, but mostly I just read magazines."

"What about Mr. and Mrs. Dorrien, did they get along?"

"Most times, but . . maybe I shouldn't say."

"What's on your mind."

Her blue eyes sparkled with untold gossip and just maybe, Mike decided, with malice.

"Well, the last few months Hugh has been really grouchy. He's always yelling at one of us. Mrs. D, she's been so cheerful, happier than I ever saw her before. Anyway, I think she did it to annoy him, to drive him crazy."

"Did what?"

"Well if he yelled, she smiled all happy. Or, she would start singing and he'd walk out of the room and slam the door. Hugh told me every day to watch the kids, like they were in danger. When I asked why, he got mad at me so I didn't ask anymore."

"Did you see Mrs. Dorrien, Monday morning?"

"Sure. She was painting but insisted on coming out to kiss the kids before we took Jarrett to school. I didn't see her after Joelle and I got back."

"How would you describe her mood?"

"Oh, well maybe she wasn't as cheerful as she'd been lately, but she was all lovey with the kids. Do you think she had a premonition?"

"Did she seem nervous?"

Melissa continued chewing her hair. "She was always kind of nervous. Sometimes I thought she was anorexic or something. A type A personality—always had to be moving and doing things."

"Did she talk about meeting anyone?"

"No, just waved bye to the kids and gave me a dirty look. Nothing unusual."

"Did she mention any friends or pay special attention to anyone who visited the house?"

"No, well there was Henry. He was a caterer who worked for them once. He was sort of cute but I don't think she was interested in him."

"Where were you from eleven to noon Monday, when Mrs. Dorrien was killed?"

"Watching Sesame Street with Joelle."

"Where were you last evening?"

"It was half-price at the movies. So Safiya, she's a nanny who works down the street. She's from Kenya. Anyway, we always go out for supper and then the movies when it's half-price day."

"What time did you get home?"

"About eleven-thirty. We went to the late show. It gives us more time away from the house; makes it like a real evening out. Sometimes we go to a bar afterward, but not last night. It didn't seem right. I probably shouldn't have even gone out but Hugh insisted. He knew there would be condolence calls and he wanted to be here to answer them. He didn't seem to mind being left alone."

"When did you leave?"

"We met in time to catch the six o'clock bus."

"Where can we contact Safiya?"

"Don't you believe me? Why would I lie?" She straightened her legs and her feet hit the floor.

"Her phone number?" Mike persisted.

Grudgingly, she recited the number.

Nodding as he made a final note, Mike smiled and thanked her for her help. "Could you send in Mrs. Grimswold?"

"Sure thing." A sullen pout had replaced her perky tone.

Mike turned to Jack Pierce as the door cut off the view of the trim derriere. "Cute!"

Jack smiled but shook his head. "You're too old for that kind of action."

"Do you think Hugh Dorrien is too old?"

A sharp knock at the sitting room door cut off Jack's reply.

"Come in, Mrs. Grimswold," Mike called.

"It's Miss Grimswold, if you please."

Tall, thin, and grim were the adjectives that crowded Mike's mind as he met the cook's gaze. She fit into the room well, as thin and fragile as its furnishings, but the ropes of muscle that ran the length of her arms reminded Mike that appearances could be misleading.

A floral, bib apron partially covered her shirtwaist dress. Her large shoes sported sensible rubber soles, ideal for the lady who stands all day.

"Would you have a seat please, Miss Grimswold?"

She assessed both men then sat on the sofa, crossing her arms over her thin chest. "Was it my knife?"

"We're still waiting on the lab results. We're here to ask you some questions that we hope might help us find Mrs. Dorrien's killer."

"First, you can tell me who he is," she said, looking pointedly at Jack.

"Of course, I'm sorry. Sergeant Pierce is from the RCMP."

"I thought so. Why are they interested?"

"He is observing to see if they can link our investigation to a couple of other crimes around the country."

"Do you expect me to believe that?"

"Miss Grimswold, it doesn't matter what you believe, providing you answer our questions."

She glared at him, then shrugged. "What do you want to know?"

"You are from Alberta?"

"What does that have to do with Mrs. Dorrien's death?"

"Nothing really. I'd just like to know."

With a look that told him that she thought he was being ignorant, she named a small town near Edmonton where a large number of French-speaking Canadians made their home.

"So you speak French?"

"He insisted on it. He felt it important that his children be raised in a bilingual environment." She lifted her chin proudly, stretching her skinny neck and exposing the cords and wrinkles running the length of its hollows.

"Have you worked here long?"

"Since they arrived. They used to have other staff but he fired them."

"Did Mr. Dorrien give a reason for firing the others?"

"He wanted a Quebec flavour to the house."

"But Mr. Dorrien didn't bring a cook from Quebec."

"My parents are French Canadian and I have spent many years in Montreal. I guess that was close enough."

"Do you like it here?"

"If I didn't, I wouldn't be here."

"Well, not everyone has a choice what with having to find another job and everything."

"I worked in the oil camps up north for twenty years, it's good money and I saved. I invested my retirement funds and now I can work when and where I want."

Mike's mind flashed to Beth McKinney, another woman who seemed able to take care of herself financially.

"Did you get along well with both Mr. and Mrs. Dorrien?"

"He just wanted good plain cooking, but Mrs. Dorrien kept asking for low calorie stuff. That low-fat, low-sugar, low-cholesterol stuff is also low taste. I just told her to eat-up and not worry about gaining weight. She was so active that she didn't have to worry anyway. Most of the time though we got along just fine." She folded her hands in her lap and waited silently for him to speak.

"What about the other staff, do you get along with them?"

"Melissa is a baby herself but she's good with the little ones.

Likes to talk, rarely says anything worth listening to, but she eats good.

"Tony Bendall, I don't see often. Doesn't eat breakfast or supper here. Lunch sometimes. Something about him—I don't trust him I guess."

"Why?"

"Just like I do not trust package labels, I do not trust him."

"Did you see Mrs. Dorrien last Monday morning?"

"She had her usual breakfast, poached egg on dry toast with a half grapefruit, no sugar, and decaffeinated coffee. I kept telling her that people should enjoy their food but her, she never wanted to listen." Her lips tightened and she shook her head.

"Did she mention planning to meet anyone or seem excited about her day?"

"No, she just rushed through breakfast like always. Said she was going up to paint. I cleaned up, then took a break to read a bit and I thought I was late starting lunch when I saw her decked out in her running-suit, heading down the driveway. She usually goes at eleven-thirty and is back by one, just missing lunch. I checked the time and it was only ten-twenty."

"You're sure she didn't mention meeting anyone?"

"Like I already told you, no."

"Did she ever talk to you about her friends?"

"Never."

"Was she carrying anything when she left?"

"No."

"Where were you between eleven and noon Monday?"

"In my kitchen."

"Was anyone with you?"

"Well, Joelle and Melissa were upstairs until lunch at twelve-thirty. I don't know where Tony was, so I guess no one was with me."

"What about last night around nine or nine-thirty?"

"I was home, reading."

"Can anyone confirm that? Did you get any callers?"

"Not in person or by phone."

"Is there anything you can tell us that might help with this case?"

"Nothing."

"Thank you for your help. Perhaps you could give us the cleaning lady's name and phone number."

"Got it right here." She handed him a card. "Tony said you needed it."

"When will she be here again?"

"Thursday, before the funeral."

With that final word, she left the room.

Mike looked at the card expecting a hand-written address instead it was a printed business card for Rosa Havestock Cleaning Services Ltd. It listed a business phone, a cell phone, a fax number, a website, and an e-mail address. He silently handed it to Jack.

"The world it is changing."

CHAPTER 13

Mike had arranged to meet Beth after her run, which she refused to give up, although she did agree that Hilda could watch her from the patrol car. Mike wanted to ask her questions arising from his interviews with Dorrien's staff and Jack insisted on accompanying him.

Before their meeting, he read Jack's report on her background. It was impressive. She had put herself through school on scholarships, eventually graduating with a Masters in Business Administration from McMaster University. Then she had worked for seven years at, a prestigious accounting firm.

The firm gave her a solid reference. After she left their employ, they had referred clients wanting on-line trading skills to her. They'd also sent others who needed detailed research on companies. Apparently, whole groups of people wanted to watch over their own finances but didn't have the time or inclination to take a course in financial planning. Beth's flexible schedule and broad knowledge base met their needs.

The head librarian at the public library also spoke highly of her skill in dealing with clients. She was the person handed problem patrons and always seemed able to find exactly what they wanted.

Two years ago, she had bought her house without the necessity of a mortgage. Her latest tax records showed her annual gross was more than he made in three years, though she paid less tax than he did in one.

The report skipped over her social life or maybe she didn't have much of one. She didn't have a significant other, hadn't been exclusive with anyone for the two years since she broke up with . . .

Mike looked up to find Jack grinning at him. Obviously, his hatred of Richard Tanner was too well known.

At least she'd had the good sense to break off with him. Shortly after splitting, he had destroyed her parent's business. No wonder she was reluctant to speak to the media.

She belonged to a bunch of associations, but wasn't active in any. Never married, no kids, no criminal record, and even her driving record showed only a couple of speeding tickets. It all confirmed his gut belief that she was entirely innocent of Lisette's murder.

Magpie greeted them cordially by rubbing against Mike's leg and checking for the smell of donuts on his hand. He had neglected to bring any, but Jack pulled a partially eaten chocolate bar from his pocket. Splatter jumped from her perch on the fireplace mantel and rushed to sniff the candy, then sampled it. She turned up her nose after deciding it was not to her taste. Magpie looked at Jack with scorn, turned tail, and stalked off to resume his nap.

Sitting in Beth's sunny kitchen with fresh coffee in hand, Mike studied her surreptitiously. She slumped in her chair, rested her elbows on the table, and held her coffee mug in both hands. She didn't seem Tanner's type, though truthfully he didn't know what type Tanner preferred. The slight bags under her eyes and her pale face hinted at fatigue. Still, considering her week had started with a friend being murdered and continued with an attempt on her own life, he figured she looked just fine.

"Did you finally sleep?" Mike asked, trying to put her at ease, but also worried about how she was managing.

Her darting glance first at Jack, then at him, spoke volumes. When she met his gaze he felt warm and welcome, then a cold front moved into her eyes, freezing him back to business.

She placed her mug on the table and straightened in her chair. "I'm sorry. I shouldn't have imposed on your kindness last night. I don't usually fall apart."

"You probably don't usually have a car, or a gun, pointed at you." Was her sudden coolness because she was embarrassed he'd mentioned her weakness on the previous night?

"I was scared," she said, but her tone revealed no lingering effects from the fear.

Jack removed his fedora and sat it on the table near him. He traced a finger around the brim and peered at her. "Being scared is smart sometimes, but jogging alone just now might not be smart."

"I would be a victim if I let them force me into hiding."

Mike watched the fierce looks flying between them. Jack knew as he did, that being dead would make her more of a victim than hiding. He broke the silence by saying, "Yesterday you mentioned that Lisette didn't get along with Tony. We talked to some of Lisette's staff today and they agree with you, but they also think a spark of attraction could have been concealed under the antagonism."

Again, she turned her watchful gaze on him, studying his words before answering. "Lisette and Tony." She rolled the names off her tongue as if trying to taste the flavour and decide if they complemented each other.

Mike noticed how her crow's-feet deepened and the look in her eyes lost its focus as she concentrated on remembering the past. He was certain he could believe whatever she deduced.

"If they were involved she hid it well."

"What can you tell us about their relationship? Did she feel threatened by him?"

She paused for a long moment, again taking sufficient time to analyze and organize before answering.

"Lisette claimed he was spying on her. She caught him in her room one day and he made some feeble excuse about looking for Hugh. He followed her everywhere. He was always trying to ingratiate himself, praising her pictures, trying to be her friend, and going on about how they were both far from home and should support each other."

She paused long enough to rearrange her coffee mug and offer them bakery shop cookies.

"Did he scare her? No. Did he make her uncomfortable? Yes. I can't believe he was her type." As she voiced the last pronouncement, her gaze strayed toward the kitchen counter where the coffeepot sat, then towards Mike's empty cup.

"Would you like a second?" she asked.

Mike heard a forced note in her voice. Was it fatigue, wariness, or a desire to be rid of them?

"I'd love more, but I'll get it," he said. The coffee was far superior to the stuff at the station and he wasn't going to deprive himself of a second cup.

Mike sauntered to the counter, then returned to the table to refill their cups. As he replaced the pot on the hot plate, he spotted a patrol car driving slowly down the alley.

"We were told most of the staff was fired about two and a half years ago. That's when Tony and Melissa were hired as replacements. Do you know what led up to that incident?"

"Oh, that."

She looked even more dejected, something Mike had thought impossible.

"It was my fault in a way. It started innocently. Lisette wanted to feel needed and useful. She liked the nanny they had at the time and spent a lot of time with her and the kids, but she didn't have enough to keep herself busy. Hugh didn't want her working. He wanted her at home ready to entertain his friends and anticipate his next whim."

Beth's voice became a whisper, so Mike leaned closer to hear her words.

"She said she had put up with his archaic attitude since they were married, but that she had outgrown it. She had never had a chance to be her own person and she was tired of being pushed to do what other people wanted."

Beth stopped talking and stared toward the window.

"And this led to the staff change?" Mike asked, pulling her back to the present.

In a firmer voice, she continued her story. "Around that time,

Hugh bought a computer so that he could access his business records from home. Lisette resolved to change the confines of her world and decided to start by learning to use the computer. I gave her a book because she was anxious to start . . . "

Beth paused, fidgeting with the spoon from the sugar bowl. Then with a look in his direction, she plunged it back into the dish and laid her hands flat on the tabletop. At second later, they were tracing the embossed pattern on her coffee cup.

"Beth." Mike reached for her hand, stilling its nervous movement. He saw tears glistening in her eyes.

"A couple of days later she arrived at the lookout with a bruise on her cheek. Hugh had found her in his den and exploded. Lisette swore that was the only time he ever hit her, but I doubt it. When does a bully only hit someone once?"

She pulled her hand from his grip. "He yelled at her to get away from the machine and out of his office. He grabbed her arm and pushed her out of the den without listening to her explanation."

Mike fought to keep his disgust from showing.

"She had spirit then and packed for the kids and herself. When Hugh stalked out of his office ready to continue the fight, he found her calling a cab. She had booked a flight to Paris, intending to join her sister.

"He calmed down and tried to talk her into staying, pleading that he was upset and scared that she would damage his files. Then, because she wasn't succumbing to his charms, he changed his tactics. He reminded her that his first wife had taken their kids and deserted him. Hugh told her that he would kill her before he let it happen again."

Abusive husbands weren't new to Mike and he knew that given the right circumstances anything could set them off. "She hadn't seen that side of him before?" he asked.

"She assured me that she hadn't. She knew about his temper, but claimed he had never hit her before."

"Why didn't she press charges?"

"I tried to convince her to, but she believed his threat and was afraid to leave. Then he took her and the kids to Montreal for a holiday as a way to apologize, but when they returned a month later, she found that Hugh had fired the staff. Melissa and Tony arrived and were threatened with instant dismissal if Lisette was left alone with the kids.

"After that, her life became unbearable but she couldn't see a way out. Hugh told her bluntly that if she wanted to leave she could, but not to expect to take the kids with her. He threatened that if she left without them he would charge her with abandonment and fight her for custody. He frightened her into believing that his lawyer could keep her from seeing them again. She was afraid that with his standing in the community the odds of him getting custody were in his favour."

"Was she having an affair at that time?"

"An affair?" Beth dropped her gaze, breaking the intimacy they'd shared.

Mike blinked, then looked at Jack to gauge his reaction to her revelations. Jack had probably known about the abuse all the time, maybe even used it to recruit and control Lisette. Jack met his silent anger with a raised eyebrow and a tiny shrug. So the Mounties used whatever lever they could even the safety of a couple of kids. That was real class. May their misdeeds come back to haunt them.

Mike shifted his attention back to Beth. With a bad taste growing in his mouth, he realized that he had to continue digging into Lisette's personal life, although if Lisette had found someone decent to love it should be no one's affair but hers, certainly not something to be dragged through a murder case.

"Hugh Dorrien says Lisette was having an affair and took the little girl to her lover's apartment."

"I don't believe it, not then, not when she was happy."

"But later?"

Beth turned her cup and rubbed her thumb over a smudge on the high-gloss surface. "After that, yes she had affairs. She didn't hide them."

"She didn't hide them from you or from anyone?"

"Hugh knew. Apparently after the computer incident they lived separate lives."

"Hugh is acting like a jealous husband. Why would he lie?"

"I don't know. Maybe he's embarrassed. Maybe he doesn't want to admit to the type of life they led. Maybe he's naturally jealous and possessive."

"Why wasn't the cook fired at the same time as the other staff?"

"Maybe Hugh felt she could be trusted."

"And Hugh hired the new staff?"

"Yes. Lisette didn't know what was happening until it was too late to make choices, even if Hugh would have let her. Hugh nearly destroyed her with that move."

"Did she ever talk about her husband's business associates?"

"She and the kids were told to stay out of sight when business took place. Hugh's office has a private, outside entrance and she said he enjoyed acting mysterious, having clients creep in and out of the yard. It all sounded bizarre."

"Did Lisette describe any of the visitors?"

"I don't think she saw them. She didn't refer to them as individuals, only as a group, like they weren't real people to her. Not people she had met or wanted to meet."

Mike caught a signal from Jack. This was information he didn't want Mike to probe, but he didn't care and felt no desire to stop Beth from talking now that she was filling in blanks. Besides, he wasn't interested in Hugh's nocturnal activities unless they lead to making the murder charge stick.

"There were visitors he expected Lisette to entertain. The company was big on staff picnics and wanted their people attending conferences and training sessions. Sometimes she mentioned invitations for dinner and the symphony and opera. The company had tickets for all the sports teams and they expected the staff to support community activities. Sometimes Lisette refused to go. Hugh was furious when she did that, but she swore he never hit her again."

Mike ran his fingers through his hair, debating the wording of his next question. "You said Tony wasn't her type, but that she'd had affairs in the past and that you believe there was currently another man in her life. Why?"

Beth's mug stopped midway to her lips. She sat as if frozen, then looked away from him and toward Jack. Her words came slowly, carefully, in almost a whisper. "She had changed in the past six months. Her self-confidence had improved and her eyes held the gleam of a smile. It could have been a new man in her life or something as good. The last few weeks she was bursting to tell me something."

Beth walked to the patio door. Mike saw the blue jays quartering the yard, taunting the cats that were chattering at them from behind the glass door.

She turned to face him. "If she had told me what was on her mind maybe I could help you find her killer. Have you found Howard yet?"

"Not yet, but we're on our way to talk with Mr. Domke. Perhaps he saw Lisette with someone on another day."

Mike stood beside her and reached out, touching her arm. "Perhaps you should forget about working in the library until we catch the creeps who tried to hurt you."

"No one's forcing me to change my life."

Her words worried him far more than they should. He better arrange for continuing protection, maybe ask Super Sam to release a statement about the false media report. Would Hugh believe such a report or think they were hiding the truth and increase their efforts to hurt her?

*****

Beth watched the officers walk toward Ceretzke's black truck. They seemed so different. Mike Ceretzke with his wonderfully deep voice and wavy hair and Sergeant Pierce as worn and baggy as his overcoat, but they acted the same. She'd been taken off guard with the question about Lisette's lover. After the confusion of last night's attack, she'd forgotten her phone call to Simon, and all that she had learned about these men meeting Lisette. Now his comments came tumbling back.

Both of those men knew Lisette and knew her well. Detective Ceretzke's emotion during that first interrogation made sense if she wasn't some anonymous victim. Was he Lisette's lover or was the dowdy Sergeant who she had often met for lunch?

Beth could understand Lisette being attracted to Mike Ceretzke. She understood how his eyes could trap a woman. How she could find herself mesmerized by his voice. How she could relax while in his care. It was too easy. Whether in work clothes or sweats, he radiated strength and capability.

Sweats. Had he been wearing sweats when he arrived to investigate Lisette's murder so that he would blend into the park environment? Why had he pretended not to know Lisette?

Why didn't she have the guts to ask?

*****

Hendrick Domke's bungalow faced a quiet street several blocks away from the expensive river view lots. A veranda designed to catch the last warm rays of evening light ran the length of the house. The window screens necessary for combating insect pests were now covered with glass to block the cold winds and frosty air.

As the men walked toward the house, Jack glanced at Mike. "How long will you keep up the security patrols?"

"You guys should know better than me. Can the Mounties haul Dorrien in on anything?"

Jack shrugged his shoulders, then shook his head.

"Well, until we decide we have enough evidence to convict him of Lisette's murder, I want at least drive-by patrols for Mr. Domke. Beth McKinney is going to require major surveillance. I don't like her being a target."

From the step, Mike looked into the porch where a low table was covered with softball-size tomatoes slowly ripening to a deep red. Foot-long zucchini lay in tidy rows and bunches of herbs hung from rafters, drying for use in the soups and stews that would bring a tantalizing reminder of summer to minus forty degree January days.

A woman who Mike assumed to be Mrs. Domke turned a final tomato before she acknowledged their presence. She leaned heavily on her cane so that the hem of her flowered housedress reached the middle of her calf on her left side but only to her knee on the right. She smiled as they approached, as if unconcerned they might wish to sell her something she didn't need.

After asking to speak with her husband, they followed her through the porch and into the living room. Hendrick sat on a couch covered in a floral print fabric. His dog rested his chin on the old man's knee. One look at his long-sleeved sweater, flannel shirt, and striped tie made Mike sweat. As they entered, Hendrick moved the dog's brush into his left hand and extended his right.

"Detective Ceretzke was it not? I have been wondering when you would be around."

After shaking both men's hands, he motioned for them sit then resumed grooming the dog.

"Orff likes his daily care but if I continue grooming him, he will not mind sharing my attention." Hendrick motioned toward his wife with the brush. "Mother, will you please make us some coffee."

Mike smiled at her. "No, thank you. We need just a few minutes."

"Then if you don't need me I'll return to my tomatoes," she commented in a pleasant voice that revealed little curiosity about their mission.

They sat in silence as Mrs. Domke retreated to the porch.

"I'd like to know if you saw Lisette with anyone in the park. Anyone she spoke to, or met, however casually."

"You mean someone other than him?" Hendrick pointed the dog's brush at Jack. Jack flinched and Hendrick lifted his eyebrows and shoulders as one. "I have had a little special training and tend to notice people who look like they do not want to be noticed. I have seen you speak to Lisette often this past summer. She knew many other people, but just for a casual wave or nod. She was not like Beth who tends to talk to anyone. So if the question is, was there someone other than him, Beth, and me, the answer is no."

"You will keep the information about our meetings to yourself, won't you?" Jack asked.

"Why should I? In what did you have her involved? I fear it was something to do with her husband."

Mike watched Jack struggling to decide which facts he could reveal, hoping to learn more about the case himself.

Jack ran his finger around the collar of his shirt, gently pulling his tie a little looser. "Lisette was helping us with a criminal investigation, but we would appreciate that fact remaining confidential."

Hendrick drew himself to attention, though he remained seated. "You can trust me to keep it secret."

"Can you tell us anything else that might help?" Jack asked.

"I cannot help you for the day of the murder. I did not see anyone or anything out of the ordinary. However, twice last week, I did catch a glimpse of someone standing behind the lookout. Hindsight tells me that that person may have been checking Lisette's schedule."

"Why do you think that?"

"Well, someone planned her murder. There was nothing random about it, but I doubt he was a professional. If that were so, she would have been killed efficiently not stabbed repeatedly and viciously. No, I think whoever did this knew how to cover his tracks." Hendrick looked across to the officers and smiled slightly, but said no more.

"Can you describe the person you saw?"

"I cannot tell you what he looked like, as my eyesight is not what it was. Nevertheless, he moved easily so I would say he was young, not yet sixty anyway, and in good shape. He was not a hunter or a soldier of that I feel certain. I noticed nothing exceptional about his height or weight, however, I did receive the impression of dark hair or maybe a dark hat."

"Was it definitely a man?"

"That was my impression at the time. Why, do you have a woman in mind?"

"Just clarifying details," Jack answered.

Mike controlled his annoyance. Jack still refused to share his information, but he admitted to himself that Jack was learning more from Mr. Domke than Evan had managed to uncover. Did they respond to the obvious secrecy and mistrust in each other's manner?

"Have you found anything that you can work on?" Hendrick asked.

"We have some clues."

"I am surprised to learn that is the case." His voice was thoughtful.

"Why is that," Mike asked when Jack didn't.

Jack answered for Hendrick. "The guy was careful, the murder well planned. We shouldn't have found any clues. Our luck changed when emotion overtook the killer, making it personal and making him sloppy."

Hendrick nodded his agreement. "You are hunting a careful person with a vendetta."

They left soon after. Hendrick walked them to the door of the porch, then watched with his wife and dog as they stepped into the cool sunshine-filled day.

*****

Back at the truck, Mike asked, "Are you game for a couple more interviews today?" He climbed behind the wheel. "I want to talk to her karate instructor and then the cleaning woman."

"Sure. Want me to phone ahead?"

Mike nodded as he turned the truck toward the Alberta Karate School. Jack had barely confirmed that Arthur Howarth was currently instructing a class, when they pulled up to the storefront gym.

They waited inside the crowded gym while twenty kids jabbed, kicked, and tripped each other. The kids were about ten years old and looked cute rather than deadly in their white costumes with white or yellow belts tied around their slim waists. A quick and noisy rush to the coatroom followed the final ceremonial bowing.

As the room cleared, the young instructor looked at them, an inquiry in his brown eyes.

"Can we talk about Lisette Dorrien?" Mike asked.

"Too bad about her. She was a good student who wasn't afraid to fight back to defend herself." He shrugged. "Still, lots of people freeze if they're actually attacked."

"Had she been in your class long?"

"A couple of years. She'd recently graduated to a brown belt."

"Did you ever meet her outside class?"

Arthur pointed toward an attractive woman watching from a desk near the window. "No way, man. You see that girl over there. We're getting married next month. Lisette was an okay human, but she was just a student."

"Did she tell you anything about her personal life?"

"Very reserved. Hardly talked to anyone but she was serious about getting good."

"Did you notice anyone taking particular interest in her?"

"She looked good to a few of the guys but all I saw her give in return was attitude and some serious hits."

"Any of them named Howard?"

"Don't recall ever instructing a Howard." The door opened and three middle-aged women walked in. "I've got another class in fifteen and I could do with a break, so if there's nothing else?"

Mike thanked him and they left.

*****

"What do you think?" Jack asked as they headed back to the truck.

"Lisette was learning Portuguese and martial arts, so she wasn't only scared, she was preparing to run or to fight, whichever became necessary. And her preparations were leaving a big trail for Hugh to follow."

"The cleaner next?" Jack asked.

They drove north, connected with the Yellowhead Freeway, and followed it toward West Edmonton. The cleaner lived in a neighbourhood where large homes covered lots to the maximum allowed by law, leaving little room for trees to grow and landscaping to mature.

Rosa Havestock was pear-shaped and wore cream-coloured stirrup-pants that accentuated the bulk of her hips. A cotton sweatshirt with 'Martinique' written across the chest and white runners with cotton pompom socks completed her garb.

Jack and Mike followed her through the entrance hall into the living room. The windows were heavily draped with transparent curtains closing out both the late afternoon sun and the view of West Edmonton Mall located a block distant.

The blended aroma of ammonia and lemon wafted from her as she motioned them toward the upholstered sofa, while plopping down in a white, leather recliner. She pushed back, raising the footrest.

"I like to put my feet up when I get to sit," she explained.

"Thank you for agreeing to see us."

"No problem. It gives me a reason to relax for a minute."

"So your cleaning business keeps you busy?" Mike asked looking around the room.

Her house reminded him of a show home. The home of a cleaner shouldn't look like this, though what it should look like he had no idea, but it wasn't this.

"I clean four houses myself, but they're big places and people want me two or three times a week. Plus, I have three crews who do apartment move-outs and new home cleanups."

"You do a great job." He looked at the bare room. Not a dust collecting ornament, not a leaf-dropping plant, and definitely not a shedding animal in sight.

"I'll tell my cleaning crew you like their work." She chuckled at his expression. "I work five and a half days a week. I don't have time to clean my house the way I want it done."

"Of course, I never thought of that." Mike wondered if she cleaned lowly apartments or just houses filled by wealthy people. Maybe cleaners were ranked by the social position of those whose dirt they shovelled.

Jack interrupted his thoughts by stating. "The reason we're here is Lisette Dorrien."

"Poor Mrs. Dorrien, getting killed like that. It makes you wonder if it's safe in the parks these days. It's not like when I grew up in Edmonton. It was a quiet little city then. The Mac Hotel was the tallest building on the horizon in those days."

Mike let the words settle as he looked out the covered window, toward West Edmonton Mall and the tower that held the roller coaster. He had been at the Mall the evening the car went off the track. The image of the broken body of the young man and the horrified faces of the spectators had never left him.

Jack cleared his throat, bringing Mike's attention back to Mrs. Havestock.

"Yes, it does make you wonder what's safe, though I don't think you have to worry about the parks. Right now we would like to know more about the people in the Dorrien household." Mike was determined to concentrate on the interview, not on the world's largest shopping mall.

"I don't like talking about my clients. It's bad for business."

"Mrs. Havestock this is a murder investigation and we do need background information. We've talked to the other staff and to Mr. Dorrien. He understands that we must talk to you."

"Then I guess it's okay. What do you want to know?"

"Did you notice problems between staff members or between the family?"

"Everything seemed okay to me. I try not to pry, just do my work and get on to the next house."

"I understand you can't clean Mr. Dorrien's office unless someone supervises."

"A nuisance that is, having to get Helen or that Tony to watch me work. It's not like they help; they just stand in the doorway. Don't even talk. Not that I mind. A couple of strange ones they are. Heck the whole group is a bit off. Mr. Dorrien and his rules."

"Do you sometimes just slip in unnoticed to give it an extra tidy?"

"It isn't worth the hassle. No, that office of his only gets a good clean twice-a-year and then Mr. Dorrien takes a bunch of stuff out before my people arrive."

"You don't do all the cleaning?"

"No, just keep on top of it and I do the ironing. I have one of my crews come in April and November to do the big spring and fall cleanings."

"What days do you work at the Dorrien's?"

"Tuesday morning, Thursday afternoon and Saturday morning. Theirs is the only house I do Saturdays. That was part of the contract when I started because Mr. Dorrien wants it spotless all the time."

"When was the last time you saw Mrs. Dorrien?"

"Monday morning."

Jack interrupted. "I thought you didn't work for them on Monday."

"I don't, but I do work at the Humboldt's. They live a couple of blocks closer to the freeway along the route Mrs. Dorrien took for her run. She went running by just before I left, that was about eleven-twenty. Her usual time."

"Are you sure of the time?" Jack leaned forward, his hands clasped tightly.

"Give or take five minutes. My clients always get full-time, I'm there from nine until eleven-thirty, then go for lunch, and then to the Smith's at one."

"Was she alone?"

"Just like always."

"Was she carrying anything?"

"Not that I saw." Rosa stopped talking, wrinkled her brow, and pulled her lips tight over her teeth. "Just wearing that little wrist pouch of hers, I guess."

"You saw it?"

"No. Not really, but she always had it. It's a real cute gadget."

"Did she seem different in any way?"

"Not that I noticed. She was wearing her running suit and she was running. Nothing unusual."

"Well, thank you Mrs. Havestock." The officers rose to leave, motioning her to stay in her chair. "Don't get up, we'll let ourselves out."

"No problem." She pushed her footrest down and herself out of the chair. "I've got to get ready for the symphony anyway. They have a guest vocalist tonight and my husband hates arriving late."

Mike was quiet until they got back to the vehicle. "You know what this means don't you?"

Jack nodded. "Lisette didn't arrive at the lookout early, so Hugh wouldn't have had enough time to kill her and we're back to looking for a third party."

CHAPTER 14

It was almost eight before Mike opened the frosted glass door of the Identification Section.

Pete Humphries looked up from a stack of paperwork. "Mike, I was wondering when you'd be by to see me."

"What do you have for me?"

"The shoe impression sets the weight at around two hundred pounds. The knife thrusts say normal to above normal strength."

Mike flopped into the visitor chair opposite Pete. That description fit Hugh and several thousand other men.

Then Pete moved to the computer and began accessing files. "Let me check the physical evidence."

"Sure, go ahead and tell me if there's any good news."

It took only a moment for him to call up the file.

"Any luck matching the cast with the shoe we found this morning?" Mike wanted more data, something to tie Hugh Dorrien tightly to his wife's murder. He planned on keeping an open mind and worrying all the clues until they unraveled their secrets, but still, he owed Lisette speedy justice.

"It's probably the same type of shoe, but that's just a visual check. We still have to do more on that."

He leaned back, giving Mike a clear view the screen's data, then he pointed to one area of the file. "Foreign fibres on the victim's sweat suit include grey fleece, cat hairs, and a red polyester cotton blend that matches items in her home. The cotton fleece and cat hairs match those on her friend's sweat suit. Her friend probably has a cat."

"Two actually."

Pete nodded slowly. "Nothing unaccounted for with the fibres."

Running his finger down the screen, he stopped and touched it at the midpoint. "The fingerprint ID came back. Nothing to match to Dorrien, the only prints on the knife belonged to someone named Helenka Grimswold."

"The cook's prints were on file?"

Pete hit a few extra keys to get more details. "She was involved in a stabbing fifteen years ago, in an oil camp in the Territories. The victim, Luc St. Lucenne, died but it went down as self-defence."

"She told us she worked in the camps, but she didn't mention she'd killing anyone. Well, that's three things I have to check with Dorrien."

Pete peered over his glasses as Mike continued.

"If he has scratches on his left arm, if he owns that pair of shoes we found, and if he checked the cook's references."

Mike ran his hand through his hair, trying to straighten it into a respectable style. "Let's get back to business. What about the blood splatter pattern?"

"Your witness arrived after the attack, just like she said. No spray on her clothes just transfer smears. No chance she stabbed the victim, at least not wearing those clothes."

"What about Lisette's runners? Did they provide any clues to the route her run took?"

"We found some small pebbles and a leaf fragment stuck to a smear of tar. The leaf was maple so it could be from anywhere on her run but the tar is a mystery. Weather this past week hasn't been warm enough to soften existing patches, but city records show no new work in a six-block radius of her usual route."

"Do you have anything more on the bag and the clothes that the Park Patrol found this morning?"

"We rushed the shoe match for you but we haven't got to the rest yet. Won't your witness help? Rumour has it she saw someone in the bushes."

"Where did you hear that? There are too damn many rumours floating around this place and Tanner seems to pick most of them up and tell the world our business."

Pete shot him a look. "Mike, I'd tone that down. You don't want people thinking you're accusing them of talking to the media."

"Don't you think he has a source inside?"

"Hey, I didn't say you were wrong just that you shouldn't be so vocal. It's bad politics to accuse co-workers of misconduct."

"I didn't accuse you."

Blankness spread across Pete's face, emphasizing his solemn expression. "Just a caution." He turned to his files in dismissal.

Mike wanted to justify his words but knew he couldn't. Pete was right—no matter how much he suspected Tanner of having an inside source, until he could prove it, he was better off keeping quiet. Besides, maybe it was just extraordinary digging on Tanner's part. Maybe it was an overheard comment. Maybe he disliked Tanner because he was the prime target of the reporter's stories. Mike pushed Tanner's image aside. The time to deal with him and his accusations was later, after Hugh was in jail.

*****

At his final stop of the day Mike found Associate Superintendent Samantha Weisman working late, a usual occurrence as she was determined to earn the rank of Chief.

"OK, let's go over what you know." Super Sam shifted a pile of files to her left, then sat back in her chair.

Mike pulled out his notebook and flipped to the beginning of his case notes.

"Dorrien left the dentist at eleven-thirty. Helen Grimswold, the cook, says Lisette started her run almost an hour earlier than usual. The M.E. says the attack could have occurred as early as 11:35. We had hoped she arrived before then, so Hugh would have had time to drive to the lookout, kill her, go back to his car, and arrive at the Club in time for his noon talk. The timing was tight, but it worked." Mike looked up from his list.

"You're using the past tense. What's the problem?"

"Rosa Havestock, the cleaning woman, saw her on her usual route to the park at about 11:20. If we believe her, the earliest Lisette would have arrived at the lookout was 11:45. That time line is just too tight."

"Maybe he gambled on her being early?"

"Hendrick Domke believes someone was watching Lisette. If he's correct, Hugh knew she met Beth at the lookout between 11:45 and noon, not earlier. Of course he could have gambled on being late for the luncheon, thinking he could explain any delay on a traffic tie-up or parking problem."

"Why choose a day with so tight a time frame?"

"Maybe he tried to get her on other days but didn't have an opportunity?"

"If she was attacked around 11:45, who did your witness see when she arrived?"

"Maybe someone unrelated to the crime."

"Are we looking for a third party?"

"The Mounties are checking that angle, but the viciousness of the attack looks personal."

"A way to throw suspicion on Hugh?"

"It was certain to land there anyway, no matter what the scenario."

Peering at Mike's list, Superintendent Weisman asked, "Does Dorrien have scratches on his arm?"

"I'm checking that in the morning. The shoe size is the same as his and Pete says the cast we took from the trail matches the shoes found in the bag."

"Yes, that convenient bag. Are the shoes his?"

"They could be. I'll check the store where he shops. Doesn't mean he couldn't have bought them elsewhere, though. The coveralls explain the lack of blood on his clothing and the change of shoes would have meant no blood there either."

"What else?"

"The murder weapon was a knife from the Dorrien's kitchen. Helen Grimswold's prints were on the knife and we have them on file. She stabbed a guy fifteen years ago, in self-defence."

"Interesting. What else?" Super Sam asked.

"Tony was hung up on Lisette and I'm suspicious that Hugh has a relationship with Melissa."

"A cozy little household."

"One more thing, the Mountie's invisible informer claims Hugh is frantic to find a missing computer disc."

"What's on it?"

"No one seems to know, not even Jack's source."

"Hugh thinks Lisette took it?"

"Right."

"Find the disc, find the killer?" she asked.

"Or at least establish a motive the Mounties won't snatch away." Mike thought about the informant and clenched his fist. Forcing it to relax, he wondered about that disc. If it was important to Hugh it was important to the police and Mike didn't want it going to the Mounties, although keeping it from them would not be easy.

Super Sam looked at her watch. "Gotta go if I'm going to get to the hockey game before the first period ends."

Mike decided to follow her example and call it quitting time.

*****

"Leave it to us you said, then you mess up. How much of a look did they get?"

"We wore the Balaclavas." Nick Fontain knew he sounded defensive, but this mess wasn't his responsibility.

"No chance they can ID Jerry or me. Shaun kept the van moving so they couldn't get a good look at the license. We're clear. Look, we're getting antsy sitting out here in the bush. We want to get back in town."

"Not for another week, maybe more. You've been too active lately, the public's yelling, and the police are stepping up their investigation because of it. Didn't you learn anything about being careful after Lisette recognized you? First, that newspaper picture and now a Crime Stoppers' re-enactment. You guys stay invisible until you're old news."

"We could just kill her and the loud-mouth who was with her," Nick said.

"With your record of getting rid of witnesses, you try again and half the city will see you. Just leave it alone. They can't ID you unless they spot you."

*****

The next morning Mike waited thirty minutes before the receptionist showed him into Hugh Dorrien's plush downtown office. Hugh slouched behind his executive desk, glowering at him.

"What are you going to accuse me of now, Detective? An overdue parking ticket? A mass murder?"

Mike let the sarcasm slide. "Just a few points to clear up."

"Lisette's funeral is at two o'clock."

"You'll make it. I called your house and was surprised to find you at work today."

"I'd rather work than sit at home going crazy."

"Of course." Mike looked at him from across the desk. Hugh's tan had faded to yellow giving him a jaundiced look. Was it grief or worry?

"Your questions." Hugh abruptly closed a file folder and straightened his back.

"Could I see your forearms?"

Incredulity showed on Hugh's face. "My arms? You want to see my arms?"

"Just the forearms."

"Why?"

"Lisette had skin under her nails. The medical examiner thinks she may have scratched her assailant."

"And you think I'm that person?"

"If you just show me your arms, we can clear this up in a second."

Hugh removed his jacket, carefully folded it, and placed it over the back of his chair. He looked at Mike and shook his head as he unfastened his pearl cuff links and pushed at his sleeves. Mike saw the unblemished skin as he turned his arms first toward, then away from him.

"Are you satisfied, Detective?"

Mike pushed his fingers through his wavy hair. Damn, this wasn't happening the right way. "Had to check."

Maybe she hadn't even scratched her assailant. Perhaps a third party was involved. Was the answer in that missing hour? Maybe she'd been visiting her lover and the scratches were on his back?

"Are you surprised that I didn't kill her? We didn't have an ideal marriage, but I had no reason to harm her."

"I heard you threatened to take the children away from her."

Hugh pulled a wooden pencil from a brass cube and began twisting it through his fingers. "She wasn't a fit mother."

"Did you have lovers too?"

The pencil snapped and Hugh leaned across the desk, his pasty face blotchy as blood rushed into it.

"We agreed to lead separate lives." His face closed, locking away all his emotions except anger. "That is none of your business." He looked toward the door. "If that's all . . ."

"I need another point clarified. Your cook. Did you know she killed someone?"

"Why should I know that?"

"I thought it might have come up when you checked her references."

"We got her through an agency." Hugh picked up the pencil pieces and asked, "Who did she kill, a former employer? Are you suggesting she's a serial killer?"

"No, it happened about fifteen years ago at a camp in the Territories. A man named Luc St. Lucenne assaulted her; the courts ruled it self-defense."

"That's a strange coincidence," Hugh said as he stood leaning his hands on the desktop.

"What's a coincidence?"

"St. Lucenne is Lisette's family name. Her father died up north about fifteen years ago."

"How did he die?"

Hugh's voice sounded tired, his anger gone. "I don't know, I think it might have been a heart attack. You can ask Odile when she arrives."

Mike turned to the door, then paused and turned back. "The shoes you were wearing Monday morning, did you find them?"

"I haven't taken the time to look. Even you can understand I've had other things to do."

This time Mike did leave. He spent the rest of the morning checking alibis for the Tuesday evening attack on Beth.

Safiya confirmed Melissa's story of dinner and a movie. Tony's neighbour, Margaret Steeples, remembered that he had left later than usual. She had to ask him to leave around midnight because she had an early staff meeting.

Calls to people on Hugh's list confirmed that he had been home Tuesday night and could not have been personally involved in the attack on Beth.

Mike's last trip of the morning was to the Dorrien house to talk to Helen. She was busy directing the caterer in the placement of tables and flower arrangements. When he walked into the room, Helen was sending her helper to the kitchen for a different serving tray. She looked up, startled by Mike's presence.

"The door was open and one of the workers told me where I could find you," he explained.

"I'm too busy to talk right now. Caterers never get it right unless you supervise every step."

"Just one thing." He kept his voice low. "Is there somewhere more private we can talk?"

Shaking her head, she looked at the staff who seemed completely engaged in turning the room into an efficient place for people to mingle. "You have to be quick," she said as she led him into the sitting room and closed the glass door.

Feeling her eyes on him and sensing her growing unease, Mike delayed saying anything until she seemed ready to explode, then he said, "Helen the only prints on the knife were yours and they're in our records."

Mike watched as her rigid expression deepened and crumbled, like a building imploding. The foundation shuddered, brick and mortar relaxed, and she ended in a heap on the fragile sofa.

He touched her shoulder, but she shrugged him off.

"You killed Lisette's father. I would like you to tell me about it." Mike was guessing, but from her reaction, he had guessed correctly.

Squaring her shoulders, head held high, the iron rod returning to her spine, Helen asked, "Why? It has nothing to do with her death."

"I can request the files, but I would rather hear your version."

"Oh, what the hell. He was a pig. Thought he was a big man, irresistible to all women. I had always made it plain—no men at the camps—it leads to problems when your lover is a fellow employee. Not that he had a chance anyway."

Mike nodded, encouraging her comments.

"He started spreading rumours about me being a lesbian—like I said, he was a pig. Kept taunting me. Sexual harassment is what they call it now, back then all you could do was quit, and I refused to do that.

"I thought I was handling it, then one night I was cleaning up after supper. The men were playing cards and boozing. Luc came into the kitchen and started grabbing at me. Said he wanted to change my mind about men. I picked up a knife and told him to back off.

"Luc was big—a foot taller and a hundred pounds heavier than me, so he laughed off my threat. I grew up with four brothers—I'm the youngest and I learned early to defend myself. Anyway, he grabbed my wrist.

"I stabbed him in the chest—the judge agreed it was self-defense."

Her bitter tone fought with the pain apparent in her eyes. "Is your curiosity satisfied? I suppose you told Mr. Dorrien and he plans to fire me? Can I at least get back to arranging this reception? I don't want to miss the funeral because I wasted time talking to you."

He stretched a hand toward her. "No, don't go yet. Why are you here? Why Lisette's household?"

She studied her fingernails, then looked at her watch. Finally, she said, "You don't kill someone and then forget him, not even someone who deserves killing. At least any normal person doesn't.

"For months after that night horrible dreams invaded my sleep, finally, I decided to stop them. My lawyer advised against my plan; so did my therapist. Who knows what I thought it would accomplish, maybe I just saw it as some kind of atonement. I hired a detective to track down Luc's wife and two daughters in Montreal. Planning to do what I could to help out, I got a job in the city and kept an eye on them.

"She pushed them, Lisette's mom did. Dragging them to modelling classes and then to photo shoots. Always a bottle handy and a guy close by, though rarely the same one. I felt bad for the girls, but their dad had been no better than the men she took up with.

"When Lisette decided to marry Hugh, I checked him out and learned he was associated with Neil Karlek. Even then, the police were watching Karlek. When they moved west, I came too. Odile had moved to France and her mother had drunk herself to death, so I had no reason to stay in Montreal.

"I saw the ad for this job and applied with some crazy idea of being close if she needed help."

"Did she?" Mike asked.

"Did she . . ?" A tormented soul peered through Helen's eyes. "Did she need help?"

"Sometimes. Hugh Dorrien is not a good person. He hurts people; he hurt her sometimes. Now he'll fire me and who is going to watch out for the little ones?"

"Does he abuse them? We can stop him, if he abuses them."

"He doesn't hit them, at least not often and then it's just what you'd call discipline. No, instead he rages at them, then picks them up, cuddling them to apologize. They've got to bear his sarcasm and his put-downs. Lisette was almost destroyed by him, but she was an adult and could fight back, they're just kids."

"But she didn't fight back."

"Of course she did. He may have held most of the aces but she told him point blank that if he hit her or the kids she'd call the police, then," she said, her eyes sparkling from the dark hollows surrounding them, "she tormented him in a hundred ways. Her mother taught her how to be a bitch and she was good at it.

"You want to know what she did?" Her voice held a hint of laughter.

Mike pulled a tiny stool over with his foot and sat in front of her. "Yes. What did she do?" Maybe Helen could help him figure out who the real Lisette had been. The easily intimidated woman Beth spoke of, the round-heeled tramp that Hugh ranted about, or someone entirely different.

"Lisette pretended to have a lover. I overheard her ordering flowers complete with steamy messages. She'd tell Hugh she was going to be somewhere, then not show up. When his friends visited, she barely spoke to them."

Mike felt the weight of guilt land on his shoulders. Had she told Hugh of their investigation and flaunted her betrayal? If they hadn't approached her, would she be alive?

"Why didn't she just leave him?"

"She knew he would find her no matter where she hid but that proof of abuse would help with a custody hearing."

Mike let the information distil a minute, then asked, "Did your dreams go away?"

"They lessened, until Lisette's murder. Now they're back with a twist. I keep dreaming that I could have done more, helped her find a way out."

Mike leaned forward to pat her hand, but she pulled back.

"If that's all you need to know, I'm going to check on the

caterers. It's the last thing I can do for her and I want it to be perfect." She looked at her watch again.

"Tony should be back with Odile any minute now. I must ensure everything is ready for her."

Helen unfolded as she stood, reminding Mike of a preying mantis with its armour again intact. She opened the door to the clamour of breaking glass. "Caterers, why can't they hire decent help," she said, hurrying into the chaos.

Was that what this case was about? A domestic dispute brought on by a goading wife and an abusive husband? Had Lisette spoken rashly about the police investigation and brought about her own death? Had so many bad feelings built up that Hugh decided the only way out was murder?

"Detective, what are you doing here?"

Tony's harsh voice interrupted Mike's thoughts. Twisting to face the doorway, Mike found himself staring at Tony's companion. Her honey blonde hair was pulled back into a knot. In her sculptured face, Mike recognized Lisette. The family resemblance was remarkable. They could have been twins. He rose and extended his hand.

"I'm Detective Ceretzke, Ms. St. Lucenne."

"Call me Odile." She grasped his hand in a firm grip.

Odile's years in France had turned her French Canadian lilt into pure Parisian and made it more noticeable.

"Allow me to convey my sympathy on your sister's death. It was a tragedy."

"I asked what you're doing here—or do you have another search warrant?" Tony crossed the room, placing himself between Odile and Mike.

Mike held his hands out, palms forward. "Slow down Tony. I'm done here for now. We'll talk later, Odile."

He left the room, pondering the identity of the informant. Helen would have been easy to recruit if Jack knew her background. In fact, her story could be a cover; maybe the Mounties had recruited her then got her the job.

Still, Tony was closer to Hugh and his business associates. Though, if he was working for the Mounties he should be nicer to cops, or was that part of his cover?

What about Melissa? Sometimes a luscious body . . no, not even the Mounties would stoop that low.

Rosa then. People didn't notice cleaners. Maybe she did slip into Hugh's office without supervision. People threw amazing things away.

By the time he reached his truck, Mike had come full circle. Unless Jack decided to tell him, he would probably never know the informant's identity.

CHAPTER 15

Beth looked around the crowd of well-dressed mourners who filled the chapel. Two couples sat in the pew directly before her, the women whispered loudly enough that people on all sides could hear. "Poor Hugh, left with two little children."

Her companion turned to her and in a quieter voice commented, "At least he still has their nanny. It's hard on kids when their nannies leave. The last one we hired got homesick after two months and caught a plane back to Australia, didn't even give us notice. No consideration at all."

"What did you think of Lisette?"

"I hardly knew her, but they have a great cook. Her Chateaubriand was the best I've ever had. Do you think Marjory would suit Hugh? Maybe I should arrange a dinner for next week? No, that's too soon, I'll make it the week after. What about you, were you close to them?"

"No. The usual business dinners, but Joseph pretty much met Hugh on his own. It seemed Lisette didn't like Hugh's business associates."

"It's a shame when a wife can't help her husband's career."

"Why don't they get on with this? My decorator is due at four. Swatches for the living room. It's been three years since I redecorated—the damned recession. Next thing you know I'll be working to keep bread on the table."

Their husbands nudged them into silence and pointed to the back of the chapel.

Beth turned to scrutinize the group just entering. An elderly man, overly thin in his black suit, and an equally elderly woman, led the way. Two men followed them down the aisle.

"Mr. Karlek." The whisper filled the room.

Hendrick and his arthritic wife, Freda, had already been seated when Beth arrived and she had slipped in next to them leaving little room at the aisle edge of the pew. Now Beth felt Hendrick's hand cover her tightly clenched fists. She slowly relaxed her jaw muscles. Whoever this couple might be, she was glad their presence had silenced the gossips in front of her. Lisette deserved respect at her own funeral.

Beth's gaze followed the elderly couple to a pew across the aisle. As the commotion of their arrival died, she turned her attention to the family. She recognized Hugh from photos, although she could see little but the side profile of his bulbous nose, heavy eyebrows, and full moustache. When he turned to face a dark haired man on his left, the overhead chapel lights highlighted a bald spot on the back of his head.

The dark haired man must be Tony. He constantly scanned the room. Beth agreed with Lisette's assessment of him. He was attractive, in a traditional Greek god kind-of-way.

The blonde on Hugh's right had to be Lisette's sister, Odile. They shared the same sculpted features, thick hair, and long slender bones. Beth also saw Lisette in the way Odile tilted her head to the side and used her hands to emphasize her words. She felt tears gathering in her throat and swallowed hard.

Lisette's children sat on either side of a young woman. Bored, they peered over the pews at the crowd. Joelle played peek-a-boo with the elegantly dressed older lady who had arrived with Neil Karlek.

When Joelle's giggle attracted her father's stern glance, the nanny put an immediate stop to the game. Then the music changed, heralding the beginning of the service. Voices quieted, demeanour became solemn.

Detective Ceretzke touched her arm and motioned for her to move slightly, so he could sit in the small space left between her and the aisle. The Minister began the service.

Beth sensed Mike scanning the chapel. Sitting so close, she inhaled a faint hint of his after-shave, not spicy, but enticing.

The minister's words caught Beth's attention. It was obvious from the beginning of the service that he had not known Lisette well, but was simply repeating clichés and platitudes.

She remembered her Uncle Gregory's funeral where the minister had told stories of Uncle Gregory's love of hunting, of fishing trips into the foothills, of his willingness to listen to any hard luck story and to offer a helping hand. No such remembrances played a part in this service. She felt unfulfilled when they played the last hymn and people began filing out.

Mike placed his hand on her arm as she studied the people leaving the chapel. His blue eyes looked steadily into her brown ones; his thumb caressed her wrist.

"There's someone here I think you would like to meet."

Mike nodded toward a woman who stood beside Sergeant Pierce. She wore a pearl grey suit with a blouse that swirled a storm of wild reds and oranges, a hint of its colour reflected onto her drawn face. She was approaching old age and appeared not to be fighting hard to avoid it. Her face was strong, but ravaged by an emotion that seemed only partially grief.

"Wait a minute," Beth said, as the women who sat in front of her gathered their husbands and waited for the chance to escape. As they turned to join the stream heading down the aisle, she stepped in front of them. "Lisette was a fine person. Just because she refused to play her husband's game doesn't mean you have any right to gossip about her," Beth said, wishing she'd had the courage to speak up before the service.

The women looked at each other, their eyes widened and their heads drew stiffly erect. Then with a look over their shoulders, they allowed their husbands to hurry them into the line of people leaving the chapel.

"Good for you." Hendrick spoke from behind her. "Someone needs to speak for Lisette."

After the mourners had left, Beth moved into the aisle to meet Jack and his friend. Freda rose with Hendrick's help and gathered her cane to follow.

Mike introduced them to Mary Carpenter by saying, "Mary was also a good friend to Lisette." He seemed to be addressing the words directly to Mary.

Beth scrutinized the woman. What secrets did she share with these police officers? With only that second of reflection, Beth recalled how much Mary had meant to Lisette and extended her hand in greeting.

"Lisette told me how much she enjoyed painting."

Mary took Beth's hand in both of hers. "As she spoke of savouring her times with you." Looking at the departing crowd, Mary added, "I never realized how truly alone she was."

Beth read anger mixed with regret in Mary's intense look.

"If only I had known how bad it was. These people weren't her friends. She deserved more."

"We were her friends." Beth placed a hand on Mary's grey silk jacket and one on Hendrick's tweed covered arm. "And she had her children to love."

Mary looked pointedly at Mike. "Friends don't put each other in danger."

Mike seemed suddenly anxious to rush them to the doorway where Hugh and Odile were accepting the condolences of his friends and associates.

As they approached, Hugh placed his hand on Odile's elbow and moved her out of a group of men. Beth appraised the ex-athlete whose muscles had long since softened and slid to his waist. He was pale and the deep lines that ran into his drooping moustache emphasized his fatigue.

"Detective, I didn't expect to see you here and in such interesting company."

Beth hung back, not intending to speak to the brute who had tormented and killed her friend. His gaze roamed over the others until he skewered Beth with a penetrating look.

"You are Miss McKinney? The one who found her? I don't believe Lisette ever mentioned you."

"We knew each other for nearly three years."

Mike rocked forward on the balls of his feet. "Mr. Domke," he pointed at Hendrick, "was also a long-time friend. He came upon the scene soon after Miss McKinney. Mrs. Carpenter instructed the painting classes your wife attended."

Beth felt relieved that Mike's tone allowed no question of their status as Lisette's friends.

"Lisette obviously kept many things from me." Hugh's words were abrupt and he turned, dismissing them. Pausing, he turned back. "I apologize if I was offensive, Miss McKinney. You must understand that I have not been myself lately."

Odile used his pause as a chance to introduce herself. "I am Odile. Lisette's sister." Her voice flowed in a melodious rhythm.

Beth saw the sorrow in her face and her resentment melted. "I'm very sorry about Lisette. When I reached her, she was near death and I couldn't help her."

"I am sure your presence was a comfort. I would like to talk with you more." She drew back to include them all in her gaze. "With all of you. After I moved to France, Lisette and I corresponded only occasionally. I would like to find out the kind of person she became. Perhaps you wish to come back to the house for a while, so we could talk."

Beth felt animosity radiating from Hugh. Odile didn't seem to notice or perhaps she chose to ignore it. She glanced at her watch. It was already two-forty. "I can't. I'm sorry. I must be at work by four." Odile's obvious disappointment made her add, "Perhaps we can meet over the weekend?"

"That would be wonderful. I will contact you to make arrangements." Odile turned to the others and asked, "You will join us?"

Hendrick and Mary nodded their acceptance.

Hugh bulled his way back into the conversation with a question directed at Mike. "Have you made any progress finding the murderer?"

"The lab work is being done; however, we have nothing new to tell you."

A heavyset man approached Hugh and reached his hand toward Hugh's shoulder. Striking out with the speed of a viper, Hugh's assistant intercepted the hand before it reached its destination. Hugh glanced over his shoulder at the sudden movement and smiled. At his nod, Tony backed off. "Arthur, good of you to come."

Beth kept the image of Hugh's handsome bodyguard in her mind as they walked away from the chapel. Was Tony the man in Lisette's life? Was she wrong to think Mike was the lover Lisette hinted to her about?

"That man is a bore." Hendrick echoed her own opinion of Hugh Dorrien.

"Grief can sometimes affect people strangely, but I agree with you." Beth could find no charity for him in her heart. "Odile reminds me of Lisette and not just physically, she has the same graciousness."

Mary looked back; sorrow filling her eyes. "She is a lady, just like Lisette."

Reporters lined the sidewalk opposite the chapel. They had been barred from the service, but the story was too big to ignore. Beth spotted the cameraman, Chuck, but not Richard.

*****

Hugh pulled the Windsor knot of his tie loose, then unfastened the top button of his shirt to free his neck from confinement. The funeral had gone well. Even Mr. Karlek had made an appearance and he had brought his wife. Hugh appreciated the honour. Although Mr. Karlek had not stopped by the house, just shaking hands with him was public recognition of his status in the organization.

Hugh shifted his gaze through the window to the looming darkness of his tree-filled backyard. The wind dragged a branch over the window, screeching like a fiend demanding admittance.

He lowered the blind. Which of Lisette's new friends could have his disc? Which was the one she would most likely have trusted with it? Perhaps she still had it when she was killed, if so the woman who found her must have taken it.

He shook his head. The police would have retrieved it and if they had it, they would be after him. Was it possible Lisette had given it to someone before she reached the park?

The phone buzzed, interrupting his thoughts. The caller was Mr. Karlek.

After thanking him for coming to the funeral, Hugh felt confident enough to confide his worries. "Trouble might be in the offing. Apparently, Lisette had friends I didn't know. What if she talked to them about our operation?"

"You overstepped your authority by eliminating your wife without my permission." Karlek's voice carried a deadly coldness.

"But, I . . ."

"Enough! If it was necessary, it was. I don't want to know details. You once assured me that your wife knew nothing worth passing onto the police. Are you changing your story now?"

Hugh heard menace in Karlek's controlled tone. A phantom disc floated before his eyes, followed by the image of his boss giving the order to dispose of him. Hugh fumbled with his tie, finally freeing it completely and throwing it onto his forest-green duvet.

"No, of course she couldn't have known anything." He wiped drops of dampness from his forehead. "Mr. Karlek, about tomorrow's meeting, is it still on?"

"No, Hugh. You have a spotlight on you right now. We will meet in Calgary next month when things are calmer. You shouldn't worry about business now, look after your family, and take some time to rest. We will move you to Grande Prairie in the spring. Things are beginning to open up in the northern market."

Panic rose in Hugh's throat. Karlek was cutting him out of the information loop. If he stopped being important he would be replaced and rumours said Karlek's method of replacement was permanent.

Was he already considered a liability? He had to recover that disc. It was his get-out-of-jail-free card.

*****

The garage door rumbled open spilling light onto the wet driveway. One wall was lined with an array of yard tools, including the snow shovel Mary knew she would soon put to use. The garage was new, the only structural change to her home in the fifty years she had lived under its roof.

Her son had insisted it would make her life easier. Well, it had been a thoughtful gesture and she certainly didn't miss scraping ice and snow from the car windows during the winter months.

She waved at the police cruiser that had accompanied her home from her class at the community college and drove into the garage, using the remote control to shut out the arctic wind.

Mary appreciated Mike's precautionary escort but knew it was unnecessary. Still the officers were good people who had detoured from their regular patrol to satisfy Mike's nagging worry.

Mike suffered from a compulsion to look after his friends and those he saw as needing his strong shoulder. It was part of his charm and part of his problem. She saw the way he had watched Beth McKinney at the funeral. Did the poor girl realize he had staked a claim on her future? Mary doubted it, though Beth had seemed comfortable with Mike watching over her. Well, time would tell. Perhaps theirs was a true match.

Beth certainly had been a good friend to Lisette and it seemed the Domke's had been too. If Mike and Jack Pierce would get busy and arrest Hugh, they could all get on with their lives and stop wasting the time of officers with more pressing concerns than escorting an old woman around town.

Mary gathered her class notes and painting paraphernalia from the seat beside her. Night classes were challenging because the participants were tired from their daytime jobs. Her favourite classes were the afternoon sessions at the senior citizen's leisure centre. She enjoyed providing a way for Betty Wilson to spend a few hours interacting with others in a day that might otherwise seem too long. Or for Pete Cameron to express the way he now viewed the world, very differently after a massive stroke left him partially paralyzed.

However, she especially enjoyed Martha Weatherspoon who had started her painting career only after she retired from nursing. She empathized with Martha because during her own working years she had given her energies to the police department and allowed painting to be a weekend diversion.

Mary climbed the three wooden steps to the door of the house. Giving it a cursory glance for signs of tampering she unlocked it, flipped on the hall light, and reached to disarm the alarm system.

It was not activated.

Mary froze, listening for sounds of an intruder. Had she forgotten to set it when she left? She couldn't remember. She leaned her cases against the wall and stepped into the hall.

Still no sound.

She should backtrack and call the officers. But what if she had just forgotten to set it? Better to check than be considered senile.

Still, with so many burglaries lately, perhaps staying in the house was foolish. She should call the officers who waited outside.

She edged her head around the wall, deciding to take a cautious look into the kitchen. If anything seemed wrong, she would retreat.

Food containers lay scattered, flour filled the sink, and spaghetti spilled off the counter. Drawers of utensils were overturned onto the floor.

A gloved hand reached out and grabbed her by the shoulder. The room spun around and Mary tasted blood as her nose hit the wall.

A muffled voice whispered in her ear, "The disc, where is it?"

She fought to inhale air into her crushed lungs and cried out as a sharp pain radiated through her chest. "I don't know what you want."

The assailant slammed her into the wall again and then grasped her arm and twisted it toward her shoulder.

Mary's breath came in shallow gasps. Bright colours streamed before her eyes.

"Tell me where it is and I won't hurt you."

"I don't have your disc," she muttered through clenched teeth. Why had she walked in on this? How could she be so stupid?

*****

"The players are being greedy, they're just going to keep asking for higher salaries until the team folds," said Cst. Tom Wong, a fan of the Oilers since coming to Edmonton five years earlier.

"The owners are the ones making the big money and it's coming out of our pockets. Just look at the Gretzky trade to Los Angeles, it's a prime example of the owner's greed," Cst. Harry McPherson rebutted. "Just cause you're a fan doesn't mean you can't admit that it's turning into big business."

Harry watched the house with one eye, while carrying on his debate. "I think we'd better check. She should have turned on a light by now."

He picked up his radio and called Communications. "Can you phone Mrs. Carpenter to make sure everything's okay?"

"Sure can."

"I still think the players are to blame for the ticket prices. You can't take your family to a game anymore without re-mortgaging your house."

"You don't have a family," Harry said, wondering what was taking so long. Mary should have waved out of her window by now, giving them an all clear signal and freeing them to continue their patrol. Maybe he should have walked her to her door, but hell, she had an attached garage and they saw her drive inside.

"No one is answering." The words squawked from the radio.

Harry tumbled out of the car before Tom finished asking for backup. Creeping toward the front of the house across the flat carpet of grass, he peered inside the living room window but saw nothing. He shook his head at Tom and pointed for him to go left while he went right.

Leaves deposited by the wind, rustled as Harry prowled between the house and fence. The orange glow of alley lighting brightened the night enough to pick up signs of forced entry. He spotted none.

Harry rounded the corner of the house at the same time as Tom appeared from the other direction. With a shake of his head, Harry let Tom know he'd been unsuccessful. Then Tom waved him toward the open patio door while he sprinted toward the alley.

Drawing his pistol, Harry crept across the tiny patio. He slid into the dining area through the open window, keeping his back to the wall. Light from the street lamp illuminated legs covered with dark slacks.

Mary lay crumpled on the floor. He studied the shapes he could interpret and the shadows where the light didn't penetrate. When Tom moved up beside him, Harry pointed to Mary.

"Anyone in the alley?"

"No."

"I'll go check her." He crouched to take advantage of the protection of the island that grew in the centre of the kitchen.

Her pulse reassured him that she was alive but a spreading stain of blood in her white hair alarmed him. He revised his backup call to include an ambulance and started checking the rest of the house.

Once satisfied the assailant was gone, they turned on the lights and assessed the damage. Slashed furniture, overturned tables, and uprooted plants now decorated the small home. Little had been spared total destruction—less had escaped some sort of damage.

*****

Mike hurried through the door moments behind the ambulance attendants. "How did this happen?" he demanded of the first officer he spotted.

"He must have been waiting inside when she got home. Sorry Mike, I know she's a friend."

Mike glared at Harry. "You're sorry! You were supposed to look after her. Why was she even in the house alone?"

"Hey, Mike, enough already."

Running his hand through his hair and over his face, Mike breathed deeply. "You're right. I didn't do any better keeping Lisette safe."

Mary lay still and deathly pale but the ambulance crew worked on her without undue haste. Mike searched for and found the rise and fall of her chest.

He took a deep breath, then asked, "Why didn't her alarm sound?"

"They knew what they were doing." The officer shrugged. "Whoever disarmed the system did a good job, but I'd say this isn't related to that string of B&Es. They don't usually make this kind of mess. They know what they're looking for and target it."

When the paramedic straightened up, Mike stepped to his side. "Is she going to be all right?"

"That's a serious bash on the head for anyone but for someone her age it could have been deadly. Be glad her heart's strong."

Mike watched as they wheeled his friend away, thankful that she hadn't been killed. Why would anyone hurt Mary? He had only asked Harry to keep an eye on her on a whim or maybe it was instinct? Had he missed something that his subconscious had caught?

He ordered the extra officers out of the house and waited for the Crime Scene Unit to arrive. The fewer feet trampling evidence, the better chance of saving a workable clue.

Eventually, Pete Humphries and his crew arrived. Pete stretched his bowed frame up to slap Mike on the shoulder. "If there's anything to find, we'll find it." Then he shook his head as he surveyed the destruction. "You would think she'd know better than to walk into something like this."

With another shake of his head, his shoulders returned to their normal hunched posture. Pete looked around. "Where exactly was she found?"

•

Harry again described what he had seen and surmised about the forced entry. Pete nodded and made notes while his assistant took pictures.

Mike listened to the officer's story again knowing he would still read their reports later. He had to ensure he had all the details. Once Pete had the scene controlled, Mike left for the hospital.

The earlier storm had calmed leaving a cloudy, winter quality to the cold. As he drove, Mike's mind flew over the events of the past few days hoping to shuffle them into a readable pattern. He parked near the hospital's main entrance, then navigated the corridors to the emergency ward.

The nurse at the emergency room counter assured him that the doctor in charge of Mary's treatment would speak to him when there was something to tell.

Rather than forcing the issue, he headed for a row of vending machines. The coffee machine offered a number of exotic blends, but he settled for a strong, black, Colombian brew. He would give the doctor until he finished drinking it. Then he would hunt him down.

Mike slouched in the waiting room chair watching the flow of injured and ill. Eventually, a petite, brown-skinned woman approached him. She held a chart clasped against her white lab coat. He swallowed the last of his still warm coffee and stood to greet her.

"Detective Ceretzke?" she asked, peering at him over her half-glasses. At Mike's nod she continued in a low voice, "Mrs. Carpenter has suffered a concussion and has lost a considerable amount of blood from the wound in her scalp. She also has a dislocated shoulder, three cracked ribs, and severe facial bruising, but those are things what will heal."

"She'll be all right then?"

"We're hopeful she will make a full recovery; however, she has yet to regain consciousness."

"You mean she's in a coma?" Mike felt the floor tilt and steadied himself against a wall.

"Not at the moment. We'll be monitoring her signs closely, hoping for rapid progress. She should come around in the next few hours."

"Can I see her?" Mike had to know Mary was alive and healing.

"We've finished with her and your lab people have taken what they needed and have left. You can wait in her room, but let her rest. Does she have relatives we should contact?"

"I'll look after that," Mike said, knowing Mary wouldn't want her son hovering at her bedside unless she was dying.

*****

Jack lay still, testing the air in the room, hunting for the sound that had disturbed his sleep.

The hardwood flooring in his den sighed under the weight of a footstep. Someone was in the house.

Jack reached across the bed to the night table and fumbled with the arms of his glasses. The glow of the clock radio came into focus, 2:34. He eased open the drawer of the night table where he'd put his gun when he undressed.

He clutched the gun and rolled off the bed.

Another creak. Closer. In the living room a desk drawer whispered.

Jack stifled a groan as pain shot through his knees. He fought their arthritic stiffness and tried to cross the broadloom silently.

Was there one thief or more? His ears wouldn't tell him. Instinct told him that at least two people were robbing him.

One was at the desk. One was near his bedroom door.

Jack slowed his approach, controlled his breathing, and waited for a sound to point him in the right direction.

The night was black, thick clouds covered the full moon and he heard drops of freezing rain tapping against the window.

A movement to his right. Toward the living room. He swung his gun ready to warn, ready to capture.

A voice whispered, "First you. Then the cop. Then no one will know."

He recognized the voice.

CHAPTER 16

"Mike. Your Mountie friend is dead. Killed in a break-in."

Mike held the receiver between his shoulder and chin as he listened to Evan Collins. He reached for the pants he had just removed and pulled them over his legs.

"Neighbours phoned to report a gun shot at 2:40. By the time the patrol car got there, the burglars were gone. Same kind of weapon, same kind of entry as that rash of B&Es the Analysis Section is tying to the Shotgun Gang. Thought you'd want to know."

It was 3:15. Only minutes earlier, Mike had arrived home from the hospital where Mary lay unconscious and unable to answer his questions. He picked up his jacket and keys on his way through the door.

"You think it's a break-in gone wrong?" he asked, as he descended the apartment stairs two at a time and raced toward his truck. At least he'd left it parked on the street and not in the crowded underground garage.

"It's their M.O. I'll be here if you want to come down."

"I'm on my way. I should arrive in about ten minutes, maybe less."

"No problem. The M.E. isn't here yet; neither is Ident."

Mike hit the disconnect button on his cell phone and turned his attention to driving down the quiet streets. As he drove by the hospital, he punched its number into his phone. Mary's condition was still serious but stable.

Mike glanced toward the lookout as he crossed the wet surface of the bridge leading to the south side of the river. The freezing rain was turning to snow as the temperature dropped. Slick road surfaces would turn the morning rush hour into a curling match with cars careening off each other like rocks on ice.

Jack's bungalow was south and west of the park. In a quiet neighbourhood where people flocked to raise their families. His wife had died of heart failure three years ago and his only child, a daughter, lived in Vancouver. Mike dreaded having to contact her.

He pulled to a stop across the street from the house. A crowd of neighbours, police, and media blocked the sidewalk. Mike flashed his badge and walked inside. Feminine touches lingered in the form of floral drapes and embroidered toss cushions. The piano held an array of family pictures showing Jack and his wife as they aged. Recent pictures of very young children stood in the front row. His grandchildren? Mike didn't know.

Jack's wife wouldn't have appreciated the splatter of blood covering the wall by Jack's body. Or the pool of deep red staining the beige carpet and outlining each crack and crevice in the adjoining hardwood floor.

Jack lay sprawled in the doorway of the bedroom. He wore only jockey shorts and faced the ceiling. Half his face was a bloody pulp.

Stomach lurching, Mike turned away and for the first time spotted Toby Wright, an assistant in the Crime Scene Unit. Toby looked about sixteen years old. Mike looked around for someone who had the experience and skills to investigate the scene properly.

"Where's Pete? Why didn't he come himself? Why did he send an assistant? Doesn't he know this is important?"

"He's finishing up at Mary Carpenter's—then calling it a night."

"Shouldn't he be here? He's the senior person in the lab."

"I'm qualified for the job. Pete trained me himself, so lay off."

A hand on his shoulder and Evan's, "Calm down, it's under control," made Mike realize he was acting like a jerk. Yelling at investigators twice in one night—was it becoming a habit?

He put his hands in his pockets and shrugged. "Sorry Toby. You're right. I'm an idiot to question your ability."

"I get that crap from civilians all the time, but I don't expect it from other cops."

"I said I was sorry."

The Ident man shook his head and continued dusting for prints. Mike scanned the room. The furniture seemed untouched except for a partially open desk drawer.

"Tidy thieves."

Evan's voice remained strictly professional as he answered. "I don't think anything's missing. The only thing that looks disturbed is the desk."

"What's in the desk—records?"

"Hard to tell. The guy wasn't organized."

"He was a good cop."

"Yeah, sure, just not a file clerk. You gonna check his stuff or am I?" Evan pointed at the desk.

"I want to go through it. If you find anything in the rest of the house that relates to Dorrien or Jack's informant, let me know."

"Sure Mike, anything I find is yours."

The next hour of careful searching turned up nothing that could help Mike with the case. If Jack kept records, they were at RCMP Headquarters.

At 5:30, Toby and his crew were still collecting evidence and checking details.

"You want to grab breakfast, Mike?" Evan asked.

Mike looked at his watch. "I want to go home and shower. I'll see you at the station later."

A few die-hard news vultures camped in the early morning darkness, Richard Tanner among them. He strode toward Mike, a smug grin on his handsome face. "So my info was right. The Mounties were involved. What is it, a joint operation?"

"Tanner, get out of my face." Mike liked the reporter even less since learning of Beth's involvement with him.

"This ties into Lisette Dorrien's murder though, doesn't it?"

Mike put his hand on Richard's arm. Richard drew back. Mike backed him across the snow-covered law toward the line of parked vehicles.

"Tell me about your source, Richard. Who is he? What does

he say about this case? Does he say how it's connected to Lisette's murder? How about the attempt to kill Beth? Was that connected too? Want to tell me where I can find your snitch, so I can talk to him? Such a well-informed person could be a big help."

"What do you mean, tried to kill Beth?"

"Beth McKinney, the woman you claimed saw the murderer."

"I know who Beth is. You said someone tried to kill her?"

"Didn't your spy tell you? They nearly got her when she was leaving the library Tuesday night. Your story about her being an eyewitness scared someone into trying to kill her."

When Mike had backed the reporter all the way to the road, he tired of the game, and climbed into his truck.

"You want to keep Beth safe, you let me know anything you hear from your informant. And keep her name out of your reports."

*****

Mike revved the truck engine and pulled away from the curb, wondering if he was losing his objectivity. Was he too close to the case to be effective? Was Hugh determined to kill anyone Lisette had talked to? Was Beth still in danger?

He picked up the cell phone to call her, then remembered the time. Not a social hour to phone. Instead, he swung the steering wheel sharply to the right and headed in the direction of her house. He would do a visual check of the place before he woke her.

A van backed up and followed his turn. A tingle raced up his spine. Mike turned right at the next corner. Then right again at the school. Then right a third time and a final right, returning him to the broad main street he had left minutes before. The van followed.

Trying to maintain a constant speed, he called in the license number and requested a patrol car to help intercept the van.

Maybe it was nothing but paranoia resulting from fatigue, but Jack had been a thorough professional and someone had killed him in his own home. Damn, had it been a robbery? Mike looked in his rear-view mirror. That van didn't look friendly. The chances of Jack's death being a coincidence were growing smaller.

A twirling blue and white light pulled into traffic behind the van. The van jumped ahead like a startled antelope, skidding on the icy road as it swerved to the inside lane. It pulled farther ahead of the patrol car and overtook Mike's speeding truck.

The stubby barrel of an over/under sawed-off shotgun protruded from the passenger window and swung toward Mike's head. He slammed his brake pedal into the floor.

A jarring blast stunned him as the truck's windshield shattered and the engine exploded.

Mike wrestled the steering wheel as the swerving vehicle bounced off the curb. His body catapulted forward, narrowly missing the shattered window, then bounced back as his seat belt locked.

The truck shuttered and died. The van shot through a red light, swerving around a transport truck. The transport jack-knifed, blocking the intersection. The pursuing police car rammed into Mike's truck pushing him dangerously close to the swaying truck. The van vanished in the distance.

Mike pounded the steering wheel and peered through the fragments of broken glass clinging to the gaping hole in his windshield. Steam rose from the hood.

Constable Hilda Carstairs appeared at the driver's window. "What kind of hair-brained stunt was that?" Then she looked at the windshield and the steam. She looked back at Mike. "Are you all right? You look like hell. I'll call an ambulance."

"I'll live."

"What was that all about anyway?"

"They had a shotgun."

The constable's complexion lost a shade of colour.

"Are more cars coming? Did you trace the license plate?" He reached across the seat with an unsteady hand, grabbed his cell phone, and unfastened his seat belt. Then clutching the doorframe, he stepped from the vehicle. The tail end of the truck and the front end of the patrol car were firmly welded together. The paperwork would be horrendous.

He signalled Hilda to wait with her questions while he phoned Beth, who assured him that she was awake and safe. No, intruders had not disturbed her rest. Yes, he could drop by to speak to her.

Hilda's raised eyebrow and smirk told him that his concern for Beth's safety hadn't come across as being entirely professional. Oh hell, it had been years since he'd met someone who wasn't more fascinated with police work than with him personally, or who ran like hell when they'd learned that he was a cop.

"Why were you chasing them?" Hilda asked.

"Wrong way round. They followed me from Jack Pierce's place."

She nodded. Obviously, she'd heard about the murder. "You think the same people killed him?"

"He was killed with a shotgun."

*****

Sunlight was reflecting off the white of the newly fallen snow by the time Mike stepped out of the patrol car and thanked the constable for dropping him at Beth's. His mind whirled with details and his neck ached. He would need time in a hot shower, then more with icy water pounding down his back to restore him and get his mind working again. That was later. Now he had to solve this case before anyone else was killed.

He was still no closer to having the evidence he needed to arrest Hugh. Was Jack's death another that he could lay at Hugh's feet? It couldn't be a coincidence. Why Jack? They had shared information but he had done most of the legwork. Maybe the Mounties had come up with the name of a professional killer? No, there would be no point in killing Jack because others in the force would know it too.

Unless his informant had given him some damning information. Did that mean Jack's informant was in danger too? What information could he have uncovered?

The name of the killer? Enough ironclad proof to destroy Karlek's organization? Facts that would hang Hugh? Maybe he'd stumbled onto what had happened during the time between Lisette leaving home and being killed. How had she used that time? Where was the disc Hugh was hunting? Was it the key to this case? Where had Lisette hid that disc?

*****

When Mike rang her doorbell, Beth had just finished a two-hour consulting session with Jeffrey Tupper, a chronic early riser who found 6:00 a.m. an ideal time to learn about financial planning.

Mike looked as though he hadn't slept in days. The grey in his hair was more noticeable and his skin tone had faded to match it. He skipped the niceties, giving each cat only a quick pat on the head as he explained the mission that brought him to her door so early.

"A computer disc? Why do you think Lisette took it?"

Mike closed his eyes and Beth wondered if he'd fallen asleep while standing in her foyer.

"You need some food and lots of coffee," she said, turning toward the kitchen.

"There's no time. We have to get to that disc before Hugh does."

"What makes you think we can find it? It could be anywhere."

"We have to."

"What was this morning's phone call about? All your questions about people breaking into my house. Was that about this disc?"

"In a way. Please trust me on this. I'll tell you everything later."

She met his gaze and read a compelling urgency. "Later seems to be your standard answer."

"Will you help me?"

"If it will help convict Hugh, yes I'll help."

He hurried her into her coat and grabbed her arm, practically pulling her outside. She looked at the empty street, then at him. He shrugged. "Can we use your car? I had an accident with mine."

"Is that something else to be discussed later?" she asked.

He met her inquiry with silence and directed her to drive toward the Dorrien house. She drove filling the silence with music from an oldies station. He said nothing until he asked her to park.

The centimetre of snow that had fallen during the night was already disappearing from the sidewalks leaving only frozen footprints to show where early walkers had ventured. The grassy areas remained lightly frosted with white. Tall maple and birch trees lined the road and a bushy-tailed squirrel taunted them, then scampered to safety in the upper branches of a nearby tree.

Beth's curiosity about Mike's bedraggled appearance was about to win out over good manners, when he spoke. "Rosa, Lisette's cleaner, saw her within a block of the bridge on the north side of the river, at approximately half past eleven."

"It takes at least twenty minutes to run over the bridge to the lookout." Noting his inquiring look, she said, "I've run this path on my more ambitious days."

"That leaves her with about seventy minutes unaccounted for."

"Lisette could run a long way in that time. That disc could be anywhere."

"What if someone thought she'd given it to Mary?"

Beth raised her eyebrows and motioned toward his cellular phone. "That's easy to check, just ask Mary."

He refused to meet her eyes. What was wrong? Beth knew his explanation wasn't going to be good news.

"Mary walked in on someone ransacking her house last night. She's in the hospital."

Beth stepped backwards. "Why didn't you tell me? Was she hurt badly? What happened?" She scrutinized his worn face. "Is that why you look exhausted?"

"She has a severe concussion, a dislocated shoulder, and cracked ribs from being slammed into a wall but the doctor thinks she'll be all right."

Beth turned abruptly and headed toward her car. "Pushing people into walls sounds like Hugh!"

Mike caught her arm.

"Let me go. We should be at the hospital, not chasing phantoms."

When she realized that she couldn't shake him off, she twisted toward him.

"That's not all," he said.

He told her about Jack's death. She leaned against the trunk of a maple tree.

"Are they connected?" Then seeing the pain in Mike's face, she added, "You had a hell of a night."

"Jack was a good man and a conscientious cop who should be looking forward to retirement. Damn, I want to lock Hugh away for so long that he never sees sunlight again."

He shook his head, rubbed at his neck, and breathed a deep calming breath.

"The M.O. of the two break-ins is about as different as you can get, but I'm certain some link exists," he said.

Beth stepped toward him with her hand extended. Instead of accepting her sympathy, he straightened his back and said, "We'll stop by the hospital later. They probably won't let you in until she regains consciousness anyway and maybe you can help me solve this."

Beth wasn't ready to abandon the idea of seeing Mary just yet. "When she comes around, we can ask her. Someone should be with her now."

"Don't you think I know that." He swung away from her and rested his head against the tree trunk. "She's my friend. If I hadn't been careless she wouldn't be hurt and Lisette would be alive. This case is going no where, but I have to turn it around before you're hurt to."

Beth watched melting snow glitter on a bare branch. She reached out to touch him then pulled her hand back. Exploring his guilty conscience would be better left until later. She grinned in spite of the morning's disasters. It seemed her life had become a series of things to be continued later.

"Tell me more about the computer disc and why you think Lisette took it."

Mike turned toward her with hope shining through his fatigue. "We know it went missing from Hugh's office. We also know she had a reason to take it and that she was in his office the morning of her death. What's on it we don't know, but it must be damaging. We're certain it is not in the house, so where did she put it? Where do you hide a computer disc?"

"Are you kidding? Something that small could be hidden anywhere."

Mike reached out and took her forearm in one hand. With the index finger of his other hand, he gently lifted her chin until she stared directly into his eyes. "If you had a disc that you thought might save your life and your children's lives, if you knew you had to keep it safe for several hours, where would you put it?"

Finally grasping the seriousness of the situation, Beth put on her best reference librarian expression, and asked, "Was she seen taking the disc from the house?"

"No, but Hugh ransacked the place and didn't find it."

"Well, even if you wanted to hide it you wouldn't want to risk it to the elements. Also, if it was that important she would have put it somewhere no one would accidentally stumble over it."

Beth concentrated, then conscious of how her crow's-feet deepened and her brow wrinkled, she smoothed her expression and answered, "I don't think I would risk the outdoors if I could help it. Maybe your information is right. Could she have gone to Mary's?"

"It's a couple of miles north of here."

"Lisette could have done that easily."

"But Mary was in Banff at a conference all last weekend. She didn't get home until Monday afternoon."

"Did Lisette know that?"

"I don't know." Mike ran his fingers through his wavy hair.

"You think she took the disc, planning to give it to Mary and not finding her home—Lisette did what?" He paused, as if waiting for her to supply an answer.

"She would have needed to improvise at that point. Let's follow the most likely route from Mary's to the park. See if anything comes to mind as a hiding place."

They retrieved the car and drove slowly down the quiet residential streets to Mary's house. A crime scene van sat in front of the house and Mike suggested they check on the team's progress.

They circled the small two-story building that was covered by the shrivelled blossoms of a Clematis vine. Beth stood outside the patio door and looked in at the dining room and beyond to the kitchen. She couldn't pull her horrified stare away from the shredded furniture, the spilled food, and the broken plants.

A round-shouldered investigator, who Beth recognized from the scene of Lisette's murder, spotted them through the patio door and joined them on the deck. His presence released Beth from the spell that had held her gaze and she scanned the room watching as a woman carefully examined a fragment of paper. A faint gleam of light reflected from the rubber glove that encased her hand.

Mike introduced the man as Pete Humphries. Pete nodded at her then spoke in a soft voice, his rapid-fire words spilling over each other. Beth strained to catch what he was saying.

"Too bad about your Mountie friend. I'll double-check the findings when I finish here, but you know Toby is a good investigator. For that matter, my entire team is good. They won't miss anything. I've trained them all myself, you know."

"I know and I've apologized all around. I guess I'm getting too old to remember to be polite when I'm stressed."

Pete squinted up at Mike. "Looks like you didn't get much sleep either."

"I used to be able to go for days on two hours a night," Mike grumbled and rubbed his neck.

His banter sounded strained to Beth.

"You used to look better with no sleep too. Getting older is not for the fainthearted, but I suppose you're here because you want an update." He held up his glove-encased hand and ticked off points with his fingers.

"So far no prints and whoever tampered with the alarm knew what they were doing. Still, that's common knowledge in some circles so you're not necessarily looking for a hardened burglar. In fact, judging from the lack of planning, I'd guess it was an amateur job. A professional wouldn't have trashed the place like this just for fun."

"Unless the guy was angry."

"A pro doesn't work because he's angry or wants revenge. He just takes what he came for and gets out clean."

"Okay, so he was an amateur," Mike conceded. "What else did you find?"

"A few fibres on Mary's clothes. Don't look so glum, Mike. Count on Mary to come through and ID the guy."

He retreated into the gloom of the dining room, then turned. "Oh, the weapon was probably a heavy flashlight. We found one near the alley. No prints, but blood. We'll check it out. Guy probably figured to leave all the evidence behind, maybe thinking it would be untraceable."

"Is it?"

"Damn near. Flashlight is a brand carried by the big warehouse stores. If he paid cash, the store probably won't have a record. This guy might be untidy, but he knows something about remaining anonymous."

Before the hunched investigator disappeared into the house, Mike asked, "Did you find a computer disc during your search?"

"There was no sign of a computer. Do you think they took it?"

"No, Mary didn't have a computer. If you find a disc let me know."

"Sure Mike," he said, this time dismissing them as he returned to the room.

Beth jumped, startled out of her shocked study of the damage by Mike taking her arm.

"I should have left you at the car. You didn't need to see that."

Beth was tired of being on the fringe, getting only the information Mike wanted her to hear. "That officer sounds like he knows Mary personally." She stopped walking and stood on the sidewalk waiting for his reply.

Mike ran his hand over his chin as if testing the shadow of a beard that covered his cheeks. Then he smoothed his hair. Beth felt his scrutiny and wondered what terrible secret he was hiding.

"Mary worked for the police service for more than thirty years and since she retired she's been consulting on cases. All the older guys know her."

"Mary, elderly lady who loves painting, is transformed into Mary super-detective?"

Mike caught her attempt at humour and laughed. Then he added in a voice that was so low she barely caught the words. "A tough lady at that."

"Excuse me." A young woman dressed in jeans, a sweater, and slippers called from the far side of the street. She waved to attract their attention, then darted from behind a picket fence. "Excuse me. Are you police officers?"

"I'm Detective Ceretzke. What can I do for you?"

"How's Mary doing? I called the hospital but they just say she's stable."

"She was badly hurt but she will mend. Did you see anything or anyone around last night?"

"No, at least not until all the police cars started arriving."

"No one before then?"

"Sorry, I put the kids to bed, then flopped in front of the TV. All those sirens and flashing lights sure caught my attention."

"What about earlier this week? Say Monday, close to noon?"

"I did see someone lurking around her house Monday–before the kids got home for lunch."

"Someone? A man or woman?"

"A woman."

"Can you describe her?"

"Striking. You know the kind." She looked at Beth for agreement. "Long and lean. Her hair was thick, dark red and glossy, tied back with a yellow ribbon. She was dressed in a turquoise jogging suit and white runners. If I looked that good in sweats, I'd be modelling them, not running in them."

"Did she go around the back of the house or into the yard?"

"She stayed on the front step and rang the doorbell a couple of times. Then she opened the screen door and pounded. I was getting ready to tell her Mary was gone when she left."

"Did she put anything in the mailbox?"

"No, she just walked away. When she got to the end of the sidewalk she stopped again and stared at two of the Murdock kids playing hopscotch. They were the only people in sight and I kept watching just to see what she was doing. You know, being a good neighbour."

"What did she do?" Mike prompted.

"She pulled something out of her pocket. I couldn't see what it was. She looked at it for a few seconds, then she shoved it back, and ran off down the sidewalk."

Mike's cell phone beeped. Beth watched his face as he answered. By the time he disconnected the call, he was smiling.

"A tough old bird. Mary is fully awake and wants visitors. The intruder was after the disc."

He thanked the neighbour and turned toward the car. Instead of heading north to the hospital, he asked Beth to drive south to the freeway. "This shouldn't take long. We'll go to the hospital afterward."

They drove under the canopy of trees lining the narrow streets. The neighbourhood had been built in the 1920s. The houses were small, like Mary's. The yards were filled with homeowners sweeping away the remnants of snow and with children rolling snowballs before the white stuff melted.

Plastic bags shaped into ghosts and pumpkins bulged with leaves. Cutouts of black cats and witches riding broomsticks covered windows.

Beth realized that Halloween had slipped her mind as real horrors eclipsed packaged demons. She had to remember to buy treats for the kids in her neighbourhood.

Looking at all the activity Beth couldn't help but wonder where Lisette would hide something that small and that important. "Lisette would have had a hard time hiding anything along here, too many people around to get curious about what she was doing."

"Unless she knew someone she could leave it with. We'll have to canvass the area."

"Do you see that?" Beth asked as she stopped for a red light. She pointed across the street to a strip mall. "Fun-time Computers. What if she was trying to tell me where she hid the disc, not the name of her assailant?"

The light changed and without waiting for his reply, Beth drove across the intersection and pulled into an empty space a half-block from the store. When she stepped out of the car, her runner sank into the softness of a new tar patch that ran at least ten meters down the street.

Mike laughed at her predicament and didn't seem embarrassed when she glared with disapproval.

A buzzer announced their entrance and a lean man with coal black hair and eyes to match looked at them from the counter at the back of the store. His face wore the cheerful look of a person who loves his work.

"Can I help you?"

"Are you Howard?"

"Yes, I am. Howard Li. Do you wish to purchase a computer or have yours repaired?"

Mike pulled his badge from his pocket. "Did a woman in a turquoise jogging suit stop in here around eleven Monday?"

"She was killed later, I know." He lost his smile. "She seemed scared. I didn't know whether to tell the police she was here or not. Nobody asked and it didn't seem that important. That she was here, I mean."

"Why was she here?"

"The lady wanted to check out her disc and asked to try one of my used machines. I ran a virus scan. You can't be too careful with all the viruses around lately. Then I booted it up. It was a table of some kind, but I didn't get good look because another customer came in just then. She left after a couple of minutes."

"Did she take the disc?" Beth asked.

"Why wouldn't she?"

He walked to a machine near the back of the store. It was the same model as Hugh's.

"I haven't demoed this machine since then."

He peered into the drive, pushed the release button, and out popped a disc. Beth pulled it from the drive. Nothing was written on the label.

"Is that what we're looking for?" Mike asked.

"Can you boot it up so we can see what it contains?" Beth asked Mr. Li.

A few moments later columns of meaningless text scrolled down the screen.

"Gotcha," Mike whispered.

After pocketing the disc and cautioning Mr. Li not to talk to the media or anyone else about their find, they turned her sports car north and finally headed for the hospital.

*****

Beth was relieved to see Mary awake though she was pale and her breathing was shallow. They had met only at Lisette's funeral but Beth liked her confidence and her exuberance. Just knowing Mary gave her hope for a long, productive retirement and concentrated her worry about her parents' lack of focus.

"Shouldn't you be lying down?" Mike demanded as he rushed to her bedside.

"I hurt just as much when I lie down and then I feel like an invalid instead of the idiot I am."

"You can't blame yourself for being injured."

"Don't try your pop psychology on me. If I had been smarter, I would never have gone into the house. Remember that. You can't control a bad guy's moves, but you surely can control your own."

Mike sat on the edge of the bed looking obscenely pleased. "I don't care whose fault it was. I'm just glad we didn't lose you too."

"What do you mean 'too'?" Mary asked. She looked at Mike, then let her gaze rest on Beth.

Beth squirmed under her discomforting stare.

"What happened?" Mary demanded.

"You're too weak for bad news. We can talk about it later." Mike patted her age-marked hand.

"Now, or I will just worry."

"She needs to know," Beth said, forcing him to answer though she saw he didn't relish the role of bearer of bad news.

"Jack Pierce was killed last night," Mike said, rubbing the loose skin on the back of Mary's hand as he spoke. "Shot during a burglary."

Beth saw the light in Mary's eyes dim. She sagged into the pillow; her slender frame now seemed frail. Beth feared any further blows would cause her to shrivel and disappear on the wind. Why had she encouraged Mike to give her the bad news? She should have let him handle Mary's concerns. If Mary lost her will to live, Beth knew she would always feel responsible.

"Was it the gang that's been burglarizing houses lately?" Mary asked, fatigue making her voice sound heavy and slow.

"We think so." Mike brushed her hair away from her brow. "It's tragic, but don't let it prey on you. The timing was just a fluke."

"Like my night-time assailant? Mike, I'm not a child. Are they connected to your investigation of Hugh Dorrien?"

Mike looked as if he might cry. That surprised Beth because he seemed so strong and reliable. Someone she could count on. Seeing him vulnerable seemed wrong and she longed to hold him close and comfort him.

"I don't know if they're connected."

"But you are working on that assumption?" Mary's voice grew in volume, if not strength. A faint smile turned up the edges of her mouth. "Of course you are. You're trying to protect me. You always try to protect those you consider weak, don't you Mike?"

She took his hand away from her hair and held it tight. "Ask me your questions and I'll do my best to help."

They looked at each other for what seemed to Beth, an eternity. Mike lowered his gaze first, then pulled a pen and a notebook from his pocket.

"Did you recognize the intruder?"

"I didn't really see him. It all happened too fast." Mary thought a moment then said, "He wore cologne with a musk base and talked in a husky whisper."

"Do you remember any other details—height, clothing?"

"Trying to remember is different when you're the victim." She paused as a flicker of fear crossed her face. "I never imagined myself as a victim. I don't like the feeling."

"Just tell me what you can."

"I'm trying to think. He was tall and strong." She stopped talking and raised her unfettered hand to cover her mouth, then dropped it to stroke the sling covering her other arm. "The way he whipped me around the corner and against the wall, I felt like I was being manhandled by a giant."

"Was he wearing gloves?"

"Yes."

"What about his clothes?"

"His arm was against my back. I don't remember feeling his jacket against my skin, or smelling the coat so with the rain last night it probably wasn't wool, or maybe his cologne hid the smell."

"Did the cloth swish, like a ski jacket?"

She shook her head then closed her eyes tightly raising her skeletal hand to cover them. The final tinge of colour faded from her softly wrinkled cheeks. When she opened her eyes again she held her head very still and smiled faintly. "It only hurts when I laugh—or move."

"This can wait."

"I want to help, but it happened so fast."

Beth watched tears flood her eyes. A yawn escaped, muffling Mary's words.

Mike caressed her arm. "Don't try to remember. It will come back."

"What's going to happen now?"

"The hospital wants you here at least until tomorrow. Pete's finishing with your place and we'll try to get your house back in shape once he's gone."

"How bad is my house?"

"Well, it is bad." He paused under her intense stare.

"It's fixable," Beth interjected, fearing Mary couldn't handle the truth.

Mary studied her for a moment. "Thank you for trying but you're a terrible liar." Then she added, "I guess it was time that most of that stuff went anyway. Were my family pictures damaged?"

Mike shrugged his ignorance of their fate.

"I don't know if I can go back there again. Not for a while anyway. Maybe I'll just move somewhere with lots of security." Mary faded into her bed and closed her eyes.

Beth squeezed her bony hand and tried to make her voice sound encouraging. "I've got a big house. Why don't you plan to stay with me until you decide what to do?" She thought about the damage she'd seen at Mary's home and knew it would take time to restore order. It didn't matter how long it took because she owed this woman something for being Lisette's friend.

CHAPTER 17

Mike left Beth sitting with Mary and took a taxi to the police station. He needed that disc analyzed and he needed rest. He rubbed his neck.

As he strode across the foyer of the station, Mike searched for some way to avoid surrendering the disc to the Mountie investigation. The Edmonton police would need the disc as evidence of Hugh's motive for hurting Mary and for killing Lisette. He stopped walking.

He'd forgotten about Jack's informant. How deep was the informant's cover? Would Jack's replacement share the name of his source? What approach would work best? Maybe a warning that the informant was in danger for providing the information Jack had been killed for possessing. Or, a plea for help solving Lisette's murder? Maybe he could use the disc as a bartering tool?

Super Sam Weisman was leaving her office when Mike caught her. "Mike, what's going on—Mary Carpenter hurt, Jack Pierce dead, and you damn near killed?"

"I've got the disc Hugh wants. We need it analyzed."

"What's on it?"

"A log of some kind, but it's in code."

"I'll have a copy made, then we can send it to Marvin Brown at RCMP Headquarters for decoding. What else can you tell me?"

"Mary will heal. The doctor says no permanent physical damage."

"Thank God! What about emotional damage?"

"She's already talking about moving into a secure building."

"Damn! I hope she's tough enough to get past this. The Chief is already on my back for an update on the break-in."

"Pete figures an amateur hit Mary's place, but Jack's death seems closer to the Shotgun Gang's M.O."

"Maybe Jack interrupted them? They wouldn't stay around to search the place after shooting him. What about you? Did you get checked out after the crash? Do you need time off? We can assign someone else to this case."

"The EMTs at the scene diagnosed minor whiplash, nothing serious." He massaged the ache in his neck. No one was taking this case away now.

"What is this about, Mike?"

Mike read concern in her pursed lips and clenched fists. He sought an answer he could defend because Sam only respected instinct if it was well supported by fact. "I'd bet money they tie into Lisette's murder. Coincidences like this don't happen. If Karlek or Dorrien are behind it, then Jack came too close and was eliminated. They must have known he was Lisette's contact and are tying up loose ends. Mary was her friend and therefore dragged into the search. I think we have to watch over Beth McKinney and Mr. Domke to ensure they're not next."

"You will have to be careful, too. You're obviously marked as a danger. What's your next step?"

"A few hours of sleep. Then I'll check Ident's findings and visit Hugh to ask him about the disc. Maybe I can convince him to deal."

*****

Mike rarely saw his apartment in daylight, especially during the six winter months. The place wasn't exactly messy, but the sunshine exposed dust on every surface. He had no problem keeping the place tidy, but when he compared it to Beth McKinney's home, his place ranked far below ten on the designer scale.

Mike removed his jacket and dropped his holster on the coffee table beside his newest pile of mail. He fell back on the sofa, his arm across his eyes, and tried to ignore the growing stiffness in his neck. The harsh buzz of his phone caught him on the threshold of sleep. Mike raised his arm to check the caller display. It wasn't the hospital or the station so he let the machine take the call.

A deep voice with an eastern accent asked him to pick up the phone. Mike ignored the request. The man continued speaking, as if certain he was present.

Was someone watching his home?

"Detective, I realize your day has been long and eventful, but Mr. Karlek is returning to Montreal tomorrow morning and feels it is to your advantage to meet with him. Mr. Karlek will be available to you between three and four at the Russian Tea House."

The machine clicked to a stop. Mike closed his eyes and let his mind wander. Why was it to his advantage to talk to Karlek? Probably a more important question was why did Karlek want to talk to him. It was two-thirty. He could grab a ten-minute nap, shower, shave, and meet Karlek at three-thirty. No point in looking too eager.

First, he had to call Super Sam to let her know about the invitation. The RCMP surveillance teams would get excited if a local police officer met with their crime figure.

Mike caught himself just before he drifted into a deep sleep. He rolled off the sofa. If he gave in to sleep now, it wouldn't be for a ten-minute nap and he didn't want to wake to find that his chance to grill Karlek had evaporated.

He reached for the phone.

*****

The Russian Tea House was not a restaurant Mike frequented, but it was convenient and he'd been there before. They served a variety of teas, light meals, and exotic desserts. A display of silver Russian samovars sat on a shelf that encircled the restaurant.

Mike took a moment to let his eyes adjust to the artificial lighting. Then he requested Karlek's table and followed the waiter to the raised smoking section that provided a view of the entire restaurant.

Most of the tables were occupied. Mike scanned Generation Xers wearing coloured leggings and oversized sweaters. Business types in three-piece suits kept to the dark corners of the room, probably embarrassed to be caught in a teahouse. Pairs of tea drinking ladies were waiting to have their tealeaves read or their palms examined by Magda, the resident psychic.

Karlek sat alone at a small table decorated with arrangement of fresh carnations. His slight frame was well suited to the narrow-backed chair. A brightly painted teapot with a matching cup and saucer sat in front of him.

Mike perused the nearby tables. Two expensively dressed businessmen sat close by, their chairs angled so they could watch both Karlek and the door. Evan sat in the farthest corner of the restaurant, his back against the wall, his line of sight unimpeded.

Replacing his cup on its saucer, Karlek rose halfway out of his chair and extended his hand. "I am glad you came, Detective. Please, join me. What kind of tea would you prefer? Would you like a piece of cheesecake?"

Mike declined the hospitality and Karlek waved the waiter away.

"Your message mentioned information. What is it?"

"No amenities?" Karlek's sigh was theatrical. "That is the problem with young people today and police officers particularly. You do not take time to enjoy what is going on around you. It is always right to business."

"Two people have been killed and one seriously injured. I intend to get the matter solved."

Neil Karlek traced his index finger across the palm of his open hand then raised his eyebrows and asked, "Do you like this city, Detective?"

"What's that got to do with anything?"

"I find it enjoyable. In fact, I have thought of moving here. Perhaps when Quebec finally separates I will do so. Festivals run from the beginning of June until September. A growing community of artists adds depth to the place. Gambling is legalized so corner pubs, sports bars, pool halls, and even off-track betting can thrive. Yes, it is a delightful place.

"Mrs. Karlek and I brought three of our grandkids with us. They begged to stay at your West Edmonton Mall so they could visit the beach and the fair contained within its walls. They especially enjoy the dolphins.

"Still, you have more here—you have parks where families feel safe to walk and picnic. It is too bad Mrs. Dorrien was killed in such a park. Crimes of violence do damage a city's image."

"Our image is just fine and we want to keep it that way. We don't need your kind of business moving in."

"I am hurt Detective. Can I call you Mike? No? That is all right. We will observe the formalities. Do you think I would move my family, my grandchildren, to a crime-riddled city? A city where school children carry knives for protection? I don't claim to be able to stop crime. Young people do sometimes grow up bad and kill their miserable next door neighbour. Drugs are also around. Alas, I am like every other grandfather in that I want a good home for my kids and their kids.

"But a city needs business and you must be careful your city fathers don't hear you discouraging business people from coming to your city." Karlek's gaze rested on the bowl of carnations in the centre of the table. He pulled one from the vase and smelled it. "My corporation dabbles in a wide range of business ventures and could bring many good things to your city. We employ thousands of people." He paused to replace the flower, then sipped his tea. "Did you know getting upset, like you are doing right now, is bad for your health?"

"Is there a point to this meeting?" Mike had missed sleep to be here, his neck hurt, and he didn't appreciate spending time listening to the rambling of an old man.

"I just wanted you to understand that my hope is that your city remains peaceful. My companies will do business here even if it is not, but the violence that has occurred lately with all those robberies is something I want ended."

"We're working on it."

He turned his teacup around on its saucer, then poured a drop more from the pot into the cup. "I have been advised to pass some information onto you." He looked directly at Mike, his bright eyes gleaming. "Do you ever consult a psychic? I find they unravel difficult problems. Ah well, I see you are impatient to get on with your day so I will give you my information without further delay.

"It seems the gang of thieves you have been hunting, I believe your media calls them the Shotgun Gang, have been seen on an acreage I own near Elk Island National Park."

Mike leaned across the table finally hopeful the meeting would have a positive result, though not the one he had expected.

Karlek pulled an envelope from the attaché case propped against the leg of his chair. He handed it across the table, painstakingly avoiding the remains of his tea. "Marked on the enclosed map is the location and legal description of the property. My lawyer has enclosed a letter authorizing a search and the arrest of any trespassers."

Mike scrutinized the shrunken little man who answered his next question before he asked it.

"In line with my duty as a good citizen, I thought I should let you know."

Mike turned the envelope over. Why was Karlek doing this? He didn't believe the good citizen story for a heartbeat. Maybe the gang didn't have his permission to commit the robberies? Was this Karlek's way of getting rid of the competition? Setting the cops on them would make others think before treading too close. If Karlek wanted to use the police Mike decided he would garner payment in the form of information.

"While you're in a helpful mood, Mr. Karlek, do you know anything about the break-in last night or the murder of RCMP Sergeant Pierce?"

"You know better than I do, young man, that being an officer of the law means you deal with some untrustworthy people, people who are often not loyal to their friends."

Of course, disloyalty would rank high on Karlek's list of punishable offences. Was he trying to convince him that Jack's informant was the person who killed him? Was this old guy trying to discredit a snitch? Could he believe anything Karlek said?

"Yes, dealing with unsavoury characters is just one of the many drawbacks of your dangerous job. About poor Mrs. Carpenter, I can tell you nothing except that I was sorry to hear about the assault. One should not suffer such indignities at her age. Do you have a suspect?" He paused to sip more tea then spread his hands, palms upward. "I see you're not willing to share and I can understand your reluctance. Well, I think I've told you what I can. It is getting late and I promised I would go to the mini-golf course with my grandson while the girls shop."

He patted his mouth with his napkin. One of the business types jumped up and pulled out the old man's chair. The other held his overcoat and retrieved the attaché case.

"It has been a pleasure, Detective. I hope you are successful at keeping your beautiful city safe for me."

He again extended his hand; Mike took it.

Mike watched as the three men wove their way between the tables. He was only mildly surprised when Mr. Karlek nodded to a pair of legging-clad debutantes. As he made his way into the bright sunlight, one of the women rose and headed toward Mike, arriving at the table just as Evan pulled out a chair.

"You heard?"

Both nodded. The debutante pulled what looked like a Discman from her oversized bag. Evan removed a tiny hearing aid from his right ear.

Mike turned his attention toward the woman. Years of aerobics and diets had given her the look of a greyhound waiting for the start of a race.

In answer to his hard look of inquiry, she said, "Constable James, RCMP Criminal Intelligence Division. I'm taking over Sgt. Pierce's investigation."

"What do you think that was all about?" Evan asked.

Mike handed him the envelope containing the map. "Someone is infringing on his territory and he's using us to get rid of them."

"You think he was telling the truth? Why would anyone be stupid enough to use his property as a hideout?"

"How do I know? Maybe they didn't know it was his place, or maybe they thought he wouldn't mind?" He added in a slower, thoughtful tone, "Maybe they thought they were working for him? Just double-check his ownership and get a warrant before we go arrest them."

Mike rubbed his neck and wished for sleep. Being used by a bad guy, even to catch other bad guys, made his stomach burn.

"I can't arrest them just because Karlek says they're the Shotgun Gang. I need proof," Evan said, pointing out one obvious roadblock.

"It's his property so we'll arrest them for trespassing then get proof of the robberies," Mike said, not bothering to keep the exasperation from his voice.

"What about Jack?" the woman asked.

"You heard what Karlek said about the people you meet as a cop. Is Jack's source a killer or was Karlek sowing distrust?"

Her face closed, sealing off all expression. Damn, no help was coming from her.

"We don't know who his informant is," she said, refusing to meet his gaze as she continued speaking. "Jack neglected to share that person's identity after his partner died."

No wonder she was ticked off.

She added, "As someone who was working with Jack, you might be approached by the informant."

"If he didn't kill Jack."

"Well, yes, although I think we can safely assume Karlek wants to discredit our informant. I'll check with Marvin about our role in taking these guys." She handed Mike a card, then loped across the room to rejoin her companion.

Evan put his hand on Mike's arm to hold him in his chair until the women were gone. "We've had calls resulting from the

Crime Stoppers' re-enactment of the trust company hold-up. One in particular will interest you. Remember the incident in the library, the one that involved your witness, Beth McKinney? Her friend, Carla Wright, phoned to say she's sure the man on the trust company surveillance tape is the same man who attacked them."

"Unlikely. That attack was the result of news broadcasts about Beth witnessing Lisette's murder. The Shotgun Gang had nothing to do with that."

Evan folded and unfolded the linen napkin he'd carried from his table. "If they were tied together, the gang and Lisette's death, it might explain Karlek's interference. Maybe Hugh is a rogue operating his own outfit under the cover of Karlek's protection."

Mike interrupted, filling in the gaps of Evan's theory. "If Lisette threatened to tell Karlek, Hugh might have had her killed. Of course, Hugh knew about Karlek's land and would feel safe using it as a hideout for his gang."

Evan continued the hypothesizing. "Hugh has the gang kill Lisette, then they go after Beth McKinney who they believe is a witness. I suppose real estate managers know the security arrangements of a property. We'll check with the victims to find out if they're Dorrien's clients."

Mike saw a neatly wrapped package but something about it stunk. "I can't see Hugh risking his position with Karlek for the kind of money those robberies are generating. It doesn't make sense but let's go arrest this gang and ask them to explain it to us." Mike added, "Tomorrow we can bring Beth McKinney in to see if she can confirm Ms. Wright's identification."

"Another thing," Evan said as he looked around the room. "A photographer came into headquarters today claiming to be the person Ms. McKinney saw in the bushes. He's been using the trails, hoping to catch the definitive picture of autumn in the river valley and thinks he was around there at the time of the murder. He's about the right height and says he usually wears a brown leather jacket and cap. Claims he saw nothing but it does tie into the M.E.'s timeline. I told him you would probably be in touch."

CHAPTER 18

By six that afternoon they had obtained a search warrant and were following a city police van toward a ten-acre plot near the southeastern corner of Elk Island National Park.

The bureaucrats had debated heatedly about jurisdiction and timing. Eventually, they compromised and the City Tactical Unit received the okay to move but a Mountie presence would be felt with two officers acting as observers.

Mike pushed for the early assault because Lisette's death had taught him the importance of acting immediately on new information.

Speeding down the divided highway, he saw a half dozen buffalo grazing behind a high, wire fence. Their winter coats had filled out so that they'd lost their patchy summer appearance. Most of the fields were bare because the dry autumn had allowed farmers to finish harvesting early.

The convoy included the Tactical Unit van, a RCMP patrol car, and Evan's truck. They turned off the four-lane highway onto a paved, secondary road and then again onto a gravelled road. A kilometre from Karlek's cabin, they pulled to the side of the road and established a command post. The house was located in an isolated spot and surrounded by dense brush.

Three members of the Tactical Unit, with rifles at ready and night vision scopes dangling around their necks, headed through the ditch and into the thick bush to conduct a preliminary surveillance of the property. The sun was near the horizon and Mike worried about the delay.

"Calm down, Mike. Karlek's giving them to us. What can go wrong?" Evan asked.

"Almost anything." Mike felt his mouth twist into a lopsided grin as he replied to Evan's remark. A few days ago, he wouldn't have been so pessimistic. "Maybe Karlek forgot to tell them to co-operate with us. Hell, maybe they're not even your guys."

Mike turned his back to Evan and planted his boot on the truck's rear bumper. With his elbow on his knee and his chin cupped in his hand, he listened as the evening sounds filled the darkness. Dried leaves rustled as they skittered across the road, insects clicked in the dense shrub and bullfrogs croaked beside a nearby pond. In the distance, a bull elk trumpeted a challenge. Mike raised his night vision scope and scanned the bush, but couldn't locate the elk.

Mike was stretching out of his resting position when two members of the team rounded a turn in the road and headed in the direction of Staff Sergeant Peterson, the head of the Tactical Unit.

"A clearing about twenty-five metres wide encircles the house," one of the men said. "The house itself is on a small hill so they have good visibility. They have yard lights, but haven't switched them on."

"Any sign of movement?"

Mike and Evan stumbled over each other asking the question. Sergeant Peterson's look reminded Mike of their observer status.

"Three vehicles in the drive. Two trucks, one van. Noise from a TV coming from inside. It's on loud, so I'd suggest we wait until they settle for the night."

Sergeant Peterson looked at Mike who reluctantly nodded his agreement. They were contained and he wanted them taken without a fight, so catching them while they slept gave the Tactical Unit the advantage.

"We'll take our time getting into position. After everything has been quiet for half an hour, we'll move in. You might as well get comfortable out here and whatever you do, don't get in our way." Sergeant Peterson addressed his comments to Mike and Evan and the RCMP unit of Constable Sally James and Inspector Marvin Brown. He didn't make it a request.

Half the group of tactical officers crept silently up the road. The others slid through the bush. Mike tried to catch some sound that would tell him what was happening ahead. Canned laughter floated on the air currents alongside the hum of one of the few mosquitoes left after the latest frost.

Marvin Brown wandered over to where Mike was standing. He cupped his hand against the cold wind and lit a cigarette, then inhaled deeply. The night was overcast and dark. Mike wanted to be with the assault team, he wanted to use his radio to demand an update, but knew he couldn't risk the operation by creating unnecessary noise.

A gunshot exploded into the dark night. A thud sounded as metal dug into the truck.

Mike dove toward the brush at the road's southern edge. Laying on his belly in the sparse grass, rough gravel digging into his flesh, he scanned the area. What had gone wrong? Why hadn't the Tactical Unit caught the shooter?

Marvin Brown lay exposed, crumpled in the centre of the road, holding his thigh. His cigarette glowed faintly where it had fallen.

Mike squinted and made out dark shadows moving in the ditch on the opposite side of the road. One of the shadows looked like Evan. He and Sally James must have made it to safety.

A second shot roared. Bits gravel exploded as the glow of Marvin's cigarette died. Marvin crawled toward the protection of the vehicle.

Mike pulled his pistol from its holster. Only the wind shuffling through the brittle leaves broke the silence but it successfully hid any sound the sniper made.

Sergeant Peterson's voice came over the radio. "What's going on? Do you need help?"

"They must have seen your men and got out. Inspector Brown has been shot. I'm trying to spot them."

"Stay put. We'll backtrack."

"No! We'll handle this."

The Inspector had crawled behind a wheel and crouched in its protective shadow. Mike raised his night scope and looked at Evan. Mike pointed down the road telling Evan he would circle behind the sniper.

He crawled through the dry grass of the ditch, trying to keep the sound of his passing to a whisper. Maybe the wind would work for him as well as it had for the sniper.

Five metres down the road and close to the spot where the shots had been fired, Mike peered out of the ditch. When you were the hunter, you could wait for the prey to come to you. As the hunted, he didn't have that luxury.

The scope showed him an eerie green and black view of the world. Aspen poplars dominated the woods. The stumps of hundred-year-old giants lay scattered between saplings. Mike saw no movement and no man-shaped shadows. Rushing up the slope to the nearest fallen tree would be his best chance or suicide if they were watching him through night scopes.

Mike held his pistol pointing toward the ground in front of him. The leaves were damp and released a musty smell when he crushed them under foot. He crouched against the trunk of a fallen poplar and scanned the bush, the night scope clutched in his left hand, the pistol in his right. Nothing moved in the green night.

He darted to another tree and again waited as the moon peeked through the cloud cover. Once satisfied no one was hiding nearby, Mike widened his search. Something crouched in the bush across the road, directly behind Evan.

Was the shooter on that side of the road? Was it a stump?

Through the night scope, Mike detected a slight shift in the shadow. The dark shape rose. The man swung the rifle toward Evan.

Mike took aim. He called out for surrender. The man twisted, swinging the barrel away from Evan's back and toward Mike's voice.

Mike fired. His shot exploded into the darkness. Two shots followed; the man collapsed. Mike watched as Evan approached the fallen man. No more shots rang from the underbrush.

Mike called the Tactical Unit. "We've got one shooter."

"It's quiet here. Too quiet. When the shooting started, I called for them to surrender. They haven't responded. Should we wait for them to make the next move?"

"Check that they're in the cabin. If one got through your line maybe the others did too."

"I'm sending a man closer."

Mike continuously scanned the bush through his night scope. Nothing moved. Had the others escaped?

Peterson interrupted Mike's thoughts. "We have a situation here. You better come in."

"What's the problem?"

"Both men are dead."

"Damn."

Mike walked toward Sally James who looked up from applying a compress to Marvin Brown's leg. "I've called for an ambulance. Have they arrested the others yet?"

Mike shook his head. "They're dead. Damn, they're all dead."

He climbed into the passenger seat of Evan's truck and they drove toward the cabin. There was no longer a need for stealth.

The night sounds were returning by the time Mike trudged through the doorway of the cabin. A single lamp illuminated the scene. Newspapers spilled over the top of a cardboard box, logs were stacked near a pot-bellied stove, and dirty dishes lay scattered and shattered on the counter that acted as a kitchen.

A dirty pillow and tousled blanket had turned the sofa into a bed for the man lying sprawled along its length. His chin rested on his chest; a square of gauze was taped to his forehead. A thin collar of blood was the only sign of violence to his person. A second man rested his head on the scarred table, his blood dripped onto the cracked linoleum and congealed in a pool beneath his chair.

"Damn it." Mike turned to Sergeant Peterson. "We wanted them alive."

"They were dead before we got here." Then, as he turned to leave, he said, "I'll radio this in."

Mike muttered as he brushed his hair back. "Three dead, one injured. That's a blown assignment in my books."

Using his pen, he lifted a woollen object from the arm of the sofa. A Balaclava. It had been tossed onto a navy, wool jacket. At least that matched the witness' descriptions of the Shotgun gang. They might have to thank Karlek for ending a crime spree.

Standing at the table, he pulled on rubber gloves and lifted the corner of the scrap of paper that lay under the dead man's head. The guy had been clipping news articles when he died.

"Mike. Come in here," Evan called from the bedroom where he was sitting on an unmade bed. The drawer of the bedside table was open and Evan held up a picture.

"Nice group photo of Hugh and our buddies." He motioned toward the dead men in the other room.

Mike took the photo. It showed three men sitting one row behind Hugh, Lisette, and Tony at the baseball park. Two of the men were now lying dead in the other room; was third man their sniper? From Evan's expression, it was a good bet he was. The snapshot was candid and Mike couldn't tell if the group was together or if the picture included both groups by accident.

"This proves Hugh is involved with the Shotgun Gang," he muttered to himself. Looking up at his partner he added, "It looks like you were right. Hugh was double-crossing Karlek. When we get back in town, start checking his client lists against the robbery victims. No wonder Karlek was ready to give these guys to us."

"But why call us if he planned on killing them?"

"He's playing games. I don't know why or how but this is working to his advantage."

"Do you think Hugh's dead too?"

"With all the men we have covering him, he better not be dead."

CHAPTER 19

Beth watched Mike approach the reference desk. His hair was in disarray, his jeans had two inches of dried mud clinging to the cuffs, and his eyes had caved into the dark circles that surrounded them.

"You didn't get much rest did you?" she asked, wondering where he had been to get so dishevelled. "You look more tired than you did this morning."

"I've come to escort you and Carla Wright to the station, to see if you can identify the men who tried to kill you."

"Did you catch those creeps?" Carla asked, looking up from the information package she'd been compiling.

"We may have, in a manner of speaking. However, I want you both to look at the Crime Stoppers' video."

"I saw the tape and like I told the other detective, it was the same man."

"Humour me. Look again and maybe examine some photos." Carla glanced at her watch and Mike added, "We will make sure you get home safely."

"I'll have to call Fredo, my boyfriend. He worries."

Mike had a patrol car waiting, so the trip to the station took only moments. He ushered them into a room and motioned toward the sofa and chairs. A narrow counter held a drip coffee pot and a stack of Styrofoam cups. A television and video-player combination sat on a cart and faced the sofa.

"Watch the footage first, we'll talk afterward."

Mike played the Crime Stoppers' re-enactment of the bank robbery, then the actual convenience store surveillance tape. Beth leaned toward the TV, studying the way the men moved, trying to recall if their profiles matched those of the men in the library. One was similar.

"Finally, she shook her head. "They could be the same men. But it was dark and I can't be sure."

"That's okay, you tried."

"Well, I am sure," Carla spoke in a loud, carrying voice. "Look at the way that guy crouches, like he's nervous. And just look at the nose on the other one." She looked at Mike who hovered near the door. "I study noses and that guy for sure is the same. Look Beth, I know it's the same guy. Put them in a line-up and I'll point to them."

Beth looked at Carla with her set jaw and jutting chin. It was plain that Carla thought Mike didn't believe her. Trying to smooth over her friend's injured feelings, Beth said, "Carla, I'm sure you're right, but I just can't be certain they're the ones." She looked up at Mike. "Maybe a line-up would help."

Mike's grin radiated pain. "Can't do that. They're dead."

"Dead! What happened?" Carla asked.

"You'll hear about it on the news. We had a tip and raided a house near Elk Island Park. Something went wrong and an officer was wounded. Two of the men were dead when we arrived. The third shot at us. When we returned fire, he was killed."

"God, the media will love this. The 'Police are Villains' groups will be out in force," Carla said, her voice overflowing with barely concealed excitement.

"The public won't remember that these men have killed people and robbed homes and businesses for months, only that they were killed when we tried to arrest them."

Beth sensed bitterness and fatigue in his voice. "Go home Mike. We can take a cab back to our cars."

Beth rose. Carla followed, but turned and asked, "Was it necessary? Was there no way to arrest them without blood being shed?"

Mike's shoulders sagged. Beth knew that if Carla who was one of their victims questioned the police action, there was little hope of convincing other people they had no choice.

"We didn't plan to hurt anyone, but luck wasn't with us." His eyes pleaded for understanding, but Carla refused to meet his gaze.

"Come on," he said, "I'll get you back to your cars."

Mike drove them back to the parking garage and parked his loaner between their vehicles. Carla gathered her bag and rushed over to her battered station wagon. Beth wondered if she was hurrying to spread the news.

Beth remained in the passenger seat of Mike's car, trying to think of something comforting to say. "Why don't you follow me home, have some coffee and a brownie, and play with Splatter and Magpie? They help me unwind."

She sensed relief in his shuddering exhalation.

"You don't think it was our fault? If we had waited until morning it wouldn't have played out differently, except that one of them would have escaped. The other two were dead before we were within five miles of the place."

She touched his arm and asked, "Did you take what you thought was the best course of action?"

"They waited with Lisette because it seemed the right thing to do and she died. I hoped by acting quickly this time no one would be hurt." He covered his face with his hands. "Did you mean it? Can I come over?"

"Get in my car. I'll drive. You're too tired."

He didn't argue, but crawled into the passenger seat and was asleep before they exited the parkade.

The drive home was an easy one because traffic had dropped off and pedestrians were few. As she drove, Beth wondered what he'd meant about Lisette dying because they had waited. More was going on here than she knew and she again resolved to find her answers, tonight.

And Carla, sometimes her comments were anti-authority, but tonight she had seemed ready to lay all the blame on the police. On the ones who tracked the criminals and risked their lives to apprehend them. Somewhere inside, Beth felt a twinge that whispered no one should have died. She looked at it without blinking.

Of course no one should have died. Unfortunately, if humans were involved, people would die—the cops, or the criminals, or the innocent bystander.

The flood of bright light from inside her garage woke Mike. He looked around, reorienting himself. Rubbing one eye he said, "Sorry, I must have fallen asleep."

"Come on in." She opened the door of the house. "Go relax in the living room. Turn on the stereo and I'll bring us some coffee."

Beth started the coffee and set out a tray with bakery brownies. Splatter jumped to the back of a kitchen chair and watched her preparations. Faint piano music floated from the living room. She popped into her den to check for E-mail messages. Just one cry for help, a simple question asking whether putting a mutual fund or GIC into a tax shelter was the better strategy. It could wait.

Her phone showed three callers, her sister, a charity to which she regularly contributed, and Richard Tanner. Even with an hour time difference, it was too late to call Myrna in B.C. The charity would call back and Richard could burn in hell.

When Beth returned to the living room, she found Mike asleep on the sofa. Splatter had found her way to the top of a tall, glass-enclosed bookcase where she lay, her eyes half-open.

Beth pulled a spare blanket from the hall closet. After covering Mike, she returned to the kitchen where she poured herself a cup of coffee and bit into a brownie.

"Well Magpie," she addressed the sleeping cat. "I guess I won't get my answers tonight either."

*****

Beth looked at Mike through the steam rising from her coffee mug. He had borrowed a pair of her dad's sweat pants and spent forty minutes in the gym lifting weights and riding the stationery bike through a five-mile, uphill program. Now showered and wearing his mud-splattered jeans and wrinkled shirt he poured himself coffee.

"I think it's time I knew what was going on," she said.

Mike pulled a chair out and sat across from her.

"I want to know why Lisette was killed and why that disc is so important."

"I can't give you that information."

"Someone tried to kill me. I think I have a right to know."

"We'll protect you."

"You've got a lousy track record for protecting anyone."

"A leak could hurt our case."

"Who am I going to tell?" She reached across the table and took his hand. "I promise it will go no further than this room."

"What about Tanner?"

"Richard? What's he got to do with this?"

"He's a reporter. If you talk to him . . ."

"It will be right after hell freezes over. I know his tactics and the damage he can do. Believe me, I wouldn't direct him to a bus stop, much less to a news story."

"The Mounties are investigating Hugh," Mike said, with a sigh of resignation. "Some months ago they received word that his marriage was rocky and that Lisette was getting desperate to leave the relationship. They checked out her background and discovered Lisette knew Mary and that Mary had worked in law enforcement. Mary asked them to work through the city police. Eventually, they worked out the details and we set up an 'accidental' meeting between me, Mary, Jack, and Lisette at the Kozy Kitchen."

"That's why Simon offered condolences? He told me you knew each other and met for lunch occasionally."

"Yes we did—Jack, Lisette and I. Lisette didn't convince easily. She was afraid of Hugh's reaction if he found out, but eventually she agreed to update us with any information that came her way. Her regular running time and route were well established, so she made contact with Jack in the park. A lunch hour runner is nearly invisible."

"Why were they watching him? What kind of criminal is he?"

"He's part of a criminal organization run by a man named Neil Karlek."

"I thought the bikers had a monopoly."

"In some areas. Other areas are dominated by ethnic groups. Karlek's organization deals with money laundering and industrial espionage. The construction arm has big question marks all over it and rumour has it that Karlek dominates a few unions."

"And Lisette uncovered evidence and they killed her."

"That's the theory we're working."

"Hugh as in property management. That's doesn't sound like it fits into that operation."

"Most of his business is legitimate. We believe he acted as a clearinghouse for information and laundered money through his real estate transactions. Also, he owns and manages many properties and can easily arrange to have an office or house available whenever and wherever needed. Sometimes he provides a place for criminals to hide until they can get out of the area."

"Like those people last night?"

He winced, making her feel guilty for reminding him.

"Hugh managed Karlek's Alberta properties. He must have felt it was a safe spot for the gang to hide out. Karlek didn't agree."

"If most of his business is legal, why did he get involved with criminals?"

"Sometimes retired athletes have trouble readjusting to ordinary life. Sometimes old friends forget your name and Hugh Dorrien's name wasn't big enough to open many doors. Besides with his reputation as a fighter, fans might not associate him with a reliable product. Add to that the economic downturn and he may have felt he had no alternative but to accept their offer to set him up in business. Agreeing to be their front man must have seemed worth the price."

"Why did you involve Lisette? She had enough problems."

"The Mounties already had someone close to Dorrien, but they knew she would be closer. Besides, it offered her a way out."

"And she was killed because she was working for them?"

"Probably. Word was sent Sunday night that she was in danger and they tried to get her out during her run Monday."

"Why didn't they get her out the minute they knew about the threat?" Beth heard her voice rise in anger. Was that the delay that he'd meant the previous night?

"Their informant assured them she would be safe for a few days and they decided they could save the investigation by making it appear she'd left on her own."

"Did Hugh kill her?"

"He probably hired someone. I've checked his alibi and it's tight."

"That's who I saw?"

"No. You saw a photographer who was in the area around noon. The M.E. says Lisette took about twenty minutes to die."

"But you have other evidence—a motive . . ?"

"We can't prove he knew she was working for us or that he'd discovered she stole the disc to give us. All we know is the weapon came from his kitchen and we have a shoe print in his size."

"But," Beth said.

"It's circumstantial. She had skin under her nails but it's not Hugh's. We have found no one to put him at the scene and his prints aren't on the knife. We did find shoes and clothing at the scene. The lab is trying to find trace evidence proving he wore them while he killed her. I have to tell you, it's possible that he will get away with this."

"What about the disc? Isn't that enough evidence? You thought it was important yesterday."

"We can't prove the disc is his."

"What does the data on the disc mean?"

"We hope it is a record of his dealings for Karlek, but the Mounties are having little success deciphering it."

"Did he ask those men to kill me?" Beth shuddered at the memory.

"We have a picture that indicates he knew them, but with them dead we have no other evidence linking them."

"Are you going to be able to convict him of assaulting Mary?"

Mike shook his head. "Forensics might help us with fibre

matches, but he was careful. Unless Mary can identify him we have nothing."

"What if I talked to Hugh, told him I had the disc he wanted so badly and that it was for sale to the highest bidder? If he agreed to buy it back, wouldn't that tie him to it? Maybe I could get him to admit he ransacked Mary's house and murdered Lisette."

"That kind of stunt only works in movies. Besides, I refuse to risk another civilian on this."

"You don't have much choice if you want to prove it's his," Beth pointed out. She hated the idea of bringing herself to Hugh's attention, but if he had killed Lisette and hurt Mary how could she do otherwise?

Mike ran his hand through his hair and pursed his lips. "We could get an officer to impersonate you."

"That won't work. He knows me."

"From a distance we might fool him."

"I'd have to get him to take the disc and admit ownership to satisfy a jury."

Mike eventually nodded his agreement. "We would have to inform Superintendent Weisman and maybe the Mounties, but you're right, at least we'd have that much."

"Just let me know when you want me to phone and what I should say. I don't want him getting off totally free, even if you can't prove everything."

Beth listened to Mike's side of the phone conversation. She wasn't sure she wanted him to be quite so compelling, but it didn't take long to get the go-ahead. Then he notified the Mounties of the plan and agreed that in return for using the disc, RCMP observers could be present.

Finally the time was set, the location chosen, and the script written. Beth held the telephone receiver in her shaky hand. She met Mike's gaze and matched his encouraging smile with a weak one. This had to be the dumbest thing she'd ever contemplated doing.

"You can still back out," Mike said. "No one will think badly of you. It shouldn't be dangerous, but I can't guarantee a thing."

"No. This was my idea. I won't put anyone else at risk. Besides, we agreed it wouldn't work if I didn't meet him."

Mike looked as if he was going to grab the receiver from her hand, but she turned away and with quick stabbing movements, she punched the number that Mike had written out for her. When the receptionist answered, Beth pressed the intercom button so that Mike could hear both sides of the conversation. The receptionist directed the call to Hugh's assistant.

"I would like to speak to Mr. Dorrien."

"Can I tell him the nature of your business?"

Remembering Mike's coaching about giving out as little information as possible, Beth said, "It relates to Lisette. Please let me speak to him."

"He doesn't want to be disturbed. Is it urgent?"

Beth looked up at Mike, who nodded.

"Yes, yes it's important that I speak with him right now."

"Can you tell me what it's about? It might make him more willing to take the call if I can give him a few details."

Mike shook his head.

"No, just tell him I need to speak to him."

An abrupt click signalled that he had put her on hold. Country music flowed from the speaker. Mike paced and Beth tried to quell her hope that Hugh would refuse to take her call.

"Ms. McKinney. Mr. Dorrien asked me to take a message. He said he would try to return your call later today."

Beth looked up at Mike's face. His frustration was apparent. She blurted out, "Tell him I know everything and that I have his disc. Tell him I will be at the lookout where Lisette died, at noon, to discuss terms for selling it back to him."

*****

The cold wind carried with it thin flakes of snow and a ten-degree temperature drop. The ground was rapidly turning white, the weather office promised six centimetres before the sun returned.

From his observation post in the thick undergrowth, he watched Beth huddle on the concrete park bench. She pulled her collar higher on her neck and adjusted her earmuffs. Mike mumbled, wishing he had thought to wear his long underwear but held his position. He hated involving Beth. He had been unable to protect Lisette and now Mary's life had been turned upside down by this case. Who did he think he was to risk another person?

However, Beth had volunteered to act as a decoy and there was no real need to worry about her safety. Enough men were hidden in the underbrush to protect her from a direct assault and unmarked cars practically lined the street. Still, the way this case was unfolding something was sure to go wrong.

Hugh was already twenty minutes late. Mike pulled his collar higher, stamped his feet to restore circulation, and cursed Alberta winters. Moments later, Hugh's dark blue sedan cruised to a stop.

Mike watched Hugh slide out of the car and pull his overcoat closed in a bid to defeat the wind. He trudged across the dry, brown grass and stopped in front of Beth. His shoulders were bowed and deep worry lines etched his face.

"I understand you have something of mine." He uttered the words in a slow monotone.

Beth pulled the computer disc from her pocket and waved it at him. "Very interesting information. It seems like a valuable commodity. What are you going to offer me for it?"

His gaze remained on her face. "A finder's fee, of course. Not keeping a backup copy was foolish of me, but who would have thought my private property would disappear like that? How did you get the disc, Ms. McKinney? Did Lisette give it to you?"

"I was the person who found her. She spoke to me before she died and she gave me this disc when she told me you stabbed her," Beth said.

Mike ground his teeth. She was veering from the script they had agreed to follow. Damn, why was she risking herself like that? Accusing Dorrien was a sure way of provoking him to violence.

Hugh's reaction to her taunt was swift. He lunged, grabbing

the disc from her hand. Mike forced himself to stay still. The men hiding in the bushes held their positions, waiting for his command to move.

"Don't lie to me. Lisette never told you that because I didn't kill her. How did you find out about the disc? Who told you I was looking for it?"

Mike held his breath as he silently urged her to ignore Hugh's question.

"You might have that disc, but I copied it before I came here. For that outburst the price just doubled and if you don't pay me, I will take the copy to the police. Your freedom's a bargain at fifty thousand, wouldn't you agree?"

Mike admired her calm response and her confident smile. He felt a surge of pride in the way she could think on her feet.

"I don't understand what you're trying to do, but get this straight," Hugh said, sliding the disc into the pocket of his overcoat. He glared at her, his fists clenched, his shoulders hunched. "I did not kill Lisette and without the key to my code, the data is worthless. Just a warning that you don't deserve, destroy the copy. If the wrong people get word you have it, you might end up dead too."

Hugh turned away and started across the field.

Mike couldn't let the plan shatter into useless pieces. He stepped out of the trees and called out, "If the disc is so valuable, maybe you better talk to me before your boss decides to get rid of the threat."

Mike wanted the upper hand and looking at the wreck before him, he figured he wouldn't have to fight hard to make him crumble.

Hugh looked from Beth, to Mike, to Constable Sally James who now appeared on Mike's left. He shook his head and released an abrupt bark of laughter. "Ms. McKinney, I am disappointed in you. This whole thing was a set-up to get me to confess, wasn't it? Is this even the real disc?"

"It's real. By coming here you've proved it's yours and that it was worth hurting Mary to get it."

"Without me to translate and testify about the information it contains, you have nothing."

Mike caught a hesitation in his voice. "You're just a small fish, perhaps we should let you swim away and see who eats you for lunch. After last night I'm certain you know Mr. Karlek is downsizing his troublesome staff."

That caught Hugh's attention.

"Is that a threat, Detective?"

"I'm just hypothesizing. We have no proof, but I did talk to your boss yesterday. He asked me to keep the city crime free." Mike decided a little tough cop tactic might help. "We know you killed your wife. Confess to that and we'll protect you from your business associates."

"Like you protected those poor sods you tried arresting yesterday?"

"I'm sorry that turned out the way it did. We were hoping those particular friends of yours could be encouraged to testify against you."

"Friends? All I know about them is what was on the news broadcasts and in the papers. They were shot in a police raid without being given a chance to surrender. Are you planning to use the same tactic with me if I refuse to co-operate?"

Mike felt anger churning in his stomach. He couldn't afford the luxury of surrendering to his emotions. He had to nail Hugh solidly and this could be his best and only chance.

"We have evidence that links you to them. Mr. Karlek knows it all, he gave us your friends."

"What kind of crazy bluff is that? I don't know those people."

"We know you killed Lisette. The murder weapon came from your house and given time we'll find the store where you bought the flashlight you used to hurt Mary Carpenter. It might take a while, but we'll find proof. Give it up Hugh. It's just going to take routine police work to nail you."

Mike fought to keep his expression confident. He commanded his hands to remain motionless. This was no time to betray his uncertainty. Still, he knew they would be lucky if just one of his predictions came true.

"You get me killed and I won't be able to give you the information on the disc. The Mounties won't be too happy if they don't get that." He looked across to Constable James.

"We're willing to talk to you, Mr. Dorrien. Your disc might even help our investigation but don't think it's so important to us that you won't have to deal with the local charges."

Mike held his breath. Were the Mounties really backing off on the idea of making Hugh an informant, or was this a ploy?

Then Constable James added, "Unless you agree to work for us."

She was bargaining, preparing to let a murderer escape the justice system.

"Why should I deal with you? You can't prove anything. Not about Lisette, or that old woman, or anything else. If you could you would arrest me, not stand out here freezing your butts off hoping I'll confess to a crime someone else committed."

"Like I said Hugh, it is just a matter of time," Mike replied. "You figured you were smart, but someone always remembers something. Your legitimate business will nose dive when your connection to Karlek is known and you will lose your value to your boss when a forensic accountant scrutinizes every business deal you make. Karlek is already wondering about you. Why would he send us to that cabin if he didn't know you were controlling the Shotgun Gang? He doesn't like what you're doing."

"That's a lie." Hugh pulled the disc from his pocket and shoved it toward Mike's face. "This disc is my insurance against local cops like you. I'll talk to someone with the authority to promise me protection."

"You will confess to causing Lisette's death first. Later, you can buy your way into the Mountie's good graces."

"I didn't kill her. I tried to find the disc at that old woman's house, but I did not kill Lisette."

Mike looked around at the desolate landscape. Tree branches

were bare; the ground was white; the wildflowers were frozen and dead on the ground. Fall had gone; winter had arrived only seven weeks before its official date.

"Let's head downtown and talk some more and maybe you will decide to make a full confession. Then, you can tell Constable James all about that disc and about Karlek's business." Then, Mike added silently, I will watch you escape the punishment you deserve.

CHAPTER 20

Mike looked across the table to where Hugh hunched, his hands clenched, his eyes tightly closed. The Mounties would negotiate the deal just the way Hugh wanted it so that they could make a case against Karlek. Still, he would take whatever he could get. The picture of Hugh and his associates at the ballpark was his strongest bargaining tool and he planned to use it judiciously.

"Tell me what happened Hugh."

Hugh opened his clenched fists, turned his hands palm up, and stretched his fingers wide. Then he again tightened them into fists. "Lisette died and everything fell apart."

His voice seemed devoid of emotion though Mike thought he recognized sorrow in his expression.

"Why would you care if she died? You told us she had affairs; that she took your baby with her when she met lovers."

"No one said she was perfect."

"How do you know Jerry and Nick Fortain and Shaun Murphy?"

"Who?"

"The men at the cabin."

Hugh raised his shoulders, then let them fall. "I don't. You claimed you had evidence. What is it?"

Mike pulled the photo from the incident file and handed it to him. Hugh studied it, then handed it back.

"It was taken at the baseball park, but I go to most of the games. Obviously someone included us by mistake because other than Lisette and Tony, I don't know the people in that photo."

"Do you and Tony go to the games often?"

"I like to watch. He likes to bet. So yes, we go often."

"And you don't know the men sitting behind you?"

"Not even from the game, so they probably aren't season ticket holders."

"Do you expect me to believe you don't know them? This photo was taken of the six of you."

"Believe what you want. It's the truth." Hugh stared directly at Mike, who knew he couldn't yet prove otherwise.

"Why did you kill Lisette?"

"I didn't."

"She was unfaithful; she had lovers. Did she flaunt them? Make you crazy with jealousy? Did she threaten to take the kids and inform Karlek about your secret records if you fought her for custody?"

Hugh held his hands over his ears, shaking his head in answer to each question.

"You'd lost one family. Did her threats to take the kids away make you crazy? We know some of your fights got loud. Did she drive you to it? Threaten to use your affair with Melissa as a lever?"

"Melissa was nothing but a pastime. Lisette knew that. She knew I'd never divorce her."

"Why did you hurt Mary?"

Hugh stopped shaking his head. "I just wanted the disc back. Karlek would have killed me if he learned about it. Don't you see I need it for protection? For insurance. I didn't want to hurt the old woman. If she'd given me the disc, I wouldn't have had to. If I agree to testify against Karlek, you have to put me into a witness protection program. I'll take my children and we'll be safe somewhere far away. Start a new life." His voice held a note of hope.

"That's later, Hugh. Right now tell me about Jack."

Hugh turned his head slightly. The horizontal creases scarring his forehead deepened. "Jack?"

"Inspector Jack Pierce of the Royal Canadian Mounted Police. He was present when I interviewed you on Tuesday."

After a long pause, Hugh nodded. "I remember, a podgy, middle-aged, balding guy. What about him?"

"He was murdered Thursday night by the men in the picture, on your orders." Mike hoped his lie would get a reaction that would shortcut their search for proof of Hugh's guilt.

"But you said they were dead." Hugh shook his head again.

Before Mike could continue, a knock on the door interrupted them. Mike was tempted to ignore it, but it came again and he knew the interruption had to be important. Besides, the flow of questioning was already broken.

Mike opened the door. Superintendent Weisman motioned him into the corridor. When he closed the door she said, "The Mounties want him, now."

"I'm not finished with him yet."

"Are you making progress?"

"He admitted assaulting Mary."

"In the interests of inter-agency co-operation we'll have to hand him over soon."

"What do you mean, we've got him for murder. There's enough evidence . . . " Mike hoped that for once logic would surmount politics.

But Super Sam broke into his spiel. "You might have enough to charge him with the assault on Mary if his confession holds, but without a witness or a confession to Lisette's murder, a jury will let him off. With the Mounties he can act as an information source."

"Sam, you can't do this. I owe it to Lisette. "

She chewed at her bottom lip. "Confession or not, give him to them first thing tomorrow morning." She turned toward the elevators that led to the executive floor.

Mike watched the door close behind her. Would he have enough time to make Hugh crack?

"Mike." His soft-spoken name came from close to his shoulder. He jumped, startled.

"Breathing too hard to hear me approach?" Pete grinned up at him. "I've got some interesting news on the Dorrien case."

"Dorrien's confession is what I need, but I'll settle for some damning forensic evidence."

Pete hunched his bowed shoulders and muttered, "It isn't that. In fact it sort of helps him out."

"Great. Well, what is it?"

"The shoes we found in the gym bag had tissue paper stuffed in the toes."

"So?"

"It was used to make the shoe fit a smaller foot. Pressure indentations on the tissue show it fit a size nine. The interior of the shoe had indentations from a size eleven and a half, Hugh's size. And the wear pattern on the pair you brought from the house is the same as on this pair."

"So, what are you saying?"

"They're Dorrien's shoes but someone else stuffed the toes and wore them. Someone with a size nine foot."

"He didn't do it?"

Pete shook his head. "Not wearing those shoes. Sorry to blow your theory."

"No, no. I want to get whoever killed Lisette. If it isn't Dorrien, well I've got him for the assault on Mary anyway."

He opened the door and stepped into the room where Hugh was waiting. Mike sat at the table for a long moment, staring at the scarred beige wall. Hugh could still have ordered the hit, but why incriminate himself? He let his mind sort the facts into a different pattern.

"Tell me about Tony," Mike said.

"Why do you want to know about him?"

As Mike watched, comprehension grew beside hope in Hugh's expression. "You think Tony killed Lisette?"

"You tell me."

Hugh leaned forward, his hands clenched. "I don't know much. The head office sent him out to be my assistant a few years back. I never bothered checking his background, but he does his job well, and he's always around when I need him. Gambles too much, but everyone needs one vice."

"Has he seemed upset lately?"

Hugh sat back, regaining his confidence. "He has always kept to himself. I haven't noticed any difference."

"Does he have access to your client files?"

"Probably more than I do. Tony helps them with details, especially the older clients. He lists their personal property for them, even arranges to have it videotaped for insurance purposes. He sets up security reviews and encourages them to get alarm systems. Alarms have been a growing aspect of the business in the past few years and our clients seem to appreciate his personal attention.

"Even the business clients find it easier for Tony to cull security and insurance companies for them. He usually tenders the contract, then presents the client with the best bids and helps them make the final decision."

Mike was torn by the turn of events. He wanted Hugh to be guilty, but if what Hugh was saying was true, Tony knew who had something worth stealing, where they kept it, and how it was protected. He could have arranged with that gang to take the expensive items, then told them where to sell the stuff.

The money from the thefts would mean more to him than to Dorrien, especially if he had a gambling problem. But why kill Jack? Had Jack's informant arrived at the same conclusions and passed his suspicions on to Jack, thus making it necessary for Tony to kill him?

Or had Jack been ahead of the rest of them? He had known Hugh Dorrien well and maybe he'd decided that he wasn't a killer. Had he turned his attention to Tony? Had he tackled Tony hoping for an admission of guilt and ended up with a bullet instead?

Hugh cleared his throat, reminding Mike of his presence. He would finish with Hugh later, now he had to concentrate on Tony. "I'm going to call the Mounties in now, but if you don't fully cooperate with them we'll be talking again."

Mike left Hugh in the interview room and headed to the Superintendent's office. It was late, but he wanted a search warrant for Tony's apartment.

"Are you sure, Mike? Twenty minutes ago you swore Hugh

killed them, now you say Tony did it. Do you have evidence, more evidence than a shoe stuffed with tissue?"

"That's why I need to search his place."

"Mike, I have always respected your skills, but you've lost your perspective over this case. Was there something between you and Lisette?"

"No. Not like you mean anyway. She was someone I should have helped more than I did. I blew it and she died."

Sam turned her chair toward the window. Mike looked out at the overcast sky. It was that lonesome time of day when dusk threatened to turn to night before the lights of evening brightened the city. Flakes of snow fell gently. Tomorrow the sun would reflect rainbows in the white blanket covering the city.

She turned to face him. Placing her hands on her desk, she said, "I came in from my cabin because I wanted to see how you were doing with Dorrien and to see if anything could be done about last night's fiasco." She held up her hand, preventing him from justifying the previous night's disaster. "Mike, this case needs a slow, second-look and that's what you are going to give it. Tomorrow is Sunday. Relax. Take Mary some flowers. Let things settle. Monday morning we'll go over the evidence that you've gathered. If enough evidence exists to convince me Tony's a likely suspect we act, if not you keep searching until you find concrete proof."

She walked to the front of her desk. "I'm heading back to my cabin now, I can't miss the first snowfall of the season. Go home, but first call Constable James and let her know she can have Hugh."

*****

"Mike, did he confess?" Beth rubbed Magpie's ear and curled tightly into the corner of her sofa.

"He admitted hurting Mary but he didn't kill Lisette."

Mike's answer was concise and brought tears of anger and frustration to her eyes.

"Are you sure? How can you be positive he's innocent?"

"We know."

"But how do you know? Did someone confess?"

"Can we meet for breakfast tomorrow? I need a sounding board for some theories I'm developing."

"Mary is staying here and she can't get around very well, so I'd hate to leave her alone. Why don't you join us here?"

"Mary is out of the hospital already? I thought they would keep her. I really did mean to get back to see her."

"I'm only glad they kept her as long as they did. Mary was insisting on getting out this afternoon, so when I said she could stay with me the doctor discharged her."

"Thanks for your help earlier. Without you we might never have proven Hugh's involvement."

Beth paused a moment, then asked, "What will happen to Hugh now?"

"That's up to the Mounties. Maybe he will testify against Karlek. If he does, they will protect him, if not we have him for assaulting Mary. He won't serve much time for assault though."

"What about the kids? Lisette wanted them out of Hugh's control."

"I'm sorry, but it won't happen. Look, I'll see you in the morning and explain everything."

After she disconnected the call, Beth continued grooming Magpie until Splatter bit his tail, ready for a romp. Then she trudged up the stairs, wondering how she was going to break the news of Hugh's innocence to Mary. The research she had done on victims said that an almost pathological fear and avoidance of unfamiliar situations and locations could develop after a trauma. Knowing Hugh would soon be out of jail was going to make her more nervous.

Well, she would help however she could and while Mary stayed with her, she should feel safe. Beth knew her home, with its extensive video security system, made her feel safe. Mary would feel the same way and she could spend her time healing rather than worrying. Beth admitted to herself that walking through the parkade since being attacked had become an exercise of will. She also ensured she left with the majority of the other staff.

Damn those men for taking away her self-confident belief that public places were safe.

If not Hugh, who had killed Lisette? Poor Lisette, she had risked her life to get the kids away from their father and it was all for nothing.

*****

Mike greeted Mary with apologies for neglecting to visit her at the hospital and questions regarding the doctor's judgement in letting her leave. She was pale, obviously too badly hurt to be walking around. The gauze that covered half her forehead scared him. The sling holding her right arm immobile emphasized her frailty.

"I'm supposed to be the old woman here. Don't you go worrying unnecessarily about me," Mary said, brushing his worries aside.

Mike absently stroked Splatter's grey fur. He knew Mary didn't take well to sympathy, but he was delighted she was well enough to brush his concerns aside. His pleasure evaporated under Beth's questioning stare. He avoided meeting her gaze by fussing over Mary until the initial greetings were finished, then he accepted Beth's offer of breakfast. Dodging their questions left a conversational void that created an uncomfortable silence. He sipped his third cup of coffee of the day and stared out the patio door at the cloudless blue sky that contrasted so sharply with the dazzling white landscape. Pristine snow made the world seem clean and new. Mike didn't like it; it hid evidence.

Beth broke the silence by asking, "If the man I saw wasn't Lisette's murderer, why did those guys try to run me down?"

Mary answered between nibbles of her light Sunday breakfast of toast and grapefruit sections. "Tuesday, when the news reports claimed you had seen the attacker, they couldn't be sure who or what you had seen. You were a threat they had to remove. After their attempt failed and before your assailants could try again, they learned you had seen nothing important."

"How?"

"That's a good question. Mike, what is the answer?"

"We told Hugh on Tuesday afternoon that you were unable to identify the assailant. The rest of the household didn't find that out until we spoke to them Wednesday morning."

Mike saw a slight grin spread over Mary's face. Her eyebrows rose and she spoke softly. "Including their highly valued informant who was so cavalier about alerting Jack to Lisette's danger? Do you suspect double dealing?"

Mike pushed away his plate with its remnants of eggs and bacon. He waited, imagining the wheels turning in the older woman's mind. He hoped her conclusions would match his.

"Why would Jack's informant want to harm Lisette if they were working for the same people," Beth asked.

Mary patted Beth's hand. "Sometimes informants work for both sides. Maybe Jack's snitch was also keeping Hugh up to date on what he told the authorities. When the order came to kill Lisette, he had to inform Jack to keep his reputation as a snitch intact, but his warning downplayed the urgency."

"Why did you say 'his warning?' Why not 'her warning?'" Beth looked at Mike and asked, "Do you know who Jack's source is?"

Mike hedged, but Beth's steady look forced him to admit, "I have a theory, but as far as having evidence we're no further ahead. Jack kept the identity secret so unless the informant approaches us it will take time to find him—or her. It could be anyone in the household."

"Anyone?"

"The cook, Helen, has already killed one man and that man was Lisette's father."

"What!" Mary said, stopping mid-bite into a grapefruit section.

"Self-defense, but it would have given the Mounties a lever. Neither Melissa nor Tony has ties to Alberta. They were sent to

Dorrien's by an agency. The Mounties could have got to each of them before, or after, they arrived."

"Did Hugh say why Jack was killed?" Mary asked.

"Denies all knowledge of the event."

"Mike, if Hugh admitted hurting me, how can you believe he is innocent of the other crimes?" Mary asked.

Mike leaned toward her. "What if a second criminal exists? Hugh assaults you to get the disc back. Someone else kills Lisette and Jack, and tries to kill Beth because they think she witnessed Lisette's murder."

"We're back to the beginning then; why would anyone but Hugh want Lisette dead?"

Mike watched as Mary and Beth focused on the question.

"The old standbys of greed, love, hate, and jealousy still exist."

The silence grew uncomfortably long. Finally, Mike picked up the salt shaker and inspected the cut of the delicate crystal. "I think Jack's informant killed Lisette. Hugh might be innocent, but if he is someone did a good job of framing him. First, we're handed the information that Lisette is in danger from Hugh. Then at a time when Hugh should have had no alibi, Lisette is killed. Hugh's unscheduled dental appointment was the killer's bad luck.

"Pete discovered that Hugh wasn't the last person to wear the shoes we found at the crime scene. Someone with a size nine foot left that print on the path hoping we would trace it to Hugh."

"When did you figure all this out?" Mary leaned back in her chair.

"Last night."

"Who is your choice for culprit?"

"You tell me," he said.

Mary shook her head.

"Well, if you add a photo of Tony with the Shotgun Gang to our mix of facts, I'd have to say he is at least guilty of the assault on Beth and maybe Jack's murder."

"But he has no motive for killing Lisette."

"Tony seemed attracted to Lisette. Maybe Hugh ordered the

hit and Tony decided to plant evidence pointing to Hugh as a form of revenge."

"Are you going to talk to Tony?" Mary asked.

Mike ran his hand through his hair. "The Super isn't as certain as I am. She wants me to present the facts tomorrow morning. If it's good enough to get a warrant, okay. If not, we're back on the treadmill."

"You were hoping I could help," Mary said.

"You've always been the best at analyzing criminal behaviour."

"Maybe my brain is scrambled. Your logic sounds just fine, though I can't seem to think beyond it without my head hurting. Maybe I can help more later."

Mary had lost the little colour she'd regained since he had seen her lying on her kitchen floor. Her smile didn't rank above a one out of ten and the tear streaking her crepe paper cheek forced him to apologize for expecting too much from her.

For the first time since the day he'd met her, Mike saw Mary as elderly. He shrugged away that uncomfortable thought and patted her hand. "Don't worry. You'll be back to playing Sherlock before you know it. Until then I've got about twenty-four hours to find enough evidence to convince Super Sam my theory is solid."

He pushed his chair away from the table. "I'm going to talk to Tony's friend again, the one who provided the alibi for Tuesday night. Then I think Odile deserves a visit, maybe Lisette wrote to tell her about her fears."

"And I," Mary said, slowly standing, "am going to lie down for a long while."

CHAPTER 21

"Tony," Odile called to him as he passed the sitting room doorway. "Can we talk for a little minute." The picture albums she had been looking through were spread over the floor around her and one lay open across her knees. "Have the police told you when they're releasing Hugh? Have they even arrested him? It has been nearly twenty-four hours since he phoned from the station."

Tony hesitated in the doorway. "There's just been the one call, but the lawyer should have him out before long. Is that all you wanted?"

"No. I want to talk to you about Lisette. She wrote me many letters, but I feel we lost contact after I moved to France. Tell me what was her life like."

Tony shifted his weight from one foot to the other. "Why ask me? I'm just Mr. Dorrien's assistant. Anyway, I thought you were going to meet with her friends and talk to them."

Odile ran a manicured fingernail along her full bottom lip. She raised one perfectly arched eyebrow. "You were more than that Tony. Lisette's last letter told me about your dalliance. I was surprised she would be unfaithful as she hated our mother's string of lovers and swore she would never follow that path."

Tony stepped into the room. "She shouldn't have told you; she promised she'd never tell anyone."

Odile felt a stirring of apprehension at the fierce anger she read in Tony's eyes.

"She was unhappy, but she wouldn't say why. Was Hugh abusive?"

"He didn't hit her, though he came close. She just hated him telling her what to do and when to do it. She especially hated him for keeping her at arms length from her kids."

"In one letter she hinted that she planned to bring the kids to France and stay with me. I thought she was going to leave Hugh, but that was many months ago and she never mentioned it again. Are you the reason she abandoned that plan? Did your relationship give her courage?"

He leaned backward and glanced down the long hall toward Hugh's office, then he stepped into the room. "She never listened to me, but she was afraid he would hunt her down if she took the kids. Look, you're not going to tell Hugh about the affair are you? He'd," Tony shrugged, "I don't know what he'd do."

"I will not sully the children's memory of her, but please help me understand my sister."

"Our affair wasn't any great passion. Do you know you look like her? You could be twins."

"How long were you lovers?" Odile asked, steering the conversation back to Lisette.

"She came onto me last winter when Hugh went to Toronto for some meeting. They'd had a fight about his fling with Melissa just before he left, so I figured she wanted revenge."

He sat on the sofa across from her and leaned forward. "Did she tell you about Melissa?"

Odile pulled back. She didn't appreciate him crowding into her space.

"It's not just your face." Tony leaned closer and inhaled deeply. "You smell like her too."

Odile nodded and leaned further back. "She suspected Hugh was sharing Melissa's bed?"

"She'd have had to be blind and deaf not to know it, with Melissa throwing out hints like she did. At least we were discrete."

"Did you love her?"

"Love?" His gaze slid away from hers. "Maybe. She didn't love me though. She was desperate and was hoping I'd take her side against Hugh. She told me how Hugh threatened to take the kids away. He's a lousy father just like he was a lousy husband, but I wasn't ready to commit suicide so I convinced her that provoking him was too dangerous a ploy." Tony touched her hand. "You know your accent is nicer than Lisette's."

Tony looked around and cleared his throat before starting again. "I shouldn't tell you this, but I work for the Mounties."

"What!" Odile closed the photo album abruptly and leaned toward him, then pulled back again when she realized how close their heads were. "She did not say you were a police officer."

"I'm not. Not really. My gambling debts started to pile up. Nothing a big win wouldn't fix, you understand, but I couldn't get past a big losing streak so I robbed a store. You have to understand that I had to get enough to pay off some guys who wouldn't wait longer."

Odile felt his demand that she and agree with his action. She nodded, just a tiny movement of her head to say she'd heard him, but it was enough to satisfy him.

"I went to a small town north of here. The storeowner came at me with a shotgun. Shotguns are very effective for making people do what you want. Anyway, the Mounties hauled me in. They checked my background and learned that I worked for Hugh. Then suddenly another guy is talking to me, Sergeant Jack Pierce. He offers me a deal. I help him; they overlook my indiscretion.

"Hell, I didn't owe Dorrien a damn thing. In fact, if he'd advanced me the money I needed to cover that gambling debt, I wouldn't have been forced to rob the place."

Sensing her disapproval, he protested, "You'd do the same thing if you were in my spot. Lisette did."

"Lisette robbed stores?"

"No! She worked for the Mounties and she was good at it, even planted a little voice activated recorder in Hugh's office. He talks to himself all the time. That's how we got the combination to his safe. She passed the cops more information than I did."

"Why? Why would she do that?"

"I told the Mounties she wanted out of the marriage. They contacted her somehow; it wasn't through me. We weren't supposed to know about each other, but Lisette couldn't keep a secret.

They promised to get her to safety after she gave them enough to arrest Hugh. Lying bastards. They keep promising to let you go, but they always want more."

His voice rose. He jumped up and started pacing. "She would have left me too. I know that. Just sell me out to the cops and run off."

"You mean Hugh," Odile corrected him. "She was informing on Hugh, not you."

He looked at her through narrowed eyes. "Yeah, I mean Hugh. How could she sell me out? It's not like I was doing anything wrong. Hell, I was reporting to the cops and they sure wouldn't complain about that."

His laugh grated across her nerves. A flicker of movement in the doorway made her shift her gaze from Tony.

"Are you sure she wasn't selling you out, Tony?" A deep voice came from the doorway.

Hugh stepped into the room. Odile exhaled the breath she'd been holding. She was glad they were no longer alone. Then she saw the gun Hugh held.

"I should kill you." Hugh's tone was matter of fact. "Still, then I'd have to kill Odile and I wouldn't want to do that."

Odile shivered.

Tony raised his hands. "Hugh, Lisette was informing on you, not me."

"I've been listening to your pathetic story. You betrayed me and corrupted my wife. The cops knew Sunday night that someone planned to kill her. They figured it was me, but that's a joke. Why should I kill her? You killed her and you tried to frame me but it didn't work. The cops know I'm innocent. They let me go."

"How did you get here Hugh? I didn't see you come in," Odile asked, hoping to turn the conversation onto a less dangerous road.

"I came in through my office a couple of hours ago planning to get some sleep so my kids wouldn't see their dad worn down by police questioning. I love those kids, now I find out Lisette was scheming to steal them from me."

"Hugh, it's over. Lisette is dead. You don't have to worry about anyone taking the children," Odile said, fearing that his red face and heavy breathing were warnings of an impending stroke.

"No, it's not over Odile." Hugh kept his attention and his gun focused on Tony. "Stay out of this."

She tried to sink into the sofa, hoping to escape unscathed.

"The cops showed me a picture of that gang of robbers who were killed Friday night. They thought it was a picture of me with them, but you were in the picture too. Have you become so desperate to pay your gambling debts that you stooped to petty theft?"

Tony stepped closer to Hugh. "Some of those banks paid us well. So did the houses. It's handy to be the one arranging the insurance on people's valuables. I helped pick out their security systems too. I'm surprised the cops didn't catch onto that long ago, just shows you how stupid they are. They never did figure out that your company arranged the installations. It was a good scam."

Tony shifted a tiny step closer to Hugh. "Yeah, I got enough to pay my bills and give a share to the other guys. Who was hurt? Insurance companies and banks. Big deal."

"People were killed."

"Stupid people who weren't smart enough to stand back and let us do our job. They wanted to be heroes. Now they're dead heroes."

"Was Lisette going to tell the police about your sideline?"

"Yeah. She saw Nick on that security tape they put on television and remembered seeing him talking to me at that baseball game. And what does she do? She starts sneaking around, pawing through my stuff and asking me questions I don't want to answer. Questions about how well I know the guys we saw at the baseball field and about the security systems in the houses that were hit and didn't some of the addresses seem familiar. She wondered if we had dealt with them. So, I figure she's decided to turn on me. I couldn't let her tell Jack because it would give him such a hold over me that I'd be spying for him until I was ninety, or until Karlek killed me. I had to stop her."

"Did you kill the men in the cabin too?"

"That was a good trick. I got Shaun to kill the Fortain brothers. They wanted too big a cut of the profits, besides they were getting careless. As usual, Shaun's timing was off, but I like to look at the bright side, at least I didn't have to dispose of him."

Odile watched Tony inch closer to Hugh with each unbelievable statement. Should she warn Hugh? He must realize his danger.

Then Tony lunged.

Odile froze.

Tony grabbed Hugh's wrist with both his hands and twisted Hugh's arm, trying to wrench the gun from his grip.

Hugh held on, his face contorted with strain.

Tony gave a final twist to Hugh's arm at the same time as he hooked his leg behind Hugh's knee. Tony jerked the gun from Hugh's hand as he fell backward and held it in both of his. Hugh fell hard, hitting his head on the hardwood pillar. He lay still, stunned by the impact of the fall.

Tony pointed the gun at Hugh's head, his chest heaving as he looked down at the dazed man. His lips thinned to a slit; his eyes narrowed to a squint. Hugh looked up, raising his arm across his face.

In a single fluid movement Tony kneeled beside Hugh, put the gun barrel against Hugh's temple, and fired.

Odile screamed as the loud retort rang through the empty house.

Hugh wore a look of surprise as his arm fell to the floor and a tiny dark spot appeared in front of his ear.

She had to escape. Tony was insane. Odile stumbled toward the dining room door, but Tony crossed the floor and grabbed a handful of her hair. She stumbled against a side table. A porcelain lady fell to the floor. The hard metal of the pistol barrel caressed her cheek.

"You understand I have to kill you now, don't you Odile?"

"It was self-defense. Tony, you do not have to kill me. I will tell them he was threatening us and you killed him."

"You'd tell them the rest too, wouldn't you?"

"No, I will go back to France. I will take the children. You will never see us again."

Tony looked around as if expecting the kids to rush into the room but the house remained quiet. "Where were the kids going, Odile? I saw them leaving as I arrived."

"Helen and Melissa took them to Sunday school." She feared she had said too much. "They will be back at any moment."

"No. They were just leaving so they'll be gone at least another hour, probably two. That's enough time."

He pulled harder on her hair, forcing her head back. "You're like your sister and she was going to run to the cops. They should have blamed Hugh for her murder. I had everything planned. If he hadn't run to the dentist with a sore tooth, it would have worked; he'd be in jail and I'd be in the clear. Now he's dead and I need a new plan."

He pushed her onto the sofa then returned to Hugh's body. She hoped to escape when his back was turned, but he watched her from the corner of his eye as he kneeled to examine Hugh's wound. He fumbled through his jacket pocket and removed a small metallic wristband that he wiped on his slacks before pushing it into Hugh's shirt pocket.

He looked at his wristwatch, retrieved the gun, and in three steps, was at her side. "Come on."

She stumbled as he forced her to walk ahead of him to the kitchen. Pushing the side door of the house open, he propelled her to the driver's door of Hugh's sedan.

The stinging cold penetrated her blouse. She exhaled a tiny cloud into the frigid air.

Tony shoved her across the seat but the gun stayed pointed at her waist. Odile shivered, uncertain whether the cold or her fear caused it.

"Where are we going?" she demanded, touching the door handle. Could she jump out at a stop light or even while the car was moving? She would be hurt, but alive.

"Sit still and shut up. Don't get any ideas about getting away because I'd just have to kill you sooner. Right now I need you."

"Why?" Her voice came out as a squeak.

"Because Beth McKinney will let you into her house."

*****

Helen and Melissa were called out of the church service because Joelle wouldn't stop crying. Relieved that she was finally showing signs of grief, they drove home and saw the side door standing open. Helen changed gears and backed the car out of the driveway. She drove down the street to a neighbour.

She dug Mike's card from her wallet and thrust it at Melissa. "Call the police. I'll watch to see if anyone comes out of the house."

Helen left the car and backtracked to the hedge that surrounded the Dorrien property, leaving a clear trail of footprints in the new snow. She crouched in the mound of powdery snow that had blown against hedge and peered through the bare branches to the Dorrien's driveway. She studied the door and the windows, but saw no one. Was Odile still in the house or had she escaped?

Helen pushed through the shrubs. She had not succeeded in saving Lisette but maybe she could help Odile. She crept to the kitchen window. What was delaying the police?

Cautiously, she slid along the wall to the open door and listened. A dash into the house and she reached the counter where the knife block sat. The police had the chef's knife, but the five-inch slicer would do.

Peering around the corner, Helen saw the dining room was empty. She slid through the door, crouched beside the sideboard, then crossed to the living room. A figurine of a slender, blonde lady lay near an overturned table. Its outstretched hand was broken off at the wrist and lay inches away.

Helen widened her visual search, her knife pointed upward at ready. She saw Hugh. He was staring at the textured ceiling. Forgetting caution, she rushed forward.

Somewhere in the background, she heard a siren.

*****

"Helen."

Mike removed the knife from her grip. He had been on his way to talk to Tony's neighbour, who lived only a few blocks away, when Melissa's call reached him. Now he had another body. Had Helen killed him? But Hugh had died of a bullet not a stab wound, so whatever she was doing with the knife it wasn't murder.

"Helen, what happened?"

"I don't know." She looked around frantically. "Where's Odile?"

"She wasn't with you?"

"No, she didn't attend church."

Mike helped her stand and walk toward the kitchen. When other officers arrived, he directed them to search for Odile.

"Who would have done this? I thought they arrested Mr. Dorrien. Why was he here?" Her hand went to her mouth. "Oh God, did they kill Odile too?"

"We will find her. Was she alone in the house?"

"She was when we left, but we saw Tony driving this way. He waved at the kids."

"Is his car here?"

She looked down the empty driveway to the street where Mike's loaner and three patrol cars were parked. "Yes, it's the fancy one parked across the street, but I don't see Mr. Dorrien's sedan. What do you think happened?" Helen asked.

"From the look of the room, there was a struggle and Hugh was overpowered. Maybe Odile can tell us who he was fighting. I'm sure we'll find her nearby, but I'll put a call out on Mr. Dorrien's car in case she used it to escape."

Mike held her arm and helped her creep toward the undamaged kitchen. He hoped Odile would still be alive when they found her.

*****

Beth checked her security monitor before opening the door and was surprised to see Odile standing on the step. Her arms hugged her body, proving that her thin blouse was no protection against the cold. Her face was pale under her expertly applied makeup and her hair was in disarray. She looked weak enough to faint.

Beth felt guilty about not having contacted her to arrange a more congenial meeting, but with all that had happened since Lisette's funeral, she had put Odile's concerns aside. Now the poor woman looked frantic.

Beth disarmed the alarm system, opened the door, and reached out to draw the shaking woman inside. "Are you all right?" Even as she asked, Beth saw that Odile was far from all right. "Come in. I'll make you some tea." Then looking at her again, she added, "Scotch would be better."

"That sounds good, Ms. McKinney. Why don't you pour us all one?" Tony stepped into view from behind the cedar that grew between the house and garage. His face was flushed and he waved a gun at her, motioning her to step backward.

"Let's relax a minute. You can get us a drink and then we can talk about what you and Lisette really discussed. And how much of it you told that cop."

With his gun held against Odile's side, Beth saw no choice but to retreat into the house. He checked the living room and pushed Odile onto the oversized couch. Eventually, he perched on the arm of a high-backed chair that sat between the doorway and a tall bookcase.

"Odile has told me all about the letters Lisette sent her. After your call to Hugh yesterday, I realize you also know too much and will have to go. If not, I'll always wonder what Lisette confided to you."

Beth turned away from Tony to look at Odile; her face wore a wild, terrified look.

"He killed Hugh. They were fighting and then he got the gun

and just killed him. Now he wants to kill us," Odile said, in a high pitched whisper.

"Why are you doing this Tony?" Beth forced her voice to remain calm. How could this have happened in her home? How could her safe, secure home be invaded as easily as the parking garage at the library? What terrible thing had she ever done to deserve having people try to kill her?

She pushed the fear away, refusing to give in to it. Her wits had served her well all her life, she could only hope they would suffice now. But, if she got out of this alive, the first thing she would do was cut that cedar down.

If she could somehow set off the alarm or start the video cameras, but Tony stood between her and the control panel and she doubted he would let her wander freely around the house.

"Why do this?" Tony scoffed. "Because Odile knows that Lisette and I were having an affair and that we were going to testify against Hugh."

Beth looked at the gun in Tony's hand. Mike had been right. Where was he now? Did he know that Hugh was dead? "You're the informant?"

"Good guess. Hurry up with that Scotch."

He waved his gun, pointing it at each woman in turn.

Beth went to the bar hidden in a built-in cabinet beside the fireplace. After a moment of searching at the back of the cabinet, she pulled out a bottle of Scotch. She took a glass from the rack that hung above the bottles, poured an inch in the bottom, and extended it toward Odile. Then she poured another glass and placed it on the table in front of Tony.

Odile took a large swallow. Beth moved across the room and sat beside the girl, keeping her hand on her slender shoulder. Turning her head to watch Tony, Beth asked, "Did you kill Lisette too?"

"As if you didn't already know."

"But the police arrested Hugh." Odile's voice squeaked. "They must have had reason to think him guilty."

"Hugh couldn't plan lunch without help. Lisette found out I was masterminding the robberies. She got upset when that guy was killed—the damn idiot shouldn't have tried to be a hero. It was his fault he got killed, but she was gonna tell the cops. Lisette made love to me, but she was going to turn me in. I know she was. They wouldn't arrest me because I'm too valuable to their investigation, but Jack would never have let me go."

"Did Jack know you killed her?"

"Of course not. He was stupid when he told me no one but him knew my identity. I saw my chance at freedom and got rid of him. He shouldn't have told me that. My guys tried to get the other cop too, but he was lucky."

Beth felt her stomach churn. "You tried to kill Mike?"

"Cops think they got the guys, the Shotgun Gang. What a laugh. They're just bozos I hired for the dirty work. But I'll let them think that and I'll prove to the cops that Hugh killed Lisette and you guys too. When they find him dead, a suicide, they'll think he did it all and the case will be over. With Jack dead no one will ever know about me."

"Why would they think Hugh committed suicide?"

"Because I'm going to take this gun back to his house, after I kill you with it, and put it in his hand. Then I'll write a note on his computer saying how he couldn't live with his guilt."

"The police will know. They can tell if someone committed suicide."

"I know that. What do you think I am, stupid? I have it all planned. The gun was right against his head when I shot him. I'll make sure his fingerprints are on it. You must realize that I plan my actions. If you don't plan, things can go wrong."

"Why not just leave. Go somewhere you won't be found. You don't want to hurt anyone else."

"The Mounties protected me when I helped them investigate Hugh, but if Karlek finds out what I was doing it won't matter where I go. He'll find me and kill me. So I've got to kill Odile and you too, because Lisette told you about us."

"But she didn't . . ."

"It's too late to stop now."

From where she was sitting, Beth saw a car slow, then continue down the street. It was marked with a Channel 6 logo, Richard's channel, but he didn't stop. Damn that Richard, the one time he could have helped and he drives right by. When would the patrol be around again? Could she attract their attention?

Catching her staring out the window Tony twisted to look, but the road was clear. Only Hugh's sedan remained in sight.

*****

Richard hadn't slept well. He kept seeing his career and reputation dissolve before his eyes. It wasn't a picture he liked.

He paced through his galley kitchen. His cigarette burned to a stub. He lit a second one. His stomach churned acid. The last thing he needed was the station finding out Beth hadn't seen the murderer. Damn it, if only he could talk to her they could straighten out their problems.

If he could convince her to co-operate and allow him to film an exclusive report about the attack at the library, his career would revive. If she denied him, or worse yet told his boss why she'd been targeted, he would be blamed for messing up again.

How had his future come to hinge on her good will? She was still hurting; he knew she would enjoy retaliation. How had their loved turned so sour?

And that cop—what was his role? It must be personal. No, she couldn't prefer a cop to him. She must still have some tender feelings, even if they were so well hidden she didn't see them herself. He had thought it was over between them too, until he saw her again.

Perhaps he could reawaken her love. If he got through her anger, she would be his again.

Driving to Beth's house and yelling his apology into her security camera was a positive course of action. Let her get his grovelling on tape, anything as long as she agreed to do an interview his way.

As he drove, he kept one ear on the police radio. The call to be on the lookout for Hugh Dorrien's car interested him. The last he'd heard was that Hugh was being questioned about Lisette's murder.

He would follow-up, but first he was going to win Beth to his side. Richard turned onto Beth's street and spotted a dark blue sedan parked in front. He slowed and drove by, noting the license number. It was Dorrien's car.

He parked half a block away, then picked up his phone, and dialled the Channel Six news desk. He needed Chuck and his camera pronto. Then he dialled again, alerting the police to the car's location.

*****

Mike was driving toward Tony's apartment when he heard Richard's call reporting that Hugh's car was parked in front of Beth's house. He turned his truck around and sped across the freeway. Long before he approached her quiet neighbourhood, he killed the siren. Not wanting to announce his arrival, he parked a block away. Mike was the first on the scene. He didn't know what was going on inside, but with Hugh dead and Tony missing, he had no intention of waiting for the Tactical Unit to take charge. He had to do something.

As he stepped from his car, Evan pulled up, and Hilda Carstair's patrol car slid to a stop behind them.

*****

"They'll think Hugh killed you. That's why I brought his car, so they'll see it when they drive by. See, I do know about the surveillance. I pay attention to details—that's why the house break-ins went so smoothly. I checked my file on each house so we knew what alarm system they had and what was valuable enough to steal."

"How did you frame Hugh?" Beth asked, hoping that if he kept talking she would find some chance for escape.

A police car glided down the street. Beth saw Hilda's silhouette out of the corner of her eye, but this time she forced her gaze to stay focused on Tony, not wanting to alert him to the event that would trigger the next phase of his plan.

Tony's gaze flickered between the women. "Get me another drink and I'll tell you my grand scheme." He glanced at his watch. "There's still a little time before good, old Hugh, famous hockey player and sleaze bag, needs my attention. I want to have the scene staged long before the ladies get back from church."

Beth knew giving alcohol to a man with a gun was a bad idea, but refusing to pour the drink was also dangerous. She carried it back to him, debating her chances of throwing it at him and running. Still, Odile was in a daze and Beth doubted she would follow her lead. Beth knew she couldn't escape and let Odile remain in Tony's power.

He took the glass and saluted her with it. "Something went wrong, though. It would take more than the weak alibi of a dentist's appointment for the cops to release him. Do you know what went wrong? Did that cop tell you?" His voice rose, his eyes narrowed as he waited for her answer.

Beth was losing hope of rescue and Tony seemed beyond reasoning with. She let her gaze search the room, wondering what more she could do to help them. Splatter peered down at her from the bookcase beside Tony. Her liquid eyes were half-closed. Magpie watched from the fireplace mantle. Beth wished she had accepted her parent's offer of a large, aggressive watchdog.

Her gaze rested on the staircase and she remembered Mary sleeping in the upstairs guestroom. Would she wake and call the police? Would she try to investigate? Would Tony kill her too?

"After the police patrol sees Hugh's car I will shoot you and return to the house where I will write a tragic suicide note expressing

Hugh's anger at you for trying to blackmail him. He wants only to scare you, but poor Odile panics and grabs his arm, causing the gun to fire. Odile is accidentally shot and dies. He realizes he has nothing to lose because the police will blame him for Odile's death, so Hugh kills you too. It is only later, when he stops to think that he knows he can never escape and to save his children the shame of a trial, he ends it all."

Beth looked out the window again. How much time did they have? "What if they don't believe Hugh killed himself? What if they start asking questions about you?"

"Don't worry about me. I will have an alibi, if they even bother to ask. My neighbour loves to give me alibis."

"Tony, you don't have to do this, we won't say anything," Odile pleaded. She looked at Beth. "Will we? We will forget this ever happened."

"I won't hurt you, Odile. It'll be quick. Just one shot in the head. You won't feel anything. Damn it, I won't wait any longer for that stupid patrol. Stand up. If you're shot sitting down the angles will be wrong and my scenario will be difficult to believe."

Tony raised his gun.

Odile screamed and covered her face with her hands.

Startled awake, Splatter jumped from her resting spot high on the bookcase, and landed on Tony's shoulder. His arm jerked upward. His shot went wild.

The living room window turned opaque as the glass shattered.

Tony swatted Splatter away. Beth grabbed Odile by the arm and pulled her to the doorway. They fled down the short hall toward the back door.

"Get help," Beth ordered, pushing Odile ahead of her.

She grabbed a soapstone sculpture from the hall table and threw it toward Tony. Maybe it would slow him down enough for Odile to open the door and escape.

The back door burst open. Beth turned at the sound. People wearing black vests and holding guns pushed into the hall. She flung herself at Odile's back, knocking her to the floor. Then she rolled them into her den, hoping to stay out of everyone's line of fire.

A shot, then silence.

Hands touched her hair. Familiar, caring hands. She looked up into Mike's eyes. He cradled her gently.

"Is he dead?"

"He's injured, but he'll live."

"He was going to kill us." She pulled away and looked around the room. Odile lay crumpled beside her. She stared at Odile's long, lean limbs, so like Lisette. Her face was pale, her breathing ragged. Beth continued staring but she saw no blood. If she turned Odile over, what would she see?

Beth watched as Mike checked Odile for injuries. "I think she fainted, but the ambulance is on the way."

"Thank goodness the security company phoned you," Beth said, looking at the officers milling around her foyer. "Are they outside?"

"We stopped them at the first perimeter."

"You were here first? How did you know Tony was here?"

"The cook found Hugh dead. With Odile and Tony missing, we put out a call on Hugh's car. We weren't sure what was happening until Richard Tanner spotted it."

"Richard phoned you? He saved us? Why was he here?"

"You'll have to ask him. Anyway, we called for backup and Hilda checked the front of the house while we approached from the back."

"I didn't see you. I was watching out the window all the time, hoping the security company would arrive and give us a chance to escape. He was going to kill us."

"You weren't supposed to see us. Sometimes we do the job right."

Beth looked down the hall to where her beautiful table was overturned and her soapstone carvings lay scattered across the hardwood. Tony moaned and held his shoulder; his blood stained her floor.

"At least he will go to jail. He admitted he killed Lisette and Jack and said his gang robbed the banks and houses. He even bragged about fighting with Hugh and killing him."

A sick look flooded Mike's face. Beth straightened her shoulders and forced herself to stand. "Tony said the Mounties would cover for him if he was caught. Do they still want him to be their informant? They can't, not after what he's done."

"Afraid so, Ms. McKinney." The words came from a slender woman, wearing a multi-coloured, chiffon skirt mostly covered by an oversized beige sweater. Her hair was pulled back and tied with a scarf that matched the skirt. Except for the gun in her hand, she looked like a child playing dress-up.

"We need an inside man and with Hugh dead, Tony will keep moving up in the organization. After all, we don't want crime taking over the country, do we."

"But he killed people and he was going to kill us." Beth felt if she spoke slowly the words would penetrate and this young woman would understand the enormity of Tony's crimes.

Mike put his hand over Beth's, holding it so that she couldn't pull away. "We'll work it out. He will not get away without some punishment."

"On the contrary, Detective, you won't let his confession leave this house and I will tell your people the same." She no longer looked, or sounded, like a kid. "I will be taking him along with me."

"Constable James, you must realize that his cover's blown. He's no good to you now."

She shrugged. "We blame Hugh for Lisette's murder and claim he committed suicide because he was unable to live with his crime. As for the robberies, well you caught the Shotgun Gang Friday night. Case closed."

She left them standing in the hall and escorted Tony toward the ambulance that was pulling to the curb.

Odile had regained consciousness and Hilda sat with her, trying to calm her weeping. Finally, she seemed to gather herself and addressed Mike. "I want to go back to the house. I am going to take the children home to France where we put criminals in jail, not free them so they can continue killing."

Mike asked Hilda to drive her home. Reporters crowded around the women as they walked to the patrol car.

"Where's Mary?" Mike asked, his voice suddenly fearful.

"She must still be upstairs."

They turned toward the stairway where Mary stood, holding the banister for support. "I must be getting old. I didn't hear anything until the shooting started. Then with this sling and my sore head it took me forever to get down here. What is this about Tony trying to kill Beth and you letting him get away with it?" Mary glared at the detective.

Beth felt she had to add her support to Mary's disbelief. "It's not fair, Mike. Mary's right and so is Odile, he's supposed to pay for his crimes. How can the RCMP step in like this?" Beth couldn't believe the justice system would cover up his crimes and protect him. What good could be served by so much injustice?

"Did he tell you anything about the murders that we can verify with hard evidence?" Mike asked.

"He was going to blame Hugh for killing us."

"If Helen hadn't found Hugh's body when she did, he might have succeeded."

Beth pulled away and stalked toward her wet bar. "I taped him. When I got the drinks, I activated the panic button to alert the security company and start the video cameras."

"You've got cameras in your house?" Mary sounded horrified.

"It was a little extra add-on for the security system my Dad installed. If the alarm goes off during a break-in, filming starts automatically but today I let them in. Thank goodness, Dad hid emergency buttons in odd places throughout the house. Maybe I'll give the tape to a reporter. If the media has it, they can't cover this up."

"That's a great idea."

Beth recognized the voice and turned to see Richard Tanner

standing just outside her shattered window. Chuck stood at his shoulder with his camera pointing into the room.

This was unbelievable. She couldn't help Richard. Damn him for sneaking around eavesdropping. He had no respect for people's privacy.

"Glad you got out of this okay, Beth. I came by earlier to apologize, again. However, I am always glad to be of service, especially if it involves a front-page story of murder, mayhem and Mountie cover-ups."

Beth studied his boyish grin. He was sickeningly overconfident. She should give the tape to a different station because even the thought of helping Richard's career sickened her. Chuck shrugged and shook his head as if encouraging her denial of Richard. Still, his call had saved them, so she did owe him both her life and Odile's.

With Mike's arm securely around her waist, Beth smiled back at Richard. Maybe it was time to forgive. A little. Maybe justice could prevail after all.

THE END

9 780738 844589